THE DANGEROUS MEMOIR
OF CITIZEN SADE

Bliss was it in that dawn to be alive

Wordsworth, *The Prelude*

Et toute la colère d'un peuple amoureux travailleur insouciant
et charmant qui soudain éclate brusquement
comme le cri rouge d'un coq égorgé publiquement

Prévert, *Lanterne Magique de Picasso*

THE DANGEROUS MEMOIR OF CITIZEN SADE

A Novel

A.C.H. Smith

LOXWOOD STONELEIGH

Published by Loxwood Stoneleigh

First edition 2000

Copyright © 2000 A.C.H. Smith
Designed and typeset by Falling Wall Press Ltd, Bristol
Jacket printed by Doveton Press Ltd, Bristol
Printed and bound in Great Britain by Bookcraft (Bath) Ltd

Illustration: the *coq* is from the *Petit Larousse illustré* of 1915, but not
the dunghill

British Library Cataloguing-in-Publication Data
A catalogue record for this book is available from
the British Library

ISBN 1 85135 033 0

Loxwood Stoneleigh is an imprint of Falling Wall Press

Falling Wall Press Ltd
225 (Top Floor) Gloucester Road, Bristol BS7 8NR, England

For Alexandra

and with deep gratitude to
Helena de la Fontaine
and Zulfikar Ghose

Contents

MEMORANDUM

To: Professor Middleton, Chair, TG/ICEP Committee
From: Zelda Butterworth, PhD
Date: Potsdam, 20th May 1991

You asked me to let you have a note about my trip to Berlin, when sending you the attached paper I presented to the 18th-Centuryists Colloquium. I am glad to write it, since certain incidents, not all of them pleasant, are worth putting on record for the guidance of any future visitors from the department. You know Berlin, so I will not waste time on my touristic impressions, which would risk appearing jejune to you. I will stick to what happened to me.

1. I was met at the airport not by Dr Schultz, as arranged, but by one Frau Dr Mader, who teaches in the Hispanic Department. She explained that Schultz had been called away to deal with an emergency in the conference arrangements. It must have been some emergency, because he never appeared at any of the sessions. Nobody offered an adequate reason for his absence. Two years ago one might have thought, ah, the DDR has decided at the last moment that he is not *persona grata* to meet people from the West. But they are selling the Wall off at two dimes a chunk, and we are all Westerners now. Perhaps you would get a sensible answer to a letter of enquiry. It was oddly perturbing, even though I have never met Schultz, of course. After our correspondence, I was expecting him to greet me as a colleague, not a visitor.

2. Dr Mader drove me out to Potsdam, and showed me to this room in what I take to be a hall of residence. The building is modern and ugly, and the passage floors are unswept, but my room is well enough furnished, except that the two lights each

have only a 60-watt bulb. I have asked if a stronger light could be supplied, but it has not been after four days now. Meals are served in a refectory at strictly prescribed times. A woman here from Naples told me she had tried to order breakfast at 9.01 and was refused, even though the food was still on the service deck. We eat huddled together, all of us foreign colloquials, at tables down one end of a bleak plastic hall. Perhaps it is more congenial when packed with students. The food is plain, which suits me but not everyone.

3. My first day was free, until registration and the reception in the evening. I took a train into Berlin, to see what I could of the city. The railway station at Potsdam is extraordinary, and it took me a moment to figure out why. The stone walls are bare. Not one poster, not one ad. It reminded me of when I was a child in postwar London: the approach to Charing Cross railway station, over Hungerford Bridge, was like that (plus human dung, tramps, garbage). The 20-minute ride to Wannsee goes past still undemolished sections of the Wall, all smothered in graffiti. In New York, it's the trains they spray. Where the railway follows the line of the wall, windows are still barred up, and watchtowers with powerful lights (no 60-watts there) stand along what was the east border. Most of the houses look decrepit but retain a dignity, like the used kitchen-knife that Brecht preferred, which is in contrast to the vulgarity (to my eyes) of much in west Berlin. But east Berlin, the old Prussian capital – that is the Hohenzollern metropolis you promised me. I wandered lonely as a crowd, gawping with other Westerners at the brown and grey grandeur of it, aware that meanwhile there would be people from the East gawping at the grandeur of the shop windows along the Kurfürstendamm. (Though I found the people in west Berlin garishly dressed, and even more elbow-shoving than New Yorkers or Parisians.) It was a chilly, blustery day, bracing after the clammy heat that I see in the *Trib* still squats on Texas. Near the Gedächtniskirche I had a coffee, and went downstairs to the toilets. The women's and men's rooms

open off one lobby, and as I came out again through the lobby a fey figure jumped out at me from a little office. It turned out to be a man, quite like Joel Gray. He gabbled at me in German, his hand out. I said, slowly and clearly, "I do not speak German. Je ne parle pas allemand. Yo no hablo alemán." I didn't have time to figure it in Latin. He understood not a word but went on jabbering, and pointing to a price-list on the wall. I could decipher that urinals cost 15 pfennig, closets 30, and the rest of the tariffs were doubtless for washing one's hands, cleaning one's teeth, picking one's nose. I gave him the first coin I found, 50pf, and left wondering if he had a bank of monitors in his office to spy on what excretions and ablutions each of his clients performed. I am not a fussy or demanding woman, but by a moment like that, or the triviality of dim bulbs in here, I am coerced into Western expectations, just as one always is in the Third World, no matter how many liberal attitudes you packed. Then I strolled past the vast Soviet embassy, with the white giant Lenin in front of it, through the vacant spaces around the Reichstag and the Brandenburg Gate, and eventually found myself in the Kreuzberg district. Right on cue – a demo, as though you had ordered it up to prove what you'd warned me about. (Like, you sent me a demogram.) Only a small demo, about a dozen skinheads in black battledress tops, all of them with insignia on their backs. Though not, thank God, a swastika to be seen. That signifier is reserved for the mindless sons of those who won the war. This lot were ugly enough, as it was. Possibly they were no more than soccer fans, I don't know, but they marched along the sidewalk, forcing the rest of us to step into the road, and they were chanting and gesturing in unison very aggressively, and whatever it was they were demonstrating I'll bet it wasn't sympathy for Turkish guest workers.

4. That evening, to distract myself from adding finishing touches to the finishing touches I've spent weeks adding to my paper (knowing all along that the best bits will be ad libs), I got into

conversation over a beer with one Frau Schniek, who is at the colloquium from Halle. She speaks good English. At first she told me about the special problems of women post-DDR. They all used to have jobs, but now their work is not required any more. The men need their jobs, any jobs. It was normal for a woman to marry young, in her teens. Crèches were commonplace. Now they find themselves stuck at home with the kids. When I asked her if it wasn't perhaps just a transitional problem, while the East is being tooled up, she raised a finger, finished her beer, and gestured for me to follow her. We walked around the garden outside here, and she talked quietly. Some say the East needs five years, she told me, some say ten. But what nobody can say is how long it will take to root out all the briars of the Stasi. It is not just the 100,000 staff spooks but the five times as many unlisted informers, most of whom were blackmailed into it and so might still be running wild and scared, and all the links too with international terrorism. She believes many of them have moved into crime syndicates. And with people from the West buying up property, and unemployment, and xenophobia, she sees the whole fabric as far more unstable than we have been told, more liable to lurch uncontrollably in some appalling direction. She is very nervous, and quite unable to break the old habit of assuming that everywhere is bugged. And yet, bless her, she's got a fine sense of comedy. She it was who pointed out to me how green the politicians are becoming: Chancellor Cabbage here, Prime Minister Watercress in Paris, Bush... Can the Democrats find a Senator Broccoli to run against him? Or maybe someone more radical – Governor Parsnip? Sorry, this was meant to be a memo for your files, not a whimsy. And I suspect I must several times have broken my resolve not to tell you things you already know far better than I ever shall. What nags at me, driving me to put it down on paper, is a sense of something congruent with what I have to say about the times Laclos and de Sade lived to see, the void – Pascal's *gouffre* – that follows a cataclysm. But that's not quite palpable: every time I look straight at it it vanishes, and I suppose it's no more than the bee in the bonnet that buzzes, for example, every time you find a new word and then the new word finds you three times in a week. The grooved mind.

5. Sanssouci. I'll make no apology here for recycling what you have seen for yourself, because you cannot have seen all I saw. I walked through the gate expecting, I suppose, something like Versailles. I was certainly unprepared for that stunning vista between the two facing palaces, and above all the surrealism of the huge, sooty statues lined up along the parapets of the old palace, as though giant insects inhabit the place and swarm up on to the roof to watch your approach. You have walked slap into a De Chirico painting. Yes, the park nods to the old geometrical tyranny of Louis XIV, a bush lined up with every bust. But it is all so much more playful, made for pleasure not pomp. The rococo jokes, the chinoiserie, the cherubs with nice little behinds, the red brick to counterpoint stone. I remembered how Frederick had sardonically welcomed Voltaire here by having the guest room repapered with peacocks, and I imagined Old Fritz in his shabby blue coat laughing to himself with that mouth too toothless to play the flute any more. More recently, perhaps Brecht laughed at a place that must have cost millions of pints of sweat to build and then called itself Sanssouci. It was a warm, sunny-cloudy day. I skipped a session that included Jenene Allison on Riccoboni (but Jenene will forgive me, I've read her paper) and wandered around the park, which is rank with nettles, daisies, buttercups, dandelions. The botanical house has wonderful succulents, and outside it a place to sit among violet-edged white tulips and reflect that the DDR must have spent plenty to preserve this imperialist pile. Near the orangery I came across a line of stalls trading in Red Army caps and shapkas, Russian dolls of Gorby and the Politburo, old DDR carplates. How soon bad memories turn into souvenirs. Nearer the palaces is a more extensive trading area. Quiet, well-behaved people, impressed by the surroundings, wait in

13

parallel lines to buy frankfurters or Hartmut Müller's Method for Success. More sinister are the Buddhist stalls, selling salvation for capitalist souls. Some sort of festival calling itself "The Power of Vision" is going on. Any lost soul who shows interest in the literature on the stalls is invited to sit among the chestnut trees, under a little vinyl pyramid on poles, and have her or his eyes opened by a cross-legged initiate. God, how I loathe those who market their redeeming visions of the world (knowing, yes, that I am paid to teach literature, I acknowledge the irony in my soul). Just to shrive my scorn, I went and sat on a carpet with one of them. He had robes and a shaven head, spoke passable English, and I recognised his power of vision when I saw his eyes constantly flickering up my skirt, which was too short to pull right over my knees. So then I leaned forward, kneeling, and said, "Your furtive lechery is merely pitiful. Your mystical sales-patter is contemptible." I doubt if he understood a word but his face was stone, pink stone. I quit the park through that wrought-iron gate with a blazing sun royally mounted on it, and walked back to the Wildpark station. On the way I passed a yard where restoration work is being done. What a great shame, they are going to replace those giant sooty insects with newly carved white ones. I leaned on the gate and gazed. Each blackened, ancient marble Apollo or Venus stood next to an exact modern copy of itself.

6. Finally – and probably all you really want from me – a note on my own session at the Colloquium. I was allocated to a chemistry lecture theatre in the old palace, with the periodic table of elements on the wall behind me. Peeling ceiling, dusty wooden floor, but an agreeable, atmospheric place, seating about 130. Every seat was filled – a tribute not to me, I fear, but to the stir that the discovery of the Laclos/Sade memoir has produced among 18th-centuryists. It was Whit Sunday, a day for tongues of flame. *Meine Damen und Herren*, I began, I am sorry that I cannot speak German, but I assume that at so international a conference my English will be understood. Then

14

I made a few impromptu remarks. I would not spend much time, I told them, in speculating on the authenticity of the manuscript. Let's wait till it comes back from forensics. For now, I shall proceed on the assumption that it is genuine, and therefore the most remarkable discovery in the field since de Sade's bitterly lamented *120 Days* turned up again behind a brick. I shall also, I told them, eschew any reinterpretation of Laclos, or de Sade, from the evidence of the memoir, because tomorrow it could be declared a fake and I would look a fool. What I propose chiefly to do is to offer an account of the rest of Laclos's life, after he left the Picpus, so as to round off the memoir. And this is an appropriate time to do so, not because of the controversial discovery, but because on 18th October we shall celebrate the 250th birthday of the author of *Les Liaisons Dangereuses*. My account will draw, naturally, upon the standard biographies by Dard, Caussy, and Georges Poisson's more recent work with its new research, but in the spirit of the memoir I shall fill in the gaps that biographers must leave by taking some slight imaginative liberties, though nothing as imaginative as those that de Sade routinely took. (Not a laugh, barely a smile on any wan face.) A literary historian need not, I believe, be tethered by the scruples of conventional historians. We deal daily in fictions, dramatisations. I have for some years now allowed my own praxis to borrow the techniques of those I am discussing. The criterion is not fact but truth, and truth is found by indirections only. For us, history is a story, a narrative. A narrative has a narrator. A narrator has a mind, a mind of her own. (The argument always unsettles a few of my students. Here, it seemed to unsettle every philologist in the room. Yet they must have known whom they were inviting, no? Or maybe Schultz had told them nothing about me. Anyway, I was committed.)

Then I delivered my paper – copy herewith, at the back of the copy you asked for of the translated memoir.

1

We toss up. The coin spins a bright silver arc through the beams from the barred window. While this second in time is the quick, living moment and any future could be seized, it might be *my* confession, taken down by him. But he wins.

I tell him that my eyes are bad, have been for years, in the Bastille I had to be visited every week by the oculist Poirier, every week on Wednesday mornings at 10.20, I wouldn't let him into my cell until that minute, every week for forty-nine weeks, I counted of course. That forty-ninth week, at 10.32, Poirier said to me, "Have you considered ceasing to abuse yourself? It might help."

I threw him out, took him by the scruff, dragged him to the door, he was spluttering, his spectacles fell off, I trod on them deliberately, ground them under the heel of my boot, hurled him into the passage and tossed his mangled spectacles after him. "I have never abused myself," I shouted. "It is you I abuse." I slammed the door on him.

They are no better now, my eyes, five years later and how many agonies of orgasm? It makes no difference to Laclos, my bad eyes. He has won, he insists. His will be the luxury of which we find we both have dreamed, in prison and out, the service of a scribe. To write without the hand cramping after half an hour so you force it to go on, go on writing, and the letters get smaller, the tiny words start to curl up on the sheet, sentences twist away into the margin like smoke, your thumb aches so much that it will not keep up with your thoughts, your imagination is on fire but only half of it can be got down in time. To speak, and see your words recorded, yes, on that we have dared to confide and to agree, if on little else.

Earlier, I had tried to draw him on our shared loathing for

Rousseau, but he would not admit to it.

"*La Nouvelle Héloïse* is the most sublime of novels," he said.

I know, I answered, *so you must detest him?*

His thin lips twitched, but all he said was, "The *Confessions* were published in the same year as my book."

Well, then, I said. *You have written, so they tell me* (never would I admit to having read his damned book), *you have written your own travesty of* La Nouvelle Héloïse, *and so have I. Now it is time, surely, that one of us write our riposte to his confessions?* And so I proposed that we toss a coin to determine who should confess and who be scribe. He was seated in the dark corner of the room, yet I could see that the idea touched him where it tickled, in spite of his haughty dislike of my company. *If we are in this place long enough*, I added, *later we will reverse the rôles.*

"Oh, we shan't be," he answered. He twitched his lips again. I could tell that he was a practised lip-twitcher.

I gasped, involuntarily. (I despise involuntariness, aspire to master myself at all times. But we are in the confessional here, bless me, and though the toss be lost, still I might palimpsest some confessions of my own over those I am supposed to be recording with a plume plucked from an angel.) Why I gasped was because I was struck by the dreadful ambiguity of Laclos's twitch. Is it the asinine, stoical twitch of a man who can see the blade chopping closer and closer to where we both sit, like a cook's knife along a courgette?

I had to distract my fears. And so I brought out a coin and spun it. He called heads, and he won.

Very well. If the story is his, the telling will be mine. I give him warning of that, as one departicled citizen to another. If we cannot speak the truth now, when shall we? I believe that every lie that could have been told in the world has been computed in these past few years. Wicked lies, wicked. Why is a lie so much more potent than a truth? Why did my mother-in-law's lies turn the key on me for so many years, when not one of my pregnant verities could prevail? I warn him, too, that my prison writings have proved to be extremely perishable. Look at what I've lost.

The best of me, my essence.

He coughs on to the back of his hand, avoids my eyes, and begins.

§ The most beautiful object in the world

"I shall start with what is most important, since we do not know how far we shall get before we are released."

A title, I say. *Should we not begin with a title? Unless even books are guillotined for bearing a title now.*

"Oh." He flaps his fingers at me. "Just head it as though it were a memorandum."

Citizen Sade's Memoir of Conversations with Citizen Laclos in the Picpus Funny Farm – how does that sound?

"Call it an asylum, to be safe, in case the document should fall into other hands."

Oubliette?

"Asylum."

I shrug. *You're the dictator.*

He makes a spire of his fingers. "The most beautiful object in the world is a 24-inch cannon. Have you ever examined one?"

I've seen them. But I was a cavalry officer.

"What rank?"

Colonel.

"Of course." He glances down at my boots. He has a curious way of moving his eyes while keeping his head as still as a mantis. "You should examine one, as you would examine a classical sculpture. They are cast in bronze, and would acquire that patina of verdigris that a sculpture has were they not cleaned and polished every day after firing practice. In the casting they are ornamented with the arms of France in relief. You can trace it with your fingertips. Bronze is a metal one aches to touch, don't you find?"

It has the texture of human skin, you mean?

21

He smiles thinly, keeping his lips closed. "There you have it." He clears his throat, and speaks rapidly. "A 24-inch cannon weighs nearly two and a half tons, and will project a ball of twenty-four pounds close on a mile and a quarter if the angle of aim be forty-five degrees."

An angle of perfection, I remark. *An angelic angle. How can you be sure of it?*

"There are calibrations, of course. You have an interest in geometry?"

Oh, more than an interest, citizen. I am devoted to all branches of mathematics, believing that in the mystery of numbers we may divine our only sure knowledge of what is, and is to be.

He nods. "My own interest in the science is no less intense, though more practical. For twenty-seven years I studied and taught geometry, mechanics, the calculus, trigonometry, three days a week, always theory on market days, when explosions might have disturbed commerce, fifty-two weeks a year, except during leave, for twenty-seven years, citizen. Not to speak of physics, the chemistry of powder, the drawing of diagrams, the study of the art of fortification, of building materials, batteries, saps, trenches, terrain, the disposition of the guns. I have been as wedded to geometry as Plato was in Syracuse."

And as Archimedes too, I add. *You know that when he was killed in the siege of Syracuse it was while he was gazing upon a diagram? I have always supposed it was the death he would have chosen, and did choose, perhaps.*

"And in those twenty-seven years, can you guess how often I commanded *Fire!* upon an enemy, in siege or in campaign?"

Many, many times, I murmur.

"Never." With a sigh he falls silent.

Through the dank smell of the room, compounded of damp plaster and the powder that occasionally puffs from Laclos's wig and drifts down the sunbeams, I detect something more wholesome – potatoes, leeks, carrots, and mutton, I guess. *Come,* I urge him, *they will be serving our lunch very soon. We must …*

"Never," he interrupts me.

But I understood that you were at the Battle of Valmy. Were you there,
as they said, only to spy on that old bugger Lückner? God rest his soul, he
was trimmed last month, so I heard.

"I was not there at all. I had left the very day before the guns
spoke. I was at the Ministry, giving Servan my account of the
dispositions, when word came that Dumouriez had outflanked
them, cut their lines of communication, Kellermann and
Beurnonville had crushed them with volley upon volley from
the cannons, the fate of France had been gloriously settled,
Brunswick and seventy thousand Austrians were trudging home
in the rain, a steam rising from their uniforms, and I – I had
been in the coach on my way back to Paris." He kneads his
eyes.

I think it proper to observe a respectful silence, as though he
has announced a bereavement.

When he pulls himself together, he continues, quietly, "With
your interest in geometry, I wonder that you chose the cavalry
rather than the artillery."

I wanted to cut a dash, I reply. *Leaning from the saddle at full gallop*
hacking into Prussian necks, that is what I enjoyed at the age of seventeen.
What men call courage. It sits lighter on my conscience than would the
delivery of death by trigonometry from a mile away. I watch him,
sadistically, and see him take it as badly as I hoped.

"You were in battle at seventeen?"

I sit back on my bench. *It was expected. I am of course merely*
Louis Sade, President of the Les Piques section, a magistrate, a thoroughly
worthy and humble citizen, who find myself confined here only through the
vindictiveness of one woman, my mother-in-law, whom I could have had
guillotined simply by divulging her particle, de Montreuil, but forbore with
a Christian forgiveness with which I astonished even myself, though I
confess there was no little pleasure in imagining her humiliation when she
heard about it, as I made damned sure she would – but, as in a bad
dream, I remember that I once had some paltry titles myself, encumbered
upon me at birth, and active service in the cavalry was what noblesse,
God save the mark, oblige. *But I digress. The pen is yours to command.*
You won the toss.

While I am speaking, Laclos stands up, turns his back on me, and is staring out of the window, his fingers writhing behind him. I wait. "You will not provoke me," he says finally, with a levelness of voice I have to admire. "I have been provoked by masters. The entire class into which you were born was a daily provocation to those like me who were not admitted into regiments of the line."

I pretend to be chastised by his dignity. I would bet that his piss comes out cold. And, besides, I don't know how much truth there is in those who say he has protectors at the very highest level, in the Directory even, else his affiliations must by now surely have led him to the Place de la Révolution with his shirt open.

He is studying me, a thing I hate. I bend my head and improve the calligraphy of a few of these words. Then he sits down again, and seems to have mastered his temper. "In what year were you born?" he asks me.

In 1740. In the Comtat Venaissin.

"Ah. A year before I came plum-coloured and bawling into this world, with only three degrees of nobility, not four. My grandfather had purchased a secretaryship to the king, but my father could not improve our title. He spent his time in Amiens forbidding the planting of vines and promoting the erection of fountains throughout Picardy. My brother was born there, and sooner or later so was I. Would that it had been sooner, or later. That was my first mistake. All the rest have sprung from that. We came to Paris when I was ten. I grew up in the Marais. Just when it was time for me to prepare for a military career, the war against Prussia was started, and you might think that compe-tence, not quarters in the escutcheon, would have been the requirement. And what did the fools decide? They put a cuirasse in *your* hand, and in mine they put Bezout's mathemati-cal manual. I cannot pretend to have foreseen the revolution, but my God!, when I think back on the aristocracy who governed us then it is as though I hear the feverish, scraping song of insects who have only one day to live. What are they –

where you grew up, in the Midi?"

Cicadas?

"Yes. Like Lafontaine's cicada, who made no provision for harder times. Although that fable will not truly apply, you know. It was the ant who cried hunger, millions of ants."

And held the cicadas responsible for the winter winds.

"Hmm. My brother read Lafontaine to me before I knew how to read for myself. And so I tried my hand at verse, later. Take this down:

> On the buds of Isabelle
> I laid my head when but fifteen.
> O tender ecstasy, you well
> Before we can know what you mean."

Without looking up from my scribbling, I remark that at fifteen I knew perfectly what that welling ecstasy meant.

I don't think he hears me. He is saying, "The one good fortune in my life, which redeems all the rest of it, is to have learned in time that true happiness can exist only within the bosom of the family. I wrote the poem immediately after reading *La Nouvelle Héloïse*, in my first year in uniform. And even today, when I read that marvellous novel again, which I do once a year with my wife, and now my children too, I am transported back thirty years. I am sitting in an armchair, my red waistcoat is hanging loose on me, a downdraught is puffing acrid smoke from the fireplace into my nostrils, but I turn the pages avidly. Until I turn the last one, nothing will interrupt me. When I finished it, I did not know what to do with myself. I remember pacing around the room, sighing aloud. And then I simply had to write some words of my own, and that is what I wrote. It is naïve enough, I acknowledge now, but by the time I had polished it I was well pleased with it. I even had the fancy of sending it to Rousseau, but lacked the audacity."

With a tap on the door, an old man comes in with Laclos's lunch on a tray. Several of us employ him as our cook. Seeing me, he says, "Ah, Citizen Sade, this is where you are. I did take

25

your tray into your room, but I found it empty, and so I left it there for you."

Would you be so good as to fetch it? I ask. *As you see, I am engaged with Citizen Laclos.*

"Of course, of course," he says, bows, and hobbles off.

"You don't mind?" Laclos asks, indicating that he will start to eat.

Bon appétit.

"Hmm," says he, chewing a potato, "I find that appetite has little to do with eating in this place. But when I was a subaltern I learned economical habits. Supper without soup."

You are spoiled by your wife's cooking, no doubt. In the Bastille I used to insist that my wife brought my favourite delicacies in for me.

"Oh," he waves his fork, "my wife sends the girl once a week here. She doesn't come herself. It's too dangerous, Paris, now. But every Sunday I get a basket with food, clean clothing, newspapers."

Those little damsons in cherry brandy, you know? I sigh. *But now there is nobody to supply me, and so I content myself with sending out for some particular indulgence when my tongue is coated with tedium.*

"A few weeks ago she even sent me a poem she'd written. I had sent her a lock of my hair, saying that she had her children's first locks so here was my last, and in return I received two touching verses. The metre was faulty, but I amended it for her while the girl waited."

Your last lock, did you say? I hear myself gasp again. *So you do not expect we shall get out of here alive?*

"Oh yes I do. But freedom, though a blessing, will not make my hair grow. Were I to remove this wig, my pate might serve you as a shaving-glass. Now, where was I?"

Rousseau.

"Ah. Well, enough of him. My daytime reading was Bezout, for ballistics, triangulation, and so forth, and Saint-Rémy's memoirs for discipline and etiquette, riding, fencing, even dancing. I was never good at dancing, but I appreciated the disciplined formations of it."

And you fought duels?

"Never. Not even that. Not even a little pistol fired in anger. My God! On my coat of arms I should inscribe: *Montreal, Pondicherry, Rossbach, Valmy,* the roll of battles in which I did not fight. I was promoted second lieutenant into the 7th Brigade, which was raised for colonial service, and sent to embark at La Rochelle, but before we could set sail Choiseul had made peace with every nation on earth, damn his eyes! Damn the eyes of every aristocratic arsehole who used to preen himself on his perch of power. Because of them I spent my time in La Rochelle defending tradesmen and fishermen."

My lunch has been fetched. I eat with one hand and continue to hold my pen in the other, so as to have done as soon as possible. Then it will be my turn. *Tell me,* I say, *just now, in your vehemence, you referred to aristocratic arseholes. Have you any views on arseholes that might entertain posterity?*

"I regret the word. I was overwrought. Strike it out and put 'fools'. There were so many fools. I served the greatest fool of them all for years, without recognising what he was. The wonder is not that the people revolted, it is that it took them so long to smell the rot in the head of the body politic, and slice it off." He removed a blade of leek from his back teeth. "When they did, it was through starvation, not indignation."

I *shall never believe it was the people did it even then,* I remark. *It was your crowd of Rousseauesque bien-pensants at the Jacobins who made a revolution of it, peace be upon them. The people would have settled for bread at eight sous.*

Those mantis eyes, glittering in his shadowed face, catch mine. "Yes," he goes on, "I've often heard that said. In order to say it, all you have to do is ignore the history you have lived through. Disregard those scandalous chronicles which, however distasteful they were, at least served notice that the stink of rank aristocracy had been sniffed throughout France. I once went into a barrack room and discovered fifty-eight soldiers spilling their seed while one, the only one who could read, was reciting from one of the pamphlets vilifying Marie-Antoinette for every perversion. Some were assisting each other. It was utterly disgusting, yet it struck me as a scene that deeply menaced Versailles. Believe me, Sade, none of it would have been possible, thinkable, without the people had already ceased to be blinded by the glint of a golden crown. There have been excesses – who will deny it? – but I am ardent for the principle of what has been done, and will never be undone."

In that case, why have they locked you up in here?

"It won't be for long." He sets his plate aside, and with a handkerchief wipes the corners of his mouth. "So let us not flag, now we have made a start. I would like to get to the end. How is your thumb?"

I will tell you when it gives out.

"Very well. We are at La Rochelle, a town that will later become dear to me. But that first tour is a hateful memory: the first visit of the vulture to feed on my liver. I thought we were marching to the real thing, but instead it is merely a different, identical polygon, three days a week, before dawn, unhitch the carriage, manhandle into position, swab the barrel, prime the lantern, plug, ball, plug, elevation, fire, and watch for the thousandth time as a cloud of dirt erupts in no man's land. Once I saw a subaltern signal fire and lose his arm as he brought it down – he was standing too close in front of the cannon, and probably the fuse had been lit prematurely – but he was a viscount and bought himself a captaincy a few months later, so no one felt sorry for him. His was the only blood I ever saw, apart from the cuts that the uncouth men were always inflicting upon themselves. They are so maladroit, most of them. I wonder we have carpenters and joiners to furnish our houses for us."

I hear that in India the English bind savages to the muzzle.

"Only as a punishment."

One wouldn't forget the lesson, I allow. *But are you sure? A nation that roasts its own children for supper when the larder is bare …*

"I found the English quite civilised when I was in London. Cold, but in the way of privacy, not cruelty."

Is there a difference? Both manners are contemptuous of what another party might desire.

"But that is true of all human behaviour, except within the bosom of the family."

I have to tell you, Laclos, that I hope never to know a more poisonous bosom than my mother-in-law's. An asp would meet its doom down there. She represented herself as devoted to correcting what she saw as faults in my temperament. O, I boil. It is not for the vicious to presume to reform vice, it can be done only by virtue, and the most limpid virtue at that. It was not for Madame la Présidente de Montreuil, cousin, niece, parent, God-daughter and foster-mother of the wickedest frauds from Cadiz to Paris, Madame la Présidente, niece to a villain sent packing from the Invalides by Choiseul for embezzlement and extortion, la Présidente, whose husband's family numbers a grandfather hanged in the Place de Grève – or should I now term it Place Grève? – who presented her husband with seven or eight bastards and prostituted all her daughters, it was not for her to repress faults of temperament of which one is not master and which have never harmed a fly. That is what I found in the bosom of my family. A nest of vipers.

"I am truly sorry for you. For myself, were it not for the contentment I have enjoyed within my family, I am sure that I would have cut my throat long ago. But where were we? Still at La Rochelle, still there. I am standing on the polygon on a grey morning, the gulls mew into an iron sky at every explosion, I am dressed in blue, red, and gold, below my tricorn my regulation eight inches of hair – ah, my own hair – tied with a black ribbon is bobbing on my collar of copper, I have awoken to the cold and stench of a barracks, and all I have to dream of is the salon tonight. There I hold myself elegant and inscrutable among the smiling and the pouting, the silences and hints, knowing that two hours from now I shall purchase a whore and spend my hope in shame."

He has half-turned his face to the light, sitting daintily on one buttock, and I see the sunbeams glint in his blue eyes. How narrow he is, I think to myself. From the waist to the shoulder he must weigh half what I do.

29

You couldn't cut a dash with the young ladies of the salon?

"I was lacking in witty conversation about the trading price of indigo, which was all the matter spoken of. Well, cotton sometimes. At La Rochelle they draw a chain across the harbour mouth at night, and I used to stand in the salon and reflect that they might as well chain up my mouth for all the traffic it would enjoy. But the words I did not speak were not lost words. I stored them up in here. My cranium was my magazine."

My thumb is aching and my eyes are sore, I tell him. *Are we near the end?*

"The end of what?"

Of your confession.

From the shadows where he sits I can perceive his eyes upon me. "We have hardly made a beginning."

As I gather up these pages, he asks me to leave them for him to look over. *No, no, Citizen,* I say. *Much of it is in my own code, which you could not decipher. At the end I will furnish you with a transcription of the whole. You will be better placed then to judge the exordium and peroration of it.*

Naturally, the truth of it is that every sheet of his soul's masturbation I intend to destroy before they come for me.

2

Something is going on, and I do not like it. Governor Coignard has been here on two consecutive days, which has not happened before in my month in the Picpus, and today he was accompanied by the slavering dog Dupommier, with two subordinate police curs cringing at his heels, yearning to be kicked. If I could accept that it were 4 floréal I might not be particularly anxious, but the unfortunate truth is that it is really 23 April, 23-4, a malign sequence. They are guillotining a dozen every day now, it's said. How do they select the ripe ones? My belief is that Dupommier has yelped at Coignard that the Picpus must supply its quota. "All the other prisons have been doing their best, Monsieur Coignard, but quite simply they are running out of heads. You must pick some from your store. Fresh, juicy heads are required daily."

Unlike some I could mention, I have no protectors in high places. I have nobody. I am completely, desolately abandoned, a 54-year-old orphan. My God, if they can murder Danton, what price a marquis accused of moderatism? Dupommier, hot saliva dribbling from one corner of his mouth, wheels around and stares up at my window, as though estimating whether with one bound he could be inside and tearing out my throat. I shrink back against the wall, remain stock still, though I thought my heart would knock its way out through my ribs.

"There is no cause for alarm," Laclos says when I ask him about it. "When did you see them take anyone from here? It is designated as a house of detention, not as a prison. Frankly, it would do no harm if they cut our numbers. I find the noise intolerable, especially in the evenings, don't you?"

That is when many of them like to have women in, I answer.

"Quite." He closes his eyes and grimaces demurely. "Most

31

of the men live two to a room, what's more."

That suits the whores. It saves them time.

"Sade ... What effect do you suppose it has on the morality of the men? Can you imagine anything more degrading?"

I have spent my life imagining things more degrading, I tell him. *As you surely must have heard.*

He shrugs. "People talk. I read *Thérèse Philosophe* when I was a young man, and I am told that what you write is in that vein of indecency, which is not to my taste. But no matter. What we write is not what we are."

No matter? My blood is still coursing hot from the sight of Dupommier's muzzle sniffing for me, and I am in no mood to indulge Laclos's refinement. *I am absolutely what I write,* I retort. *This treacherous body of mine, this blubbery gut I have grown, with a recalcitrant tool dangling beneath it, this gouty face, this fat rump jutting out behind me, even the hairs that persist in sprouting from my toes, do you really believe that this is what I am? No, no. What you see squatting here is a joke played upon me by our most malevolent of enemies, Nature. But I have conquered Nature, Laclos. I have invented a dignity for my life. Read what I have written, such of it as survived the Bastille, and then dare, if you can, to tell me that the best, the truest of me is not there, in what I have risked all to imagine.*

It is as though I have been hammering at his door and found nobody at home. "Blanchard did warn me," he says, "that it might be necessary for me to share this room, if they continue to cram new people into the Picpus. I told him that I will pay double rather than put up with that. It was vexing enough when they used to come a-visiting every afternoon – you know? I'm sure they tried to inflict themselves on you, too. As though it weren't penance enough to be shut away in here, without being called upon to converse civilly with dullards, as if it were a salon for soldiers. The most malevolent of our enemies is not Nature, as I am sure you know, but boredom, and the worst boredom of all is not inactivity but the company of dull wits. That is why I am entertaining this notion of dictating my stories to you. You may be vicious, as I have been told, but I doubt you are dull.

32

And if you are, or if I am, well, we have at least chosen our tedium. Tell me, why did you come to me with the idea?"

Because I hoped to win the toss.

"I see." He pauses. "What you said just now about your writing reminds me of the *risqué* pieces I once wrote. There was a poem called *The Procession*. A maiden called Lison is to carry a candle from the church, but her cousin Lubin delays her. She is just changing into votive robes when she hears – too late – the procession passing below. She rushes and leans out of the window with nothing on her but a chemise, then falls to her knees in dismay, her eyes modestly lowered upon her firm white breasts, rising and falling to her sighs. And Lubin cannot but avail himself of her devout posture."

He buggers her?

Laclos has permitted himself a self-deprecating little smirk at his youthful indiscretions, but my question wipes his face clean. "Of course not. Why on earth should you think that?"

The devout posture sounds propitious. And I thought that perhaps you had endowed Lubin with enough wit to know what is most delicious.

"I abhor obscenity."

Then you must abhor Nature for providing us with the possibility.

Laclos speaks deliberately. "If the revolution were to yield just this one fruit, the liberation of women from the slavery in which they have been held by men, it would all have been worthwhile. Unfortunately, I do not see much chance of that."

I am not talking about liberation. You exasperate me with your high-minded translation of human nature into fantastic dogma. It is a woman's destiny to be wanton. She must belong to all who claim her.

"If that has any truth in it, it is because men have degraded women with their obscenities. In their natural state they are much lovelier and gentler creatures than you will ever know, if you are incapable of being satisfied by the normal act of love."

With the benefit of hindsight I prefer buggery. I used to compliment my wife on the snugness of her arsehole. He is gazing at me, shaking his head, with a thin, chilly smile. I can see he is going to hiss that he feels pity for me, or perhaps for my wife, so I forestall him.

My wife and I used to adore each other. I called her the fresh pork of my thoughts. She would procure wenches for me, and it was not she who was upset when I ran off with her sister, no, it was her bourgeois, dried-out hag of a mother, the merchant's wife, who decided that enough was enough. The truth is that enough can never be enough. Excess is the only road to freedom, citizen.

Laclos has raised his hand some time before I finish speaking. "Your opinions are vile," he says, "but what matters at the moment is that they are distracting me. It is my time to speak. I was discussing my poem, *The Procession*. Please resume your note-taking."

§ Victims of Reason

"In publishing such a poem, I ran a severe risk, you realise. It was only a few years earlier that a chevalier watching a religious procession omitted to remove his hat, and he had it removed for him by the executioner's axe. What penalty might have been visited upon me, had I been identified as the author?"

Everybody knew you were the author of that novel of yours, but that didn't get you into trouble, did it?

"It is not the same thing at all. My novel offended only aristocratic libertines, of whom you perhaps were one, at the time."

Citizen Laclos, to call me a libertine is to call the Pope a churchgoer. I have the most extreme contempt for those dilettantes of the boudoir. I would find seduction more tedious than fishing for trout. You should understand at once, if you really have not understood before now, that my sole project is to invent myself, and my method is to be even more vicious than Nature herself.

He shakes his head again. "I confess, I feel sorry for you, Citizen Sade."

Keep your altruism to yourself. Let me tell you something. Every aristocratic libertine who has spoken to me of your book has done so with little climactic screeches of adoration for it, and invariably confessed himself

34

to be the model for your hero. That is how much offence you gave them.

"And the women?" Laclos asks coldly. "What opinion of it have they expressed to you?"

I have never met a woman who has read it. But the sort of woman I have known ... I shrug, no need to continue, because I have already hit my mark. I see his mouth working. Then he favours me with the following narration, which I set down as punctiliously as I can, given the pain it is causing me in my thumb, and the waves of nausea that terror produces in me every hour I spend in this place. The sooner he is done, the sooner it will be my turn, and not the least pleasure will be to watch his face as he takes down the story I have to tell.

"Some have compared my novel to *Phèdre*. That is obtuse. Of Racine's passion there is no trace in my characters. Mine are victims of reason. I shudder when I think of them. They are hateful to me, because they are heartless. But note that, in consequence, they may be judged according to their conscience. It would be absurd to appeal to Phèdre's conscience. My creatures know what they are doing, and what the outcome will be. That is why I took an epigraph from Rousseau, to advise the reader that my sole concern was with the morals of *that* time, which is no longer our time. It is impossible to estimate what contribution I may have made to discrediting the aristocracy: but it follows that it is impossible to overestimate it. You may have heard dark rumours of the part I played in the revolution. They are without substance, save in this: by thrusting the old régime's putrefaction under the nation's nostrils I compelled people to turn away in horror and consider a better way."

He covers his mouth and performs his soft little cough, more like an aspirated sigh, really. God, how this man disgusts me, poised on one haunch and profiled, a leg crossed away from me, fingers resting on the kneecap. However, he serves to keep me from brooding on Dupommier.

"It was in Grenoble that I witnessed the *danse macabre* of the aristocrats. Until then I had suffocated in the mothball morality of the bourgeoisie. But now, on the Savoy frontier, the

35

ceremony of corruption was enacted daily for me, as though I were in a vivarium. When Monsieur le Mantis raises his lorgnette and rubs his dry legs together, Madame de la Moth pouts her painted lips and flutters her powdered bosom at him, and everyone else smiles sideways at each other because they know that it cannot be long before his fingertips are tracing the cleft between her buttocks, and his beak is tasting the juices of her scented white body. And while they groan together, thigh on thigh, each will be thinking only of how best to profit, in tomorrow's salon, from bragging of this latest victory of theirs. The men call it conquest, the women call it theft from each other, but no one ever, ever calls it love. To love is to be an occupied territory: one's strategy has been defective, one has omitted to defend a redoubt for a safe retreat.

"At concerts or on promenades, at the hunt in those barbarous mountains, or in the theatre's stink that a cloud of perfume adorns like the rictus on a corpse, all the talk is raillery against the Court. A thousand subtleties are found to mock the counts who snuff His Majesty's candles and the marquises who pass the royal salt. In the salon, no less than in the barracks, Her Majesty's lewd appetite is the favourite subject. 'What she adores most is to be coated in thick cream and licked clean by three of her paramours.' 'No, no, that was last month. Haven't you heard? Now she must lie legs open and straddled by a standing Adonis, bursting to go down on her but checked by cherubs, until his cannon bellows.'

"And just how many cherubs might be required is the topic of the salon at suppertime, when a few of us have the tact not to sample the conserve of plums, in grape jelly. Most aver that an infinity of curly cherubs would not suffice. I demur: let the Adonis be twenty and the cherubs five years of age, four cherubs, a total of twenty years, will be needed to restrain each side of the lusting folder of the napkins. The answer, I announce, is eight cherubs. This absurd proposition is acclaimed as though I had cited it from Euclid himself, which is why I had put it forth, for the pleasure of watching the only true enthusiasm, that of ignorance. A callow young poet, wishing to make an impression, asks, 'But what of the King? Does His Majesty collude in his wife's abandoned behaviour?' 'The King!' shrieks Mademoiselle d'Arachnida. 'The King! What of him? He is not the man he was.' 'He never was,' remarks Monsieur the Duc de Scorpion.

"At which I feel obliged, again, to demur. Louis, it is true, is a pathetic creature, but his head was anointed with holy oil at his Coronation and we must assume that his wife has not taken a fancy to lick it all away, else the State is without a foundation of any kind. 'Mock Louis,' I advise the company, 'but do not mock the King.'

"All eyes are upon my blue eyes, which arouse discomfiture, I have been told by a confidante, as does my svelte figure in black satin, and my cold humour, and now my metaphysics. I see a muttering behind raised hands, while the band scratches over some tedious Austrian quartet. Our hostess, seeking to rally her troops, sniffs: 'Monsieur Choderlos de Laclos speaks as though he had found the truth served upon his plate, although I cannot remember supervising its preparation in the kitchen.' 'No, Madame,' I reply, never smiling, 'I respect all who seek the truth, but fear those who say they have found it.'

"My sally serves to extricate her. She allows herself a light laugh, and a turn of her fan. She would be afraid to be left alone with me, I know. That, too, my confidante reported to me. My own fear is to find myself facing her in the gavotte. She dances with a grace that can only be called bovine.

"My malady was what it always has been, and still is here, in the Picpus. I cannot tolerate tedium, Sade. I assuaged it then by my talent for asking questions."

And now? I ask. *Is it assuaged by putting me to this misery of scribble-scribble?*

"I am quite enjoying it, to my surprise. I have never dwelt on the past with anyone, except my wife, and expected that by now I would have dismissed you, and busied myself with the lessons in book-keeping that I have been giving to a couple of our

37

fellow inmates. I am also preparing a new lexicon of French grammar, which is needed, as I know from my daughter's difficulties."

You cannot dismiss me before I have had my turn, I shout. *That was our agreement.* You *cannot dismiss* me *at all. I am still the Marquis de Sade and the Comte de Mazan.*

"That is true," he answers, "but it were better whispered."

I clap my hand to my mouth, then find it moving down to my throat, forfending yellow fangs tearing into my flesh. *If there is no cause for alarm,* I murmur, *then tell me, why is Dupommier here at all? I am frightened, Laclos. I have seen too much, more than anybody should. Tell me something to comfort me, even a lie.*

His upper lip moves, revealing his teeth, and for the first time he leans, slightly, toward me. "The only time in my life I ever heard anyone speak of you," he says, "you were calling yourself the Comte de Mazan then. It was at that period when I was in Grenoble. They were looking for you. They wanted to hang you."

That is not true. What they wanted was to behead me. Before which, I was to have expiated my so-called sins at the Cathedral porch in Marseilles. And after which, my ashes were to be strewn to the wind, the only provision of my sentence which I found acceptable. They can make a stew of my bones and serve them up with dill dumplings, for all I care. But I haven't finished with my bones yet, Laclos. Can't you get Poignard, I mean Coignard, to call Dupommier off me? You have influence. Haven't you? Everyone says you have. Please.

"Yes, I remember now, you were the talk of the salon one evening. They said you had committed sodomy upon your manservant, and taken refuge in the mountains."

Not upon but with. He was there with me, not in the mountains but in the Château de Miolans, over the Savoy border. Not refuge but custody. My wife had to bribe the guards to get me out. O, I boil. What business was it of theirs, what it pleased me and Latour to do together? I would have been let off with a reprimand and covert winks of gratitude had I been found guilty of fucking all my judges' wives, severally and, to finish, ensemble.

"Please." He has raised the palm of his left hand at me. "I can feel pity for soldiers when I hear their monotonous obscenity. If you and I are to spend much more time together in here, you must restrain yourself. You have all the advantages of the class into which you were born. You must have studied rhetoric, and Greek, and astronomy. Do not trail your mind in the filthiest gutters as though it were a ruined cloak. All your timidity, your imagined terrors when a police inspector pays a routine visit here, would evaporate if you would but bend your mind to higher, finer things.

"And besides, you disgust me. Do you understand? You represent that betrayal which I despised in Grenoble. You have been educated, you have even written a book, so you say. And yet you wallow in filth like a honking pig. Remember what Shakespeare wrote: 'Lilies that fester smell far worse than weeds'."

He nods, just once, content with his ludicrous homily, so neatly pointed with an apt quotation, just as he had been taught to do by teachers who spent the whole class yearning to ram their prick between his tight buttocks. "Even in the salon," he is going on, "there were weeds, privileged weeds. A woman whose pretty eyes distracted a man from her stupidity. Them I could pardon. They were not to blame. One could even derive a rather sad amusement from them. I caused a scandal with a squib I wrote. How did it go? – take this down:

> She was born in a pit,
> Her titles are hollow.
> And Margot's wit
> Is an easy act to follow.
>
> O face divine,
> You'll pay no heed
> To words of mine.
> You've never learned to read.

"There was more. They did pay heed, believe me. At first they said that my Margot – everyone knew she was my invention, even though I never acknowledged my authorship – she must be the Marquise de Pompadour, but that didn't satisfy their appetite for scandal, because la Pompadour had died, so then they declared, no, it is a vilely witty assault on the Comtesse du Barry, whom the King had just presented at Court. The truth is that it was aimed at all of them, all those pathetic creatures who were scouted out for the royal bed.

"One of the first stories one was told at that time, on arriving in Grenoble, was that Casanova, a few years previously, had leaned over during a concert and whispered into the ear of one such ravishing little thistledown-head that it would not be long before she found herself measuring her back upon the silken sheets at Versailles. And within a year that very Mademoiselle Coupier had been transfigured into Mademoiselle de Romans and had given birth to the Abbé de Bourbon."

He pauses, looking up at the barred window, his back almost wholly turned to me. Then he says, "That is enough for today."

What? I stare at him. *Citizen Laclos, you cannot suspend your narrative at so tantalising a moment. Pray, continue, at least to conclude your account of Grenoble, now so revolutionary a city.*

"No. The memory of it has oppressed me. Tomorrow we march to Besançon.

Damn you, I shriek. *What am I to do, then? Go to my room and sit on my own and suffer a thousand tortures of fear every time I hear a booted footstep in the corridor?*

"The remedy is to hand. Concentrate your mind on transcribing those notes for me to read. I would be much obliged if you would supply me with a fair copy after each day's dictation, so that I may judge the accuracy of the work we have done together, and perceive what omissions need repair."

Oh, what beautifully polished periods you speak in when you are high on your horse. I marvel at that, citizen. All around us we hear men and women talking in rags of French, often with scarcely a main verb to share between them, let alone nicely placed subordinate clauses. And this through no lack of education, but because they are terrified, and bewildered, from the moment they open their eyes in the morning. All they dare to do is exclaim. But you – you speak as though God were still residing in Versailles and eggs were sold for twenty sous.

"I am in my fifty-third year. It is too late for me to alter the way I was taught to speak."

Even though everything else in the circumstances of your life has been altered unrecognisably?

"That is not the case."

Then you did not embrace the revolution? I had heard that you were on intimate terms with Danton, and some even say with Robespierre himself.

"Politics has nothing to do with it. I mean that the central stone on which my life is founded is my wife, and she and I have not altered toward each other, whatever storms may have been blowing beyond our hearth."

You are uncommonly fortunate. Every other hearth has had its cosy fire scattered by a gale coming down the chimney.

"You are playing with metaphors." He has his forefinger across his mouth, and is sucking on it. "It is an idle game."

He may be right. I do not care. What matters to me is that it distracted him from his request for a transcription, as though he were a debate and I merely the recording secretary.

In all he has said, one thing intrigues me, and he has not said it yet. There is something about his discontent in Grenoble twenty years ago that I can sniff. Some score being settled. I sniffed it in his book. I shall track it down and seize it in my teeth and shake it like a rat. Let him command me to transcribe that. It will be my pleasure, citizen.

41

3

I put some crumbs outside my window this morning and attracted three sparrows, but scarcely had they begun to eat when a black cloud covered the sky and the rain frightened my guests away. It has poured since. At least Dupommier may be discouraged from leaving the foul hole he will call home. In Laclos's room it is so dark that we need a lamp in the afternoon for me to write. It is on a low table. When Laclos tilts his head, as though to collect his thoughts in the back of his skull, his nostrils are illuminated, and the shadow of his nose is an eyepatch. The stink of burning oil is in my throat and my eyes; but we must go on.

§ Bad Faith

I let him ramble for a time. In 1775 – my, isn't he punctilious about dates? – after six years in Grenoble, his regiment is transferred to Besançon, where he is appalled to find yet another feeble fortification designed by Vauban, just as in Toul, and Strasbourg, and La Rochelle, and Grenoble. He will have more to say on Vauban, he reassures me. And no doubt on other piles of rotting bones. *De mortuis nil nisi bono*, I murmur. "Third declension, Sade," he clucks, "third declension."

Of his promotion to captain – after twelve years of service, he stresses (with a glare that lights up his wig) and unfailing eulogies in the annual inspection – and of his need, nevertheless, to enlist the influence of his masonic lodge in order to be given a rewarding office in his regiment, I will spare posterity a verbatim account, intending as I do to spare posterity any account at all of these conversations, once he has cast his eye over my scribbling and accepted that there is no remedy but to wait for me to decipher it. Though I shall favour posterity with the rat I have sniffed in Grenoble, if I can find a way to flush it out. Do not ask me why I am so kind to posterity, the very thought of which bores me to the same degree that history appals me. Why does any writer write? It is a more drastic act of faith than believing in God, and more painful to the thumb.

I think this rain has rusted his wits, because now he is back in his zigzag trenches for covert advance, simulating sieges with mortar fire, commanding sappers, bombardiers, gunners, telling me that men were punished with forty rifles on their backs for five hours, or for drunkenness having to drink a cask of water, but I am not to suppose that the junior officers were treated much less brutally, and their leave was only alternate winters, and the rest of their lives they spent amid two rush-seated chairs, a beechwood bed with curtains of Caen serge, towels changed weekly but bed-linen only fortnightly, a fireplace, a pisspot, a goosedown quilt, copper candlesticks – but, ah!, I see now, this has been a refutation preluding a grand peroration on the new uniform for our Royal Artillery.

O my chuck, I am not surprised to see you stand up in order to illustrate the breast-fluttering prettiness of a white waistcoat under a blue Habsburg-style coat with red trimmings, and blue trousers over that svelte arse of yours, and fleurs-de-lys and gold and red braids everywhere, and white feathers in your four-cornered hat. *My*, I say, *what a dash you must have cut. Now if only you had been so handsome in Grenoble, what a swathe you must have scythed through the demoiselles of that cultivated charnel-house.*

He sits down. "Perhaps I misled you in my account of Grenoble. A charnel-house may be what I have described, but it was not entirely without its charms for me."

Well, it is true that you have once or twice made reference to a confidante you had there. I did not suppose that you lived the existence of an anchorite.

"Oh, it was not her."

Who was not her?

44.

He shakes his head. "No."

After a while, he says, "Gambling was a popular pastime, and it epitomised the place. Pascal had bet on God; now all men had to bet on was women. There was no other risk. And their stake was their reputation, their manhood. But I have always liked women, just as Rousseau did, and I felt horror when I saw how men were treating them. And what rankled most was that the continually successful gamblers, in that game, were the very same sleek and purring aristocrats who, in uniform, enjoyed preference for promotion. They were a social plague, and I breathe more easily now we are rid of them."

He has stood up again, and is staring out at the rain, his fingers knitted behind his back. Through the window comes the smell of earth, and wet leaves. "The women had been corrupted," he continues, quietly. "They were willing agents, even enthusiastic, in their own profanation. All day they would rail ironically against Grenoble's excesses, and all night augment them. They were blinded by a bad faith. I almost said they lacked the courage to call the men's bluff, but that would not be just. It would be to blame them for not being heroic, such was their plight."

What you say is extraordinarily touching, I murmur as levelly as a confessor. *How did that bad faith express itself, in practice? Can you offer an example?*

"Well ..." He shrugs, and speaks as though to himself, still facing the window. "I remember one young woman, for whose mind I had the greatest respect. I forget her name now. She was married, to an elderly man. I was told a story of her entertaining a young poet in her boudoir, and the poet confides to her that he has written some verses in her praise. 'Please, do recite them to me,' she asks. 'I am a lover of poetry.'

"The young man is anxious not to omit or mangle a line of what he has written to her, and so proposes to go and fetch his verses. He does so, only to be met by the housemaid with the news that her mistress is indisposed. And from the boudoir he hears the sounds of laughter. The young woman, and a young man, some powdered fop

"I can assure you, Sade, that I knew that woman well enough to believe that she spoke in good faith when she asked to hear the verses. But she had allowed her spirit to be profaned.

"From that story I deduce this moral: Love levels, seduction betrays. And another conclusion may be drawn: when women are so subjugated – as they would sometimes confide to me they were, since they knew I was not one of their oppressors – then their seduction was a pathetic prize. Next day you would hear the man brag as though he had conquered Constantinople single-handed, and his friends laud him, when in truth it had taken hardly any skill at all. The chief skill required was to have been born with four degrees of nobility. In my book I pretended, in order to divert the reader, that seduction required a campaign as labyrinthine and geometrically executed as the most brilliant siege, and to raise excitement I posited as my Constantinople a devout prude, who has never allowed herself even to imagine the abandon of passion, and as her conqueror one who has undergone a long, hard training, as I had in the artillery. That was a conceit. The only impeccable campaign was one that I executed myself, in the planning of the fiction. A lesser story would not have been worth the conquest."

I have been nodding sagely, like a dog with a rat now dead in my jaws. Only through my astonishing art of self-control can I repress the most vulgar laughter, which I promise myself to indulge at length this evening, in my own room. It is beautiful, I think, very beautiful, citizen. It is so beautiful that it must be true. After I escaped from Marseilles, they executed my effigy, in the town square at Aix. But you have committed suicide on your own effigy. In your chaste, Northern, bourgeois nostrils, that stink of noble rot, which you feign to have despised, was an exhilarating musk. You dreamed of yourself in mirrors. You were drunk on secrets. And what horror, infinitely blacker than the pool of Narcissus, lay condignly in wait for you. O, you have made me happy. I cannot continue. I must go and hug myself. *Citizen*, I say, *I am feverish today. We will resume tomorrow.*

46

4

And so we do. To make up for yesterday's foreshortened labour, he rattles on from the start. Even now, it is hard for me to keep my face straight, as befits a scribe.

§ A Book without an Author

How can he convey to me, he wonders, his excitement when he heard that the American colonies had declared the Atlantic Ocean a natural frontier dividing them from the British? "I smelled a clean wind for the first time in many years, and I knew where it was blowing from: the future. Something modern, proud, was stirring in a fetid world. And I dreamed, alas, that I might soon be discharging a cannon on the field of battle.

"We were ordered from Besançon to Valence, and I was detailed to go in advance to set up our accommodations. I had done the same when we were posted to Grenoble, and won respect for the economical arrangements I secured, as well as for my culinary judgment, even if some criticised Rivière, our cook in Grenoble, for using too much garlic. For my pains they gave me a golden épaulette, and I sped by post carriage to Valence, twenty leagues a day for three days, and in that molehill of monks and nuns I did such good work that the townspeople received the regiment as enthusiastically as my comrades greeted the quarters I'd found for them. And before the year was out, that popinjay de Montbarrey, the one who kept his wife quiet by buying himself a princeship of the Holy Roman Empire, was told by his mistress, who ran the Ministry of War for him, that it had been an error. We were sent back to kick our heels in Besançon. Everyone knew that war was coming, British ships were off the Atlantic coast, one artillery regiment was sent to Le Havre, but our niche was Besançon. The frustration ... What could I do?"

I shrug. *Write a book?*

"Exactly."

I did the same. My prison of frustration was literally a prison. Is that why all the books have been written? Cervantes, after all. Malory. Have you thought of writing a book in here?

"I have nothing further to say."

Nor have I, but I intend to go on saying it.

"I wrote my book with an objective. Beyond the pettiness of military routine and the vacuity of salon gossip, I conceived that a republic of letters existed somewhere, enlightened minds who cared and reasoned about the condition of France. I wished to witness to them the decadence of the ruling class."

I'll bet even your farts smell of lavender.

"What?"

Just clearing my throat. Please continue.

"And while I was writing the book, Rousseau died, and, sad though I was, I felt as though a space had been cleared for me at the tribunal. I was even writing in the epistolary form, as though bidding to occupy his vacated seat.

"But at my writing-desk for three hours every afternoon, consumed by my own invention, I made a grave mistake, Sade. I counted on my readers to understand me. Laying siege to my subject, I was invisible in my zigzag trench. But had I stood up at every twist and blown a bugle and announced: 'These are contemptible people, dear reader. The wickedness they so admire in themselves is banal – merely the trick of controlling and humiliating their victims. But watch, and I will show you how they will all come to grief' – even then, I doubt if one in a hundred would have grasped my intention. And to make it worse, Durand printed it in duodecimo, as though inviting a clandestine reading. The effect was atrocious. The aristocrats did nothing but squabble over which of them could claim most credit as my models, and the bourgeoisie blamed me for celebrating the corrupt amusements of the aristocracy.

"It is still a bewilderment to me, a dozen years later. I thought the cause for which I fought was the belief that people are by nature good, if they are allowed to follow their spontaneous hearts in freedom, but that the old régime was pitiless in twisting and distressing human nature. Well, the régime was about to collapse, and who knows but that I may have added my straw to the camel's back? But there is the very point, Sade: who knows? Who *knows?*"

His voice has risen to anguish, his hands are grasping the air. He is falling into a pit, yet believes that someone, in the natural goodness of human nature, will surely throw him a rope in time. I reply, *Citizen Laclos, forgive me for saying this, being ignorant of the text of your book, but can you not accept that it is naïve to speak of your intention in writing it? Might it not be that your own motivations were mixed?*

"What do you mean?" He is standing to attention.

I mean nothing precise. I make only the general observation that we may know not what we do when we perform even the simplest act, and are correspondingly less likely to be enlightened about our reasons for writing a book.

"Speak for yourself, Sade."

I never do otherwise. But, if you will allow me to dwell for a moment in a sphere less elevated than yours, one of your intentions was doubtless to make some money?

He grunts. "Many assume that that is one's sole intention. I made only a little, and that paid to me late. There were of course a score of pirated editions, most of them from Switzerland, from which I did not get a sou."

And it must, further, have been your intention to make yourself noticed?

"If that were so, why would I have disguised my authorship behind initial letters only?"

To intrigue.

"Not at all. I wanted to produce a book without an author. I was, I supposed, addressing the libertine in every reader, that spirit which needs to read its own existence in the face of another. And instead of a face I offered a mirror. No one understood. They all thought like you, that I was being coy, and shortly everyone knew me to be the author.

"I had a distressing correspondence with Madame Ricoboni, who wrote to say she knew I had written the book, and how could I be so ungallant as to depict women as lustful and scheming creatures? Every woman she knew was ashamed to have read it, she said. But my book is a proof of how deeply I care about women, I tell her, and how can I care about them without conceding them a moral parity with men? Even a parity of evil, and futility? I asked her, why do you imagine I worked so hard to create the figure to whom you allude, Merteuil, who says that by the age of fifteen she had all the talents of a successful politician, and then learned more? It is to make her the equal of Valmont, to allow both of them a tender recognition in the other of how pointless their lives are. Merteuil is not crushed by misfortune. On the contrary, she knows exactly what a profanation of her grace is permitted her by rank and riches. If the law will not be the judge of such a woman – as it was not then, before the revolution – then the writer must be. I compared what I had written to a statue by Pigalle: under the flesh one perceives with dread the skeleton. If you and your friends, I concluded, believe that no such woman could exist in France, then why such sensitivity?"

Her reproaches sound like those a discarded lover might make, I remarked.

"Ha. There is that noise."

My question and his answer hang gaudily on the air for a few seconds, flittering around each other like tiny, iridescent-winged cherubs.

He shrugged. "She was a failed actress. She failed for twenty-five years. So she tried her hand at writing. Romances in pink ink about adolescent girls. I should not have responded to her at all, but I felt some obligation since we'd shared a disappointment a few years previously. In Valence, with nothing else to do, I read one of her books and was seized by the ridiculous idea of adapting it as a comic opera. Saint-Georges, that mulatto equestrian, wrote some tunes, and the thing was staged at the Comédie-Italienne, if you please, as though it were a worthy successor to *Andromaque*.

"Marie-Antoinette and the King's sisters are in the royal box. I have no idea what to expect. When Saint-Georges lifts his bâton and strikes the first beat, it is apparently a cue to the audience, because on the instant everyone begins to whistle and boo and stamp their feet and hurl artichoke leaves at the singers, and they keep that up till the end. You have to admire an audience with such stamina. One line alone wins general approval. A messenger had to call, 'Ohé! Ohé!' The entire house takes it up in unison. 'Ohé! Ohé!' they're all chanting. I see Marie-Antoinette leaving her box, and rush to introduce myself. As she comes down the staircase to where I'm waiting, she is calling over her shoulder to her sisters-in-law, *Ohé! Ohé!* They walk straight past me and into their coach, in fits of laughter, and I hear the Queen tell the coachman, 'To Versailles, ohé!'"

Oh dear, I tut. *A relatively unsuccessful première.*

"And *dernière*. I do not say that the piece was of any worth. But it might have been *Le Cid*, for all that audience allowed it to be heard."

I nod. *The audience is always responsible for the performance it sees. I have had comparable vexations from them. Three years ago, when I was released from Charenton, to distract myself from grieving over my masterpieces lost in the Bastille I scribbled some plays and had them performed at the Théâtre Molière. But your Jacobins did not approve of them because I had been a marquis.*

"Not *my* Jacobins, Sade. A fraternal society has no proprietor."

I spoke loosely, I reply. Mea culpa, *citizen*, mea maxima culpa, *and I swear to recite the name Maximilien Robespierre one hundred times after leaving here. But they were Jacobins, because they were wearing their red bonnets with the point forward, when they rose to denounce the piece, in*

51

the fourth scene. It had been going rather well, until their disturbance. I suspended all further performances, of course.

"Yes. One has one's pride, even in the theatre."

Yes. And, though an ex-marquis, one has one's head still on one's shoulders. I have sometimes wondered about that two-headed woman they used to exhibit at the Palais-Royal. Were she to take it into her heads to utter counter-revolutionary words, would they guillotine her at both necks, or only at the one deemed to have profaned? Citizen Laclos, I know that you have never in your life committed laughter, but could you not bring yourself to grease our intercourse by even a smile, sometimes, at my irrepressible frivolity? You know it springs from the terror in which I live every minute of my breathing life.

"Stop gibbering," he commands me. *Me.* "You have been a soldier, so you say. You should know that your best hope for survival is to remain absolutely calm. I have not yet explained the mission I was given at the Île d'Aix, while I was still writing my book. Are you composed enough to take this down?"

I nod. Damned if I'll take it verbatim. The Memoirs of a Retired Captain of Artillery who never Discharged so much as a Popgun at any Living Thing and whose Wife must resemble a Mammoth Frozen in Ice, as dictated by M. Pierre Ambroise François Choderlos de Laclos to his Ever Servile Clerk the Citizen Sade, né Donatien-Alphonse-François, the Comte de Mazan and Marquis de Sade, direct lineal descendant of the peerless Laure de Noves, whom Petrarch hymned.

He is saying he was officially attached to Field-Marshal the Marquis de Montalembert in order to assist with the fortification of the Île d'Aix against the threat that the offshore island of England might seize further offshore islands and use them as bases to raid France, a threat which materialised no more than our own dream of invading England, don't ask him why. This old Montalembert was possessed by a singular, violent bat in his belfry. The revered Vauban was *passé*. Advances in artillery tactics demanded a new design in fortification. The intimidating bastions within which Laclos had served for two decades, modelled by the hand that sketched Versailles, were monuments to seigneurial fear of the mob, and for soldiers defending them would serve only as grandiose coffins. What was required was a polygonal structure, within which the ingressor would be confounded by a labyrinth. "One presents one's sword to the enemy, not one's body," Montalembert devastatingly observes.

The old bird spent half his life writing a treatise on perpendicular fortification and tried to launch a subscribed edition of it, but the reading public were made to wait for that literary ravishment by the Ministry of War's objection to the disclosure of military secrets, in particular, no doubt, the confidential advice against shoving one's gut out for easy skewering. Eventually, he began to publish it, volume after volume, at his own expense. Moreover, sent to fortify the Île d'Aix, he does so according to his own notions and, to make his point about angles, rather than bastions, builds it in wood. Laclos, tail wagging, is delighted to bound around as second-in-command of something subversive. The Ministry let them pursue their folly, and when it's finished call it effrontery. One bombshell would reduce it to sawdust, they declare, a view they maintain even after 523 shells have not shaken it.

I remark that one has to admire the ministers of the old régime for their strength of character, but Laclos is in such a rage of memories that he can't hear me. Meanwhile the English have gone away again and collapsed at Yorktown, and Lafayette has gone after them, but poor Laclos is marooned with his little boy's wooden fort. He begs for more soldiers to be given him, pointing out that the fort's 286 beds could accommodate 858 men, but the Minister is cross with him. So, he says, he decides to follow the tradition of courting the general's wife, but Mme la Marquise de Montalembert coldly returns his poems (probably the same ones that had brought him no joy in Grenoble either) and refuses to receive him. Thus, he is reduced to filling the long Atlantic afternoons with the perfecting of his prose style. "I find this a convenient point at which to finish for today," he says, turning to look out of the window, where it is once again pouring with rain.

I tug my forelock at his back, and scuttle along the corridor with my sheaf of papers. I have more writing to do, for myself. A letter to the Mayor of La Coste, who is impudently proposing to demolish the battlements of my château. I shall spend some of the evening decoding the numerical combinations that Laclos stumbled upon: 523; 286; 858. I shall go to tonight's concert and buy a woman, to cheer me up. And I shall write the inversion of 999 words of my boudoir book, in which I have decided it will be amusing to interpose a lengthy tract on the civic responsibilities of revolutionary citizens, closely modelled on the speech of Citizen Laclos, between bouts in which my characters stop at nothing in order to prove to themselves that they uniquely exist, and any lapse from such efforts risks provoking the existence of God.

5

I tackle Blanchard, honest Blanchard, our concierge, about Dupommier's visit with the governor. He is as useless as Laclos, just fobs me off.

"My dear Citizen Sade, don't worry so. It meant nothing, and that's a fact. Trust me."

I have never trusted anyone yet, and that is why I am still not dead. "It is not that I am fretting, Citizen Blanchard," I say, "merely that I am incurably inquisitive. I do like to know what's going on. I am the sort who will go into the kitchen to see what the cook is putting in the broth. You know?"

"Ah-hah," Blanchard grins, "I know you are a man who loves to eat. I hope you have no complaints about the food we serve here?"

"No, none at all, it was just a figure of speech, citizen. Won't you satisfy my curiosity about Inspector Dupommier, and the governor's unwonted attention to us? "

"They tell me nothing, Citizen Sade, and that's a fact. I am to make sure that everything is kept in order, and there's an end to it."

I persist. "You did not hear them say anything about what they might have in mind for any of us in here, then? "

"No, no. All I heard them talk about was the nunnery next door."

The nunnery. I blink, and say no more. Blanchard thinks I am a man of refined manners. If he has heard about my *Justine* it will have puzzled him; but Blanchard is one of those blest souls whom perplexities do not torment. He might be stung by a thousand paradoxes and not do so much as scratch himself.

He it was who let drop a morsel I am still cherishing, in case it may come in handy one day. Some years ago, when this place was simply a convenient cupboard for families who had a skeleton to hide, a young man was put away here for having stolen his mother's jewellery and sold it. His name was St-Just – yes, the very same who only a few weeks ago was chief grand inquisitor in the condemnation of Danton. Whose tongue is perpetually sheathed up Robespierre's arse. The papers say that St-Just's denunciation was a triumph of oratory, marred only by Danton's disdaining to be there and shake at the knees before the tribunal which was his own invention, his and Robespierre's. One of the accusations was that Danton, the people's hero, the gentle Danton, had joined the enemies of the people in supporting a motion for a regency under the Duke of Orleans, which led to the slaughter on the Champ de Mars, scores shot down like poultry. And who had proposed that motion at the Jacobins? – Citizen Laclos. I do not understand how it is that the man does not have shit constantly trickling down his ankles. I, merely a moderatist nobleman, die a thousand deaths with each breath I gasp. I just do not understand Laclos. Perhaps he is already dead, galvanised from the grave by a chance bolt of lightning. That would explain much.

I tell Laclos the rumour about the nunnery. In prison, rumour is a capital asset. You trade it shrewdly. *Perhaps we are to be given the freedom of the nunnery,* I suggest.

He frowns. "Or the nuns wish to extend their premises, and we are to be moved. To nowhere as safe as here, that's for sure. No," he decides, "that cannot be what is in question. There is more demand for our cells than for nuns' cells. More are being crammed in here every day."

An amalgamation, then, I speculate. *You would look fetching in a wimple, citizen. You like a uniform.*

He ignores me, of course. The man is without fancy, even when it is imbued with serious content, as mine is. "I insist on keeping this room to myself," he says. "For my own peace, principally. But also in case my wife should be able to pay me a visit."

Why shouldn't she? Visitors are here every day.

He shakes his head. "It would be too dangerous for her to leave our house."

Because she is your wife?

"Yes." He reflects. "And her own family was of the minor nobility. I do miss her. I have not seen her for months, not since I was given liberty for a day to help her move house. We had been in an apartment at the Palais-Royal. But you know what happened there."

I nod, and say nothing. Everyone knows that the Palais-Royal was sold off to pay the creditors of the Duke of Orleans. Everyone knows that Laclos was the Duke's right-hand man and left-hand man. But I nod and say nothing, because he is trading me a measure of confidentiality. Those who nod and say nothing have the better chances of survival. In a few years from now, France will be peopled exclusively by men and women who nod and say nothing. I aspire to be one of them.

Guardedly, Laclos continues to talk about his wife.

§ A Dead Squirrel

"Hers is an impoverished family. Nothing like the Grenobility. And La Rochelle, where I found myself again after the Île d'Aix, is nothing like Grenoble. I would stand there on the quay, gazing out over the dreary calm of the Atlantic, and reflect that in twenty years I had written a novel and sprouted an épaulette.

"The place had not altered. It was poorer, with the loss of Canadian trade. My mission was to extend the arsenal. I had to negotiate the purchase of land from a dolt named Recollet, who was forever coming to me flapping increased estimates of what income he would lose from his plots of melons, cucumbers, artichokes, salsify … 'Onions, Captain de Laclos, do not disregard my onions.'

"And no sooner have we finished haggling over all of that than here he comes again, reeking of sweat, with another scrap of paper illiterately scrawled with figures discounting the value over thirty years of spinach, chervil, garlic, haricots, cabbages … 'Ah, Captain de Laclos, it is a humble vegetable, your cabbage, but where would we be without it, eh? Tell me that.' 'Exactly where we are now,' I say. I might as well strop my razor on lard.

"It was a tedious job, and the salons were homely, and I would have sunk into despair but for one encounter. I was walking in a garden and came across two young women. One of them was kneeling on the ground, and I saw she was holding a dead squirrel and, when she looked up, under her bonnet her eyes were brimming with tears. I have been in love with her since that moment. I learned that her name was Marie-Soulange Duperré, and she was unmarried, although twenty-three years of age, because her widowed mother and her eldest brother had decreed that the family could afford no dowry. There were half a dozen younger children, and more than a dozen deceased. I knelt down with her and commiserated over the squirrel, which we buried together, in a little grave I made.

"Walking home afterwards, my heart was on fire. I looked out over the ocean, and the setting sun was poised above it like a huge gong, the water was orange-coloured and black, I could hardly draw breath. That was eleven years ago, yet I remember it all in such detail, down to the laces of the shoes she wore.

"I was enchanted when she allowed an attachment to form between us. I quickly understood that she was of a nervous disposition, but when she judged that she could trust me she devoted all her tenderness to me. Her family's reduced circumstances were of little account to me, I assured her; nor did I heed the advice given us by our regimental commander, Gribeauval, that we should take care to contract advantageous marriages. Gribeauval himself had only three degrees of nobility. The irony was that her family disapproved of me for those very reasons: I was not rich, nor of high rank. We shrugged our shoulders, and paid attention to the only deprivation she had which did cause me concern, her lack of education. I helped her to read, Rousseau of course, and then to understand what we had read together. And I was inspired to write an essay on the education of women."

How strange, I remark, putting down my pen and vigorously exercising my thumb. *When I am not at your service in here, I too am grappling with that subject.*

"Ah," Laclos replied. "You must let me read it over, when you have done it. It is a subject on which I hold strong opinions. In my essay, the rhetorical figure of the argument I made was ready to hand in La Rochelle: the slave trade. I even had slaves before me in my family's coat of arms, along with pikes, which have since rather opportunely become a symbol of the revolution. I argued that as long as women are held in slavery by men, it is not in our interests to see them educated. We procure their enslavement by denying them the right to live in their natural state. Men don't cherish women, they seduce them. Thus, we force them into unnatural behaviour. We teach them to arouse our curiosity by concealment, to practise the painful art of refusal even when they would rather consent. Their only weapon is the withholding of imagined pleasure, which is always less than the imagination expects. They become enslaved to the opinion of others, brutally coerced into adopting the strategies of coquetry, adornment, and the vocabulary of teasing.

"A natural woman would know or care nothing of beauty, or passion. But what do we find? My character Tourvel attempts to transcend her slavery, and is punished. My Merteuil escapes slavery only by disguising herself as a slave-owner. 'Women,' I wrote, 'is there one among you who has ever made love without fear? Without jealousy?' There is the disreputable secret of men's power over women. Do not speak of freedom unless, first, you speak of sexual freedom."

Laclos is standing closer to me than I like, with his hands oratorically spread, and his eyes seeking mine. I bend my head over this page, scratch up inside a nostril with the quill, and remark that his argument has much to recommend it. *As you say,*

59

citizen, we should teach woman to make herself freely available to every man who desires her. Monogamy is the invention of an obsessively tidy God. The force that drives us to flower is the urge to discover and conquer new coral islands, where strange vegetation exhales fresh and delicate fragrances. How monstrously grey is a world in which, for example, a woman might be rebuked for entertaining one lover while awaiting another. It was a beautiful argument to put forth at a time when you were so sensually attracted by your wife. She must have been moved by your selflessness.

Laclos remains frozen in his oratorical pose until I have finished speaking. When he moves, now, I flinch. But all he does is close his fingers into fists, and turn away from me. "The question of monogamy is an entirely different one," he says, "and my argument made no reference to it."

I must have misunderstood you when you spoke of the tedious need to conform. How I have suffered from that tedium myself!

"We all have. Don't whine. Your so-called suffering is nothing in comparison to what women suffer."

Really? I've got him on the boil.

"You have spent most of your life in the luxury of prison."

Luxury, citizen? You call …

"I don't mean material comforts. They are trivial. The great luxury you have enjoyed is that you have been removed from the need to make choices."

I hold my breath for a second to make my face red, so as to encourage him. *How dare you?* is the best I can think of to say.

He leans over me and spits his words. "You aristocrats, you cannot change, ever. I have seen heads like yours drop into the basket gouting blood, and do you know what the expression on the face was saying? 'How dare you?'"

Corday's head blushed, they say, when it was slapped.

"They say, they say. We live in a time of terror, which means of superstition. They say many naïve things." Laclos is collecting himself. "They say Marie-Antoinette was lewd. I say she may have been depraved, but who depraved her? She was just a royal example of my general argument. Her seducers' zeal outran her imagination. Through womanly weakness, she

60

allowed those most dear to her to be supplanted by men who were boasting even as they left her boudoir buttoning themselves. She was enslaved, which left her no time to know what she truly desired. And so her palace became tedious to her. She lost herself in inanities."

Laclos is standing at the window again, with his back to me. I notice a cockroach running across the tiles past his shoes. "Well," he says, "the revolution was supposed to liberate all of us, but I am doubtful what benefits it may have brought half the nation. Have you noticed how every woman who aspires to public office is at once the subject of sexual innuendo? There is truth in what Olympe de Gouges lamented, when she said that women used to be scorned and powerful, now they are respected and excluded."

I am faithfully recording your every word, Citizen Laclos, but I beg leave to impinge upon your memoir in order to insert an amending footnote. Allow me to know better than you what my experience in prison has meant to me. That luxury of not having to make choices, though a characteristically elegant theory, is tosh. It would be the same luxury as a pig enjoys in a ditch. The luxury of being brutally subject to Nature. I thought I had made it plain — I will make it plainer still when it is my turn to be dictator — that the project of my life has been to make such choices as will permit me to dominate Nature, since Nature doesn't give a toss about us. Without that, I mean nothing, nothing at all. I might as well fling myself into the ditch.

And my torment, nothing luxurious, has been to remember every day of my life what ninnies and bigots are those powdered wigs to whom I owe my enslavement. Yes, I can use that word too, having been fucked around just as treacherously as those perfumed women whom you pity so. The chief justice enters from a night's sport with his best friend's wife and, with a glance at me, asks, 'Did this little runt seek to puff himself up by presuming to be like us? Prison, gentlemen.'

"Aye, prison," coughs President Michaut, waking up from forty winks.

"My verdict, gentlemen, is prison," screeches Beau Darval, briefly raising his head from the billet-doux *he is scribbling under his robes to a chorus-girl.*

"No question of it, prison," grunts the pedagogue Damon, his brains still addled from his lunch in the tavern.

"Oh, who can be in any doubt?" yelps little Valère in conclusion, standing up on his tiptoes and keeping an eye on his watch lest he be late for his rendezvous with Madame Gourdain. "Prison."

Bah, I boil.

Thank you, citizen. Pray, resume.

I have amused him, I do believe. At least, he has been watching me, and now speaks to me, not at me as though I were posterity. "Very well," he accepts. "I am glad to record the happiest weeks of my life. I summed them up in a poem I wrote to my beloved. Let me cite just the closing couplet.

> When people say an angel can't be seen,
> I look at you, and don't know what they mean.

"But there were shadows in our sunlight. The Duperré family opposed our match, and vowed they could afford no dowry. I had a bitter fight with them, because I was scrimping together every sou I could save from my salary in order to afford to keep a wife. In the end, we screwed a revenue of four thousand livres from them, and even that required legal intervention by Alquier, you know? – the Jacobin, later. He was a good friend to me then, though he would have preferred to be a better friend to Marie-Soulange, she confided to me. He was known in La Rochelle as the terror of husbands, though a married man himself, but he had found time for smiling at her, too. Well, even he had to stop that once she was visibly pregnant. As for my mother-in-law, she sent her youngest son away, in order, she said, to shield him from the evidence of immorality. Étienne-Fargeau was born before we could afford a married ménage, so for the time being he was registered as 'of parents unknown' and – forgive me, shade of Rousseau, but we had no choice – the baby was put out to a wet nurse.

"We had one extraordinary piece of good fortune. I discovered that the house adjacent to the Duperrés', where Marie-Soulange was still obliged to live, was available for rent, and has a secret passage under the garden giving access to a room in her house, just as though I'd had my own sappers build it for us. She makes that room her boudoir, and we are able to visit each other as often as we wish without any clacking of tongues. When Alquier gets me elected to the Academy in La Rochelle, even the Duperrés come round to a grudging recognition of me. What they don't know, because I maintain only the most formal relationship with them, is that on my occasional visits to Paris I am making valuable acquaintances.

"I spend an afternoon at the Palais-Royal with Saint-Georges. He greets me with a cry of 'Ohé!', at which I find it painful to smile, but later he asks if I would like to be introduced to his master, the Duke of Chartres, whom of course we now know as the late Philippe Égalité, once Duke of Orleans, alas." Laclos sighs. "That man ... Well, we must set aside some later days for him, if we are still in here. I am sure you know that he and I had much to do with each other, and I trust the whole world knows that in no point did he or I ever traduce the revolution. On the contrary. This memoir will serve to set down the truth."

Citizen, I say, you have more than once hinted that you expect us, both I hope, to be released soon. If you will not oblige me by explaining your grounds for hope, will you at least give me a similar security by agreeing to what would be only fair? – that tomorrow, and for a few days thereafter, I dictate my memoir to you, and subsequently we dictate on alternate days. Only thus can we be assured of a parity of scribing.

"Who spoke of parity?" he replies. "I won the toss. Between heads and tails there is no space for parity.

"Let us not finish today's collaboration while I am still sequestered in La Rochelle. Inspired by my wife's affection, I begin another essay, in response to an academic invitation to write In Praise of Vauban. My experience with Montalembert has supplied me with much ammunition that I want to fire off. I print it at my own expense, and send a copy to old Ségur, the Minister of War, in the same week as I formally seek his permission, via Gribeauval, to get married. He must read my

63

request before he reads my essay, because it is granted readily.

"Having kept scrupulous account, I feel confident that we can now afford to set up a home together, my angel and I. From the church we go together to lay the first stone of the new arsenal building. As it settles into the pit prepared and we spoon cement down on to it, our eyes meet. We have no need of words. It is the perfect symbol of the foundation of our eternal troth.

"Now we are able to acknowledge our son, and off we go with him on leave, to Rouen, visiting some of my wife's family there, and then to the Marais, to see my mother and brother. It is not easy for us to become true parents so suddenly. Étienne is by now two years old, and yet the wet nurse has not taught him any disciplines of the bowels. I undertake his training, while we lodge with my brother and consider whether we might not set up home in the Marais, so familiar to me from my own boyhood. Oh Sade, I little realised what a barrage of artillery was about to answer my mortar. That seems a good point at which to pause for today. It will keep you wondering all night, eh?"

He is in the best of humours and, walking back to my room, I spend two minutes wondering why. I conclude that his venomous assault on my patrician birth, coupled with the prospect of watching me guillotined, has been a tonic for him, a toxic tonic. Does the viper feel better after evacuating its fangs? That is a question to which I do not expect to learn the answer. There are others.

6

I tread the tiles of my room in practised patterns. Assume that they be grouped in nines, with three tiles to each side of a square, and let the middle tile in each side (viewed from my starting point) be considered west, north, east, and south, then my initial step is with the left foot on the south-west corner, followed by my right foot on the north-east tile, then my left foot on the west tile of the next group of nine, my right on the south-east of the following group, my left on the north-west; but now I am in the furthermost north-west corner of the room, and so I place my right foot on the west tile close behind my left foot, at the same time pivoting my ungainly body so that my left foot may next arrive on the north-east tile of the second group, my right on the south-west, and my left on the east of the first group; now my right foot has to be placed just in front of the left, on the south-east tile, and my body pivot so that my left foot may arrive on the north-west, followed by my right on the east of the second group, left on the south-west of the following group, right on the north-east, and here we are at the wall again; so left foot on the east, just behind my right foot, pivot on my left, and place my right foot on the north-west of the second group, left on the south-east, and right foot on the west tile of the first group, thus completing the initial adventure by having trodden once on each of the eighteen tiles in what we may term column one and column three, if I may be permitted to introduce a new term after we have come so far together in what I hope has been perfect trust. The next step is crucial: my left foot on the south tile of the first group, while pivoting so as to place my right on the north-west tile of the adjacent southerly group of nine. Then, off we go again, repeating the aforesaid formations, until we have completed two more columns. But here, you exclaim, is a pretty fix I have landed us in. For, on completing the second adventure, we find ourselves with our right foot on the central tile of the initial southerly group, and no untrodden tile available for the left foot unless the crotch be stretched measurably wider than I have so far invited you to do, and than may be comfortable in one of your age. Trust me, companionable treader of my tiles. If you will but place your left foot on the south-westernmost tile, while pivoting, you will find yourself placed to repeat both adventures again, and again, to your heart's content. But I hear you object that in such a scheme no tile is ever thoroughly trodden both by the left foot and the right. That is true: and might it not be accepted that our feet and our tiles have predestined affinities, since more incredible beliefs are celebrated every day in church? However, a more Euclidean solution is available, if you will but place your left foot on the south-east tile of the initial group, and thence proceed backwards on a mirror image of the initial adventure, following it with the left foot on the south-west tile of the adjacent southerly group, and the second adventure again, also backwards. That, you will discover with delight, delivers your right foot, finally, on the west tile of the adjacent southerly group, with all the thirty-six tiles (in question) now trodden by both feet, and your left foot available to be placed on the south tile of the adjacent southerly group; and thus an entirely untrodden group of four more columns may be explored, in the same fashion. But I hear you object again, it is all fine and dandy for you, Sade, with your seigneurial expanse of tiles in the Picpus (you jest), but just how many columns of tiles do you suppose that I, poor wretch that I am, have to tread in my stinking cell? Ah, why can you not trust me? You remember our pivoting: consider this. One may pivot clockwise or widdershins. By alternating the twist of your pivotings, you could arrive at a series of variant treadings of your tiles so multiple that I have never yet computed it to its limit. You can if you like. I have better things to do with my time.

Laclos hugs his grievances to himself as though they were a

favourite coat. Even when he is not dictating them to me, I am sure he spends his time rehearsing them in his memory, just as old soldiers fight their battles over and over again, so that one is obliged to wait for the sauce hollandaise for one's artichokes until it has finished being an entrenched line of infantry in Westphalia. My pen dawdles and doodles, while he practises perfect recall of his essay on Vauban. It opened, he states, by asserting that two important questions had to be resolved: whether Monsieur de Vauban was really a great man, and, *secundus*, whether the present generation owes him recognition. "I admit that, for a long time now, I have thought not." I will indulge the reader of this never-to-be-read memoir, as Laclos does not indulge me, with a summary of his narration and confirmation: that Vauban's brilliant conquests, redounding to the glory of Louis XIV, were built on sand; that Vauban made no progress in the art of fortification; that his forts are not impregnable, as he himself often proved by recapturing them; and that his works cost the country more than (I gloss) the ransom of le Roi Soleil would have been had that glorious monarch ever been taken captive by, let us say, the Grand Turk.

It is only because I long for Laclos to have done with this unusually tedious passage of pique that I bite my tongue and do not voice my own objections. There is, for example, something to be said for a man who calculated that a shrewd investment in the philoprogenitive pig would, within ten porcine generations, suffice to feed all of France, even – note the mark of genius in Vauban – allowing for an interim 434,874 piglets to have been devoured by wolves. If Vauban was right, certain it is that France would boast the fattest wolves in Europe.

"Had Monsieur de Vauban known how to conserve as well as acquire, his fame would be intact." (I believe we are at the refutation.) "Not knowing how to acquire, had he not taken upon himself to conserve, his fame would at least be pure. But who can praise Monsieur de Vauban, who spent his life in fortifying without advancing one step in the art of fortification? Who can praise Monsieur de Vauban, who swallowed up millions with an appalling prodigality in order to erect with one hand those very emplacements which, with the other, he would so easily overturn? Who, to conclude, can praise Monsieur de Vauban, who cost France more than half our present national debt in order to leave part of our frontiers wide open, and the other part but feebly defended?"

I, for one, will praise him, I do not say. We cannot have too many fortifications, and Vauban was at least prolific, by Laclos's own account. What is it in these revolutionary hotheads that they must forever be seeking to tear down stones and expose our vulnerability? I have only just had occasion to write to La Coste, where I have been Lord of the Manor since my father's death nearly thirty years since. My battlements there displease the civic princekins. "I ask you," I wrote, "only for the glory of sacrificing them to you myself, the Constitution in one hand, a hammer in the other. I insist that we make a municipal fête of the demolition. But in the meantime, Messieurs, let us make peace and *respect property.*" Those two words I transcribe from the Constitution itself, as it was brought down from the mountain by Robespierre. (The last phrase I did not of course include in my letter, irony now being a capital offence, like all forms of wit. Only the most sincere of us can hope for salvation.)

So, Laclos is observing, that was his mortar fire. When he had published his novel, a cold bombshell printed with tacit permission, the august heads had blinked and looked the other way. But not this time. Little Captain de Laclos questioning the greatness of Vauban! It was as though he had criticised the design of Versailles.

In our privity I could tell him that what he had wanted, above all, was to be noticed, but that only by taking the greatest care not to be noticed could any of us achieve our ends. I recognise his dilemma; but will not give him the wisdom I have suffered so much to acquire, that to be noticed is to be found out. I have, as it were, a lover's loathing for anybody who tells me they have read my *Justine.* It is as though they were saying,

Ha, now I see what you have been up to. A subtle wink with one eye, and no word spoken, is plenty. That way, my fortifications remain intact.

§ An Argument with a Cemetery

"The very day after my wedding, Ségur tells Gribeauval to reprimand me in the strongest terms. I am never again to utter such opinions without permission. My leave will be terminated, and I sent back to La Rochelle. Gribeauval, from whom I might expect a little more sympathy since we are both natives of Amiens, sees fit to enhance his own reputation by being severer still. He orders me to Metz. My first thought is to resign my commission; but I have a wife and child to support.

"On my way to Metz, I write to the Ministry. I have been married for just eight days, I point out, and my wife is ill. She sends Ségur a similar letter of her own, guided by notes I left for her. I have persuaded the Count of La Châtre to speak to Ségur on our behalf. The response to all is: 'The King does not change his mind.' Moreover, I receive abusive letters from several old fools at the Ministry, clearly put up to it by Ségur. One snivels at 'the ridiculous way in which minor men of letters, aspiring to the greatness of the writers of Louis XIV's time, seek to elevate themselves by mockery.' Fourcroy is woken up so that he might intone at me: 'The science of fortification is infallible. Any novelty proposed is a proof of ignorance.' Then they let him go back to sleep. My God, Sade. It was like arguing with a cemetery. All I had done was to enunciate an evident truth. Is it any wonder what was to happen to France? What hurt me was that Montalembert stayed silent throughout. Not a word from him."

I nod my head, and sigh with him at the frailty of comradeship in a man whose wife one has sought to ravish, all the while keeping my eye on Monsieur Cockroach, again displaying interest in Laclos's shoes. Today he is accompanied by two lesser cockroaches. He is showing them the ropes, no doubt. Probably he bred them last night.

"So there I sit in Metz. My black mood is deepened by news from La Rochelle. My eldest brother-in-law, feckless at the best of times, has been ruined by the trade treaty the English have forced down our compliant government's throat. While I am kicking my heels, Duperré takes to his, with the bailiffs in pursuit. We have never heard from him again. Everything is sold off. We go to court to claim what is ours, not the Duperrés', but they take it all from us. The family splits up. As for the cook, we find him hanged by the neck, like game, from a hook in his own kitchen. I was almost glad to get back to Metz. There I am informed that the regiment is to move again. Of all cynical jokes they could play upon me, I find myself posted back to that hole La Fère, twenty-six years after I ardently conned Bezout's mathematical manual and dreamed of besieging fortresses.

"At least Picardy is nearer Paris. I send for my wife to join me, with the boy, and for the first time we set up a home together. I show her the most efficient way to organise domestic matters, and she proves an apt pupil, though sometimes, even now, she allows herself to lapse from her own high standards. When I have to be away from home, I include in every letter an affectionate reminder of what needs to be done. Last week, for instance, I wrote, 'Please, do be sure to keep your dressing-table as tidy as we made it together.'"

He is seated in the afternoon sunbeams with his hands clasped in front of his face, as though in prayer, but with his thumbs raised to knead his brow. I think it best not to intrude on the intimacy of his reflections. The cockroaches, I notice, make it a point to avoid the barred patches of sunlight staining the tiles.

Laclos stirs himself, brushing his coat and adjusting his cravat. "In the warm bosom of my family, I reason that I have nothing at all for which to reproach myself. I cast about for a way in which to assert that confidence. Giving the go-by to

70

Ségur and the dolts at the Ministry of War, I address to the Ministry of the Marine a letter describing an invention which might prove most effective at sea, a shell hollow at its core and filled with powder that will explode upon impact. It was an idea I'd been developing since conversations I had had with a rarely intelligent colonel, one Bellegarde. He was with the regiment only passingly. There was some trouble over allegations that he had sold arms privately.

"Further, applying my geodetic ingenuity beyond military affairs, I publish in the *Journal de Paris* a notion for the better addressing of streets in the city. You must have cursed, after spending thirty minutes seeking a house with a number and a street name that is triplicated within five minutes' walk, or turns out to be several miles away. The solution would be simple. Take Paris, I wrote, and form it into, as it were, a square of four thousand units per side and divided into two equal parts by the river; the river becomes the common side of two equal parallelograms situated on the right and left banks, each with a base of four thousand units and a height of two thousand. Divide that common side into ten equal parts and, from each point of division, project perpendicular lines to the opposite side of each of the two parallelograms, which are thus themselves divided into ten other equal parallelograms, each with a side, on the original base, of four hundred units, and a height, now better seen as a long side, of two thousand units."

Hold hard, citizen, I cry. *Have some consideration for my thumb.*

"Am I going too fast for you?"

Yes, fascinating though your proposition is to a fellow Euclidean.

"The conclusion will be apparent: that every building in the city have appended to its address a geometric location derived from the vertical and horizontal axes. Does the argument persuade you, as well as fascinate?"

It would have persuaded Descartes himself.

Laclos grunts. "It clearly did not persuade the readers of the *Journal*. Nor have the enlightened minds of the revolutionary sections shown any interest, for all their municipal idealism.

The city remains a chaos."

Possibly, your argument was lacking in the common touch?

"These are technical matters. We owe them our best powers of reasoning. But no one listened to me. What contribution to the nation could little Captain de Laclos have to make? France, after all, was so splendid and wisely ruled that it could no longer afford to have a foreign policy. You remember why Ségur resigned. He wanted to send an army to support the Dutch rebellion, and they told him it was out of the question. First the Prussian war and then the American business had been very costly; you must go back to the grocer's shop and find us a much cheaper policy, Monsieur le Ministre, one that will cost us – well, nothing at all. The King of France is broke.

"I despaired, Sade. I applied for permission to go and fight for the Turks against Russia. Gribeauval, of course, wrote on the foot of my application: 'Refused.'

"The nation's problems were addressed by convoking the Assembly of Notables. All they could assemble were notable idiots, exemplary aristocratic cretins. When we brought our daughter into such a world, I felt I should go to her baptism and apologise to her. We might have named her Sorrow."

Am I to understand that you did not go to her baptism?

"I was in La Fère. Why?"

You appointed proper Godparents for her?

"I was represented by two of our servants. Why are you so agitated by the question, Sade? I had not suspected in you such a devotion to Christian rites."

God help you, I say. It has nothing to do with religion. You can have no idea of the trouble I have endured through making the same mistake, when my son was born. We appointed Godparents, they never showed up, drunk probably, or fornicating with each other. We had no choice, it was left to a servant to hold the baby at the font. She got the name wrong. She was so illiterate she might have got the wrong baby, wrong font. "Donatien-Claude-Armand," she croaked. Donatien, my first name too. Last year, they accused me of having been an émigré. It was my son, but they were going to guillotine me for it. Me.

7

One step outside my door, my heart stops. Dupommier is closing on me, only a few steps away, black bristly muzzle dripping. I can already smell the leeks and cheap red wine on his breath. Governor Coignard is just behind him, followed by half a dozen murderers carrying shovels and blades. I cannot move. I hear the last air wheeze out of my throat. Dupommier strides straight past me, pretending not even to see me. I know that trick. It is like putting you up before a firing-squad with empty barrels. I don't move or breathe or flicker an eye while they all troop past me and clatter away. When they are outside the building, beyond my hearing, they will look at each other and explode with laughter, collapsing into each other's arms and slapping backs, tears on their cheeks. What a capital game it is for them. A *coitus interruptus* before their collective orgasm when my head drops into the basket, eyes bulging, tongue stuck out.

What does it all *mean*? I beg Laclos to tell me, sobbing. Those narrow shoulders rise, once. He doesn't know, and plainly doesn't give a fig. He looks away from me, through the window, embarrassed by my frank, unashamed terror. Laclos is embarrassed by another man's anxiety not to be killed. Eventually, he admits that he, too, saw the murderous band march along the corridor. "I suppose they were going to do some work."

Yes. What work?

Another shrug. "We may know later. Meanwhile, let us resume. It will take your mind off your fright.

§ Bark Gruel

"Last night, after you left, I found myself wondering what would have happened to France had there been no revolution. And the conclusion I came to was that it was inevitable. Even the weather was telling us so. Remorseless rains, then remorseless drought, followed again by storms, hail, snow, two consecutive harvests wiped out, livestock annihilated. The people see bread double in price, beyond their means, and what does Versailles do during those dark days? Marie-Antoinette and her crew are playing pastoral games. They couldn't tell a peasant from a clod of earth, yet spend their days dolled up as shepherds and shepherdesses. Rousseau is in vogue, though none of them has actually read him."

I do not understand you, Laclos. What could the revolution do to change the weather? People went on starving.

"Of course. The real question is, what did the weather do to advance the revolution? I heard of people reduced to boiling tree bark for gruel. Put yourself in their place."

Very well. I am sipping bark gruel and starving to death.

"So is your wife. And two of your children died last week, and were not much more than skeletons when you buried them."

I might have been tempted to boil them.

"Some were. And now the door of your house is thrown open, and bailiffs tip your sick wife out of bed on the suspicion that you have salt under the mattress and have not paid the salt tax."

I might kill them.

"No. They are armed, and you are weak from hunger. All you can do is hate them. Your empty belly is filled with hatred. You can see that the bailiffs eat bread every day, and so do their masters. So why not you? On the river, grain barges pass."

I raid them.

"Of course you do. Starvation is the severest of tyrants. You do as it commands, and become a brigand. You meet others in

74

like case, and form a band of brigands. None of you has food, employment, or hope. All you have is your hunger and hatred. You roam. Now, here's a thing. You come across a village where they have some food, and before you can even beg, let alone rob, they drive you off. Why?"

To protect their own food.

"True. But why are they shouting, 'Death to all aristocrats!' at you?"

Search me, citizen.

"Because they think you are the agents of a plot. These people have survived, frugally, but things are harder than they were for their fathers, and much harder than in the golden age. That is what they talk about. They ask, 'What is to be done?' They see that Versailles has no more interest in relieving their oppression than in changing the weather. All they see it doing is to summon the Estates-General, for the first time in living memory. And in that they place all their hopes. What will a huge room full of viscounts, bishops and squires do about the weather? About national bankruptcy? About shaking out aristocratic corruption as though it were weevils to be knocked out of bread? But mark this, citizen: it is the only hope the people have. The only sign that anything at all might be changed, pathetic though that faith may look now, like any faith in a higher power. And so, they are working side by side in their fields, or conversing on a street in Montmartre, and they look up and see your ragged band approaching. Who do they think you are?"

Brigands. I shrug.

"No. You are not simply a threat to their food. You represent a threat to their dearest possession, hope. Hope in what?"

That we will push off, I reply, weary of the part I have to play.

"Think, Sade. I told you, their one hope is in the Estates-General. Who threatens that? The jealous nobility, placeholders, military commanders. Therefore, you have been hired by aristocrats to dismay the country, terrify the peasants into submission, shatter their hope, and perpetuate complacent privilege."

Citizen, if this were a play, the audience would be thinking it far-fetched.

"It was a play, and perhaps it was far-fetched, but people believed it. That is all that matters. When you watch la Contat acting Suzanne, if you believe it, while it lasts, then you will weep – or laugh. How are those tears chemically different from real tears?"

They are not.

"Exactly. *Ergo*, the peasants drive you out of their village. Excited by their gesture of defiance, they go on to the château outside the village. They seize the manorial rolls, the documents of oppression, and burn them. While they are about it, why not burn down the château? They do. What do we smell in that smoke?"

A great fear.

"Yes, yes. And?"

A revolution?

"*Quod erat demonstrandum.*"

Citizen, I have to tell you that I had the honour of initiating the revolution, from the walls of the Bastille. I've never been given the credit.

"It was I who initiated it, before the storming of the Bastille. I *have* sometimes been given the credit, unfortunately."

Citizen Laclos ...

"Enough, Sade. We can quarrel about it later. What matters now is that the revolution, the revolving, could not have been initiated at all had it not been for those earlier shoves at the wheel to release it from the grip of the mud, as I have described." Laclos is more enthusiastic than I have seen him, striking poses, finding new angles for his head, tossing powder from his wig, cueing me with a forefinger like a pistol.

"Come with me," he continues, "to another stretch of the mire. I get away from La Fère whenever I can, to Paris, in order to develop my connections, or to our house in Versailles, where my wife has moved to be near her mother. Often I coach it to the Château de Luzancy. I don't ride there, I'm awkward on a horse. Through the park, where the trees are brilliant green on a yellow field of parched grass, tip the footman, and who is in the salon today?

"My face I keep impassive as I look around, hands clasped behind my black coat. Why, Florian is accepting congratulations on his election to the French Academy. I watch him smiling with his wettened lips. He laughs precisely on the beat of any *bon mot* dropped by a journal editor, or an officer senior to himself, or a seducible woman, or an influential nobleman. I admire the trick he has of modestly lowering his lashes, which must have cost him hours in front of the mirror. Any other poet who approaches him is afforded a view up Florian's nostrils. In time, I stroll over, left hand behind my back, and offer him the other in a handshake. I would match him nostril for nostril were he to play that game with me, but he doesn't. We know each other's gall. Our eyes acknowledge that fact when they briefly meet. Mostly we are, both of us, entranced by the view over the other's left shoulder.

"We are joined by the Viscomte de Ségur, whose unique distinction in this salon is that he believes his father to be the perruqued, powdered old sot who ruined the army for years. He has never wanted for anything, the young Ségur, except a brain. But he is one of my admirers, never mind what his father thinks of me. We get on famously. My novel, he assures me, is a miracle. He is writing a play, to be put on in Paris, and would I permit him to take, for his title, a phrase from my incomparable novel: *Le Parti le Plus Gai?* It would be an unrepayable honour, I reply, which fetches a sincere smile through the miasma he has for a face. With equal sincerity, I promise not to miss the first night. Come on, Sade, you are that trio of women seated over there, talking behind your fans. What are you gossiping about?"

I shake my head. *I have never frequented the salons. You must give me my script.*

"Very well. Your subject is the Comte de Guibert. He has been your only subject for weeks now, in anyone's salon. Just fancy, though from a frankly mediocre family, he has fashioned a glittering military career, and already, so young, he has been appointed to the War Council. In his spare moments he has written some plays and won election to the Academy, and Madame de Staël is devoted to nurturing his genius. But this triple reincarnation of Thucydides, Julius Caesar, and Racine is not, surely, a breeze to flutter your fans?"

I am certain that you expect me to answer, No.

"That's right. But listen: de Guibert has lately attained the apogee of his career. When he abandoned his mistress, she let herself die. What a crown of laurels for him! Ever since, the debate has raged: would you rather be de Guibert's mother, sister, or mistress? Meanwhile, at the War Council, his declared aim to reform the army has aroused another storm of debate. It centres on what advantages a four-cornered hat can be said to have over the tricorn."

Laclos shuts his eyes and smiles at the sublime. "Would that I had been there to witness the education of young de Guibert. All his knowledge of military history could avail him nought in that battle. He was fighting an army that was the most formidable in the world when it was defending its own incompetence. Old Ségur's first act, when Marie-Antoinette told her dithering husband to appoint him, had been to restore the requirement for promotion of four degrees of nobility. It made us the grand staircase of the aristocracy. They trod on our backs to become generals, two a week, year after year. Most of them were on leave most of the time, naturally. When we hear that young de Guibert is talking of reforming an army like that, the few of us who are not painted tin model soldiers say to each other, 'Oh yes, and the sky will be dark with flying pigs, and the Bastille will crumble.' We have barely half our requisition of cannon, ten thousand are rotting in arsenals, and when the War Council are not tussling over four-cornered hats they're considering abandoning the cannon altogether. I would have let myself die. You know what they said? It got in the way of the cavalry. It got in the way of the *cavalry*, Sade."

Is he aiming his defunctive cannon at me, an old cavalry officer? I think not, just wait, pen poised. "Keep talking, citizen," I encourage him. At every pause I hear the scratching of dogs' claws on my coffin.

"Florian has been ballooning, and has scribbled several insipid stanzas on the joyous terror of it. He is pressed to recite it aloud. 'To rise, above lies, unto the skies', that is all I remember of it, thank God. I lean against a pillar, always the man in black, the cold, saturnine, methodical Laclos, and look around at the paintings of heroic lordlings. They are seated with their backs to the landscape that they own. They have no need to look at it, it is simply theirs, like the tax exemptions and public offices they have bought for themselves. And the peasants are theirs, brown blobs which cannot detach themselves from the background of earth. Florian twitters on, and I distract myself by whispering better words, that speech which Beaumarchais gave Figaro to speak to the Count: 'Because you are a grand seigneur you think yourself a grand genius. Nobility, cash, rank, property, all of it makes you so high and mighty! What have you done to deserve so much? You hardly took the trouble to be born, and there's an end to it. You're a humdrum body. While I, dammit, faceless in the crowd, need all my wisdom and wit just to survive.' I forget the rest. There it is, Sade. The voice of the revolution, be it those enraged peasants burning down the château, or mine, within the château, silent with contempt. Even His Majesty's wits detected the menace in Figaro. He stomped out of the theatre, muttering that such stuff was seditious while the Bastille stood foursquare. And off he went for more hunting and eating, our first gentleman of the kingdom. Poor Louis Capet. 'Profession: last king of the French,' they billed him at the guillotine. All this was running freshly through my mind last night. It was like remembering the age of innocence. Do you remember what people said at that time? 'Our father, which art in Versailles, give us back our bread.'"

I look up. *What I remember being said at that time was said by*

79

Rousseau. Laclos nods me on. *As you know, he wrote that Nature gives every man absolute control over his members, and so the Social Contract gives to the body politic an absolute power over all its members. And I reflected that poor, phymatic Louis had less than absolute control over his member. And perhaps we should have been quicker to draw a political lesson from that exquisitely tight foreskin. I was delighted when they guillotined him. I said so at my trial. He was not the king we needed.*

"No?" Laclos replies. "Who was, would you say?"

I wouldn't say. Does Laclos suppose I have lasted this long without being nimble enough to dodge that one?

A commotion arises in the corridors outside. We hear Blanchard's voice crying unavailingly for "Peace, my friends, peace," but the din is growing.

I drop the pen and stare at Laclos. *They are coming for me,* I gasp. *Save me, Laclos, for pity's sake.* My hands are protecting my throat. *Dupommier,* I whimper, *it is Dupommier. His yellow eye has been fixed upon me all this week.* I swallow, and feel my Adam's apple jerk under my fingers. *Please, citizen,* I say, *I know you have influence. Please, do something to help me. I was delighted when they executed the king. Surely that will count for something?*

Laclos says, "We will finish the passage. Then we will see what that noise is about. Pick up your pen."

I do so. What else can I do? He is my only hope.

"Necker was at that salon sometimes," he resumes. "I think he knew he would be recalled as the finance minister. At all events, he is the only man there worth talking to. As a Switzer, he stands outside the mire. As a Protestant, he is for speaking one's mind candidly, and acting as one speaks. You can see why the Queen hated him. I count it no accident that as soon as he is recalled I am, at last, recommended for promotion to major. Because even the War Council, in one of those terrifying moments of clarity that the drunkard knows, blinks at what de Guibert is saying, and mumbles something about professional advancement. Ha! It lasts a few days. Then they choose a new minister, and my red silken lozenges are cruelly withdrawn. That was it. I had had enough. In October 1788, I left La Fère on leave, vowing never to return. Now, let us go and see what Blanchard's fuss is all about."

Would you be kind enough to go, citizen, and come back and tell me? I know it is undignified, but I shall hide under your palliasse.

The scorn on his face is a celestial blessing on me, because he will do as I have begged. He leaves, and comes back a few minutes later. "You can come out, Sade. There is no danger."

I put my head out, and can raise my eyes no higher than his knees. A herd of cockroaches scuttles past my elbows.

"The news," Laclos announces, "is that our premises have been extended. The nuns have been moved out, to make way for new inmates. You and I will no doubt remain where we are, but with this delightful difference. The wall between here and the nunnery has been taken down, allowing us access to the garden they have there. Henceforth, Sade, we can continue our work together sitting in the shade of apricot trees."

I close my eyes and weep. Sobs so rack my body that I have to prostrate myself, legs still beneath the palliasse, one cheek on the floor, tears rolling down my nose and splashing over the cockroaches. I see Laclos's shoes move away, and imagine the distaste on his face, but I do not mind. *Thank you, Laclos,* I sob. *Thank you so very much. I am ever your humblecumdumble.*

8

With a garden to wander in, lowering his thin nose to sniff at flowers, and raising extended fingers to marvel at sparrows and gnats, Laclos is the new Rousseau. Every word he speaks will be a fresh miracle of perception. Piqued to have seen nothing yet of what he has been drivelling to me, he now insists that every morning he will scrutinise "our previous day's work together." I am to restrict myself to following him around like a dog, taking notes, and promptly writing them up for him in my room. I shall do so with a harlot's back for my desk and her arsehole for an inkwell. Since any editorial interventions by myself are thus precluded, it should be understood that his narrative as I now present it has been written under duress. I can accept no responsibility for it. Believe what you will, beady-eyed posterity. We who are about to die piss on you. I doubt if any record at all of what is happening in France will be believed by those who come after us. It will be dismissed as a gap in chronicled time. History has gone on holiday, and fiction invents us every day. In the mornings, we wake up wondering what bizarre fairy-tale we will be required to act out now. I trust that does not make it sound like an amusing experience.

As to the foregoing pages, I shall procrastinate. Why should I give him the gratification of seeing his sentimental souvenirs written down for him? And besides, to make a fair copy of them, omitting my own observations, which were all that kept me awake, is too much labour for me, who have my own book to write, on the education of a young woman. I shall entitle it, *A Philosopher of the Boudoir*, and as epigraph recommend that every mother should require her daughter to study it. That should serve to contradict any pernicious opinions that Laclos might publish on the question.

Now, hush my heart. Laclos speaks. Ear, attend. Hand, transcribe. Mind, go on holiday. Laclos speaks:

§ Two Parks

Imagine two parks, laid out for pleasure. My home is close by one of them, at Versailles. I am most often to be found at the other, in the middle of Paris.

The first park is a palace of air, beside one of stone. At my back are 375 windows, reflecting the passing clouds, as I stand in weak sunshine, eyes closed, facing the wide vistas, the terraces, the yew-lined walks, the fountains and ornamental basins, the statues, and I see the Sun King showing a select group of visitors how to look at his gardens. *One must pause* – he is reading from the guide written in his own hand – *on this terrace, at the top of the steps, in order to appraise the pattern of spume at the far end of the arcade. Next, one must turn to the left, advance five paces, and contemplate the arrangement of the marble group comprising the figures of Diana, Air, and Venus.* The Doge of Genoa, and the Princes of Persia, Muscovy, and Siam, glide along with the King as though transported on a moving carpet of air, to the sound of hautboys and fifes, drums and silver trumpets. Louis Quatorze is in his element, vaingloriously waving his hand at the impossible dream that Le Nostre has carved for him in water and marble, stone and air. *Next, one must turn left and pass between the sphinxes. One will pause to contemplate the grounds to the south, and thence one must go straight to the orangery, whence one will consider the terrain of orange trees and the Swiss lake. Afterwards, one must turn to the right and descend to the little west shrubbery, wherein one will arrive at the Baths of Apollo attended by Nymphs.* He was awoken by his valet this morning at 8.15, as he is every morning, and attended by his physician, the first gentleman of the bedchamber drew back the curtains of his bed, he was addressed by three privileged petitioners, his beard, wig and costume were prepared, before he proceeded from the vestibule to the guardroom, the antechamber, the chamber, and into the cabinet room at nine o'clock, to attend to every detail of government. None will escape him. His divine function on earth is never disordered. He governs by an etiquette that cannot be disturbed. To disobey him would be sin. *One must walk westward along the precise centre of the green carpet of grass in order to appreciate its continuation by the Grand Canal.* The heterogeneous little group glides as one along the broadwalk of the sun, between trim files of trees brought from Normandy, beds of jonquils, anemones, narcissi and tulips, another aisle of the airy cathedral to the glory of Louis Quatorze. What was sand and black mire has been imprinted with the splendour of his absolute will. Nature has been tyrannised into unity. I hate it. In a hungry land, the ostentation of taste is obscene. Even water obeys him, even gravity is the Sun King's subject. To feed his fountains in an arid plain, all the ponds of the region were trapped and culverted. But there was not enough to supply the spumes and plumes of his fantasy. Windmills, and horse-drawn pumps, were installed far away, to drive water up here for His Majesty. Still not enough. A river of water was required, the Eure, and who better to besiege it, with Louis Quatorze, than Vauban himself? Across twenty leagues of flatland, along aqueducts higher than the Romans', twice as high as Notre-Dame, through reservoirs, ports and sluices, down any little slope or terrace that led to Versailles, they ordered the diversion of the Eure, from Pontgoin to Courville, Saint-Arnoult, Fontaine-la-Guyon, Bailleau-l'Évêque, Berchères-la-Maingot. Nothing, not even nine million livres, nor twenty thousand infantrymen struck down with pleurisy, was too much to spend on beauty. The machine of grandeur remade the land. And still it was not enough. Still the Sun King has to order his fountains to play when he wishes to impress Genoa and Persia, Muscovy and Siam, moving evenly through air heavy with the scent of orange blossom. I see them coming spectrally back, now, between statues of heroic size, toward the level skyline of the stone palace, where tonight, from the Salon of Apollo, furnished in silver, the King will move through a hall of mirrors crested with the discs of the sun, to where the almoner of the day waits with a lighted candle in still air, which he will hand to the first valet, who will name aloud tonight's bearer of the candle, who will step forward, removing a glove, and lead the King to bed, while a thousand courtiers and four thousand servants, all stinking inside their clothes, bow to wish him a good night. O, I am rapt, despite myself, when I contemplate that perfection of order, that luxury and calm, unblemished by the voluptuousness of Louis Seize, who had no secrets to bow us down. And when the Sun King went to his last bed, eighty years ago, his dazzling invisibility was preserved in the eyes of his people by burying him incognito. Dust to dust, light to light, the Sun King set beyond the western horizon, and the night air, already cold, closed in upon all of our bones.

The second park, also, is laid out beside a palace, which embraces it with a horseshoe curve. At midnight, at noon, and at every other hour, it is swarming with people, like maggots in a dead sheep's belly. Some have come there for pleasure, some for politics, most could not tell you the difference, and perhaps, in those heady days and nights, there was no difference. You can taste hope, like sharp lemonade. You can get drunk on the future. Here is one declaiming for three-quarters of an hour how he would reform the constitution. Walk five steps along the arcade, and another, no less vehement, is denouncing the aristocracy. Turn to your left, and appraise the defrocked Abbot Bernard singing a bawdy song about Marie-Antoinette to his own guitar. Rivarol is here, Marat, Chamfort, Danton. Servan is reading out his own pamphlet. *If hotheads still dream of holding back the changes that millions are demanding; if fanatics wish to build a dam with their coats-of-arms, robes and necklaces, strings of pearls, hats of office, mitres and crosses – then let us, in return, offer them not our anger but our laughter.* At Versailles, history is frozen; at the Palais-Royal it is a foaming torrent. It will sweep us along, like children in small boats, to paradise. Six thousand people of all sorts cram themselves into the gardens to promenade, listen, laugh, solicit, pick pockets, learn satirical slogans, play chess or billiards, read journals. You gawp at the four-hundred-pound man Butterbrodt. You sigh at the two-hundred-years-old corpse of Zulima. You enjoy serious arguments in the Café Foy, and risqué repartee in the fetid air of the Grotte Flamande. White-faced Harlequin will wring your tears in the Théâtre Beaujolais, if you can squeeze in. Look, over there the merry Grammont family have everyone at a roar with their *poissard* patter. Pass between the magic-lantern booth and the shadow-light show, along the arcades of the wig-makers and the lace-makers, smile at the whores, bet on the knave of hearts, but exactly at noon do not fail to be beside the miniature cannon, which will be fired when the meridional ray falls upon it. Smoke hangs on the air. And the moment of silence that follows is broken by a cry of "The King to Paris!" Cheers, easy laughter. There is no rancour here, not yet. We are the children of the *patrie*. We want our King with us here, in the heart of Paris, because he belongs to us, to the people, the family that is France. He should reside at the Tuileries. No one will decry the King. So what if he has issued a ban on political pamphlets? It has served only to increase their production tenfold. They denounce the aristocrats who would fain sabotage the Estates-General. They execrate the King's wife, who sells herself for a diamond necklace. But it is, for the most part, just general denunciation. The pamphleteers denounce the state of things, as Rabelais would if he were here, or Molière. Over there, Desmoulins is declaring that tax fiefs are leeches on the body politic, and no policeman will arrest him, for this is a private place, a sacrosanct carnival, and the policemen wear no uniforms, you know them by their eyes only. Later, in years to come, we will know them better. But by then we will know, too, that the jolly Grammonts have been employed to sniff out traitors for the guillotine, and Zulima's perfectly preserved body was wax. Not yet. Now, at midnight, torchlight flickers on the sweaty faces who are watching the principal balcony, in case the most popular man in France will wave to them tonight. He is the Prince, Philippe, Duke of

Chartres, Duke of Orleans, and of a coronet of other titles which, soon, he will doff to call himself Citizen Égalité. He is the great spoon that stirs this melting-pot, in the gardens of his palace. He is the hope of the liberals, and the despair of his more numerous creditors.

When he engaged me as a private secretary, he offered me six thousand livres a year.

I inclined my head, and said nothing.

"You accept?"

"Thank you, Sire. Yes." It is more than double my salary from the army.

"You seem doubtful."

"It is my way."

"Good. It is not mine," he drawls. "I need someone for the doubtful things."

"Can you describe what my duties will be in your service?"

"Very well. Your first duty will be to deny that you are in my service, when speaking with anyone outside this establishment." As the Prince speaks, his vague eyes rest on my face occasionally. With thirty years of training, I keep myself inscrutable. "Your second duty will be to keep your ears open. Your third will be to keep your eyes open."

I nod. "Thank you, Sire."

His delicate Bourbon mouth, underscoring a big nose in a florid face, has the habit of twitching once or twice before he speaks. "I dare say I shall think up other duties, as time goes by. We shall see, eh?"

"Sire."

"Have you any further questions?"

"Two, Sire. At present, I live with my family in Versailles. Would it be more convenient for you if I were to live in Paris?"

Twitch, twitch. "Versailles is perfect, Monsieur de Laclos. Please remain there, and attend me here twice a week. Shee keeps my diary. He will make the next appointment after each of your visits."

"My second question is something more delicate. If my

service to you must remain confidential, it will presumably not be possible for you to raise me, as I had hoped, to the rank of gentleman?"

The Prince laughs, raises his heavy body from the ornate chair, and stands at the window, looking down at the crowds in his gardens of paradise. "But they tell me you are not a gentleman," he says, swivelling his neck to turn those vague eyes upon me.

I smile. To be offended would be to retreat. To smile is a step into complicity. And so I smile, and answer, "They do not know me."

"Then they have served me badly with their advice." He leans down and picks up a long-haired, grey cat that is familiar to his office. He scratches the cat behind its ears. "Not that it was on their advice that I decided to engage you. I took that decision myself."

"I am flattered, Sire," I murmur. We have met only twice, once here in the Palais-Royal with Saint-Georges, and once at a lodge. They told me he was indecisive. Perhaps they were wrong about him.

"If I find you indeed to be a gentleman, I shall be perplexed. Is the book you wrote not a scandalous chronicle?"

"That is for you to judge, Sire. I am merely the author."

"Oh," he laughs, "don't fear, I shan't read it. I have no need to expose myself to satanic influences. Besides, there is no time for me to read books. I leave that to Madame de Genlis." He is stroking the cat's ears, which are flattened.

"I will say only this, that my book, however it may be received, is a fiction."

"And so less strange than truth?"

"Possibly. But more true."

Nodding, he turns the cat upside-down in his arms, and rubs it on the belly. The cat seems to enjoy it. "Well," the Prince says, "I have another appointment now. I look forward to our meetings, Monsieur de Laclos. Please make your arrangements with Shee."

"Sire." I bow, and leave.

To reach Shee's office I had to pass through a drawing-room. Then, as it always would be, it was littered with hangers-on to the man who was seventh in line to the throne. Tobacco smoke drifts on the air, swirled by large gestures and cackles. I nod to the faces I know, several of them on leave, as I am, and make a promise to myself. I will become indispensable to the Prince. My motive, unlike theirs, is disinterested. I wish to correct morals. That has been my constant desire. Having done what I could with a novel, now I will try to use political influence.

Henry Shee was about my age. It was hard to assess him, because he spoke French with a brogue. "The Prince has tol' me o' yewer appintment. Yew most be sainin' these peepers, now." He wore a suit of clothes apparently flayed from the living sheep, and displayed an uncovered pate, freckled, and fringed with red hair. The Prince must trust him, I reflect, because of his uncouthness. Who would give credence to secrets whispered by Shee?

I sign the papers, and coach it home to Versailles with a beating heart. I know what is said of my new employer. He has more money than sense, and more debts than money. His notion of economic reform is to dissipate his huge fortune as swiftly as possible by paying interest to as many creditors as he can enlist. His investment in the Palais-Royal is being sold off piecemeal. His reputation as a liberal reformer is no more than a mask to protect the liberties he takes for himself. As though to be an inbred Bourbon were not warranty of a weak mind, he has dunked his will in debauchery. A reception at six will always be a dance at eight, a party at ten, and an orgy by midnight. All of it I have heard often, and do not care how much truth there is in it. I have become his man so that I can make him mine. In order to lay siege to the decadent aristocracy, what more exquisite engine could I find than a great nobleman? It is subtler than the Trojan horse.

Marie-Soulange is full of questions. All I tell her is that the

Prince has been kind enough to indicate certain courses it would be profitable for me to follow. I see she is disappointed for me, thinking I have been rebuffed, and so I hasten to add that the Prince and I have reached an excellent understanding, and that I will be in his circle henceforth. Very well, she says, but that will not raise you to be a gentleman, will it? I shrug. Who knows? And besides, what do I care for titles? The army cares, she answers. Yes, but I no longer care for the army. Then how do I expect to earn my living? I put her mind at rest: I am still on leave for some months, and with the Prince's influence should certainly find a position before my commission has expired. She persists: what sort of position? The artillery is the only occupation I have ever known. I put my arms around her to gentle her, and remind her that what one learns in the artillery is more than cannon practice. In the end, she smiles trustingly at me. I wish I could tell her everything, but have to keep my excitement to myself.

After three decades of tedium, I now have a purpose in noting all that I hear and see. I put on a show of the personality that till now has come naturally to me: I train myself to breathe deeply, blink slowly, and laugh never, so as not to awaken suspicion by any alteration in my appearance. Everyone else is excited too, at this time, and shows it. In salon conversation, anything seems possible, and most things desirable. When in Versailles, I am regularly to be found *chez* Madame d'Angiviller, whose ugliness is shaded by her wit. She likes to arrange for literary readings, followed by a discussion. No matter the subject of the reading, the talk invariably turns to political reform. An Ovidian pastorale will provoke ridicule of the Queen's antics with sheep, just as a piece portraying city life will at once remind a listener of Marie-Antoinette's fondness for the Grammonts' gutter slang. On fine days, our hostess leads us to her pavilion beneath the trees, where we sip wine, and some go fishing in the lake, whereupon the market price of herring will surely be mentioned, and the price of bread will have every wig shaking in confident despair.

Like a rustling in the leaves and a distant thunder, some dramatic change is presaged by the calling of the Estates-General, and every fool is blurting out his prognostication. Those that have at least an ounce of sense I commit to memory, and later write them down in the dossier I present twice a week to the Prince; anything touching directly upon what part he might himself have in government I mark up with red ink. The rest I hear and scorn: aristocrats playing with revolutionary visions as though they were the latest toys; notorious rakes piously assuring me that a contented domesticity is what every Frenchman yearns for. People I have since seen cheering the tumbrils spoke, then, of the paramount need for tenderness in political dealings, "as Rousseau has so eloquently persuaded us" the more sanctimonious ones chanted.

At nights, always in black, with a silk waistcoat, I frequent the political clubs that have sprung up like toadstools since the royal edict banning them. Men of substance, if not of sense, are to be heard: Mirabeau, Barnave, Sieyès, Lafayette, Servan, Duport, Chamfort, Condorcet, de Guibert, Desmoulins. When I make the acquaintance of Talleyrand, he flatters me by greeting me first. "Monsieur de Laclos, I have read what you write."

I incline my head, as usual saying little, listening much.

"You are" – he chooses his word – "versatile." And he grins at me with yellow teeth.

"Sir," I reply, "versatility is a skill we all do well to practise now."

He sniffs, and looks away, and for a moment I think him easily offended, but it is only his manner. He grins again. "As Bishop of Autun, I condemn your opinion. But as an atheist I commend it." He steps closer to me, on his crippled leg, and quietly asks, "Is Orleans paying you well?"

I know him to be a member of the intimate circle at the Palais-Royal, so am not perturbed by the question. "His Highness is a generous employer," I answer, wondering whether

Talleyrand is perhaps employed to spy for the Prince upon the Prince's spy.

"Particularly of other people's money," Talleyrand cackles.

I reflect that I will have to report this conversation, else Talleyrand might report that I have not reported it.

"He came into the second largest fortune in France, you know."

I nod soberly. "So they say."

"By now I suppose it is the second largest fortune in England."

"His affection for that country is no secret," I observe.

"His investment in that country is."

I am certain that I am being sounded. I say, "I have no knowledge of his financial affairs. I imagine that Shee deals with all that."

"Then you have a vivid imagination, Monsieur de Laclos. It would require a bogful of Irish buggers to deal with all the Prince's accounts."

Talleyrand watches me for a few moments, then perfunctorily nods, and limps away with surprising agility. The conversation leaves me feeling uncomfortable, but intact.

Sometimes the Prince was at the clubs, or at one of the lodges I attended. At such places, we avoided encountering each other. Within a day or two, I would be visiting him with my dossier. I was punctual, which meant that often I had to wait for hours until the Prince was back from ballooning, fencing, swimming, riding, gambling, dancing, or dallying with Agnès de Buffon, whom he kept in the house where her predecessor, Grace Elliott, still lived. (Such matters, which were in any case open secrets, I had made it my business to discover, believing that it is prudent to know one's ally as thoroughly as one wishes to know one's enemy. *Leave no opportunity to be taken by surprise* is a precept I taught for thirty years.) His wife, the Duchess, lived at the palace, and was devoted to him when they met at Tuesday lunchtimes.

Another retired mistress haunted the Palais-Royal. Madame

de Genlis had been given the post of educating the Prince's beloved children, as a superannuation, one supposed. A woman has but one season of beauty, though it may last for years. La Genlis was visibly losing her petals. The skin was coarse on the backs of her hands and under her ears. Her eyes bulged at the tightness of her corsage. No doubt she envied la Buffon's blonde curls and la Elliott her lissom English thighs, but her resentments vented themselves openly upon me.

"You will corrupt the Prince's character," she tells me, having cornered me in a waiting-room.

"What is golden cannot be corrupted, Madame."

"No. But it is easily worked."

"If there is one thing that upsets my stomach, it is a mixed metaphor before luncheon."

"I despise your sarcasms. I shall not rest until I have seen to it that you are sent packing."

"I think you should rest sooner than that, Madame, for your complexion's sake."

Such boulevard knockabout, similar to the stuff being played in the booths beneath the palace windows, was our intercourse every time we met. It was none of my doing. At first, I put it down to the spite of one who knew she could never be more than a pink-ink novelettiste, a Riccoboni with talons. But I came to realise that what goaded her was jealousy. If she could no longer enjoy the Prince between her legs, at least his ears had still been hers. She saw herself as his preceptor. My arrival threatened her position. Once I had understood that, and surveyed the terrain over which we were fighting, I found myself quite looking forward to the heavy scent of musk that entered the room before she did.

"I have told the Prince that if the author of that degrading book of yours is appointed to his household staff, I can no longer be held responsible for his children's morals."

"Did my book degrade you, Madame?"

"Of course not. I am made of sterner stuff."

"That is plain to all who have the pleasure of seeing you,

Madame." I make the tiniest *moue*, to enrage her. "But the noble children, you fear, have feebler minds than yours?"

"They are still of a tender age, Monsieur." She is grinding her teeth. "It is my duty to educate them to loathe such filth."

And, instead, to savour such rosewater as you publish, I reflect. But I hold my tongue; that is not the field of our combat. "Tell me," I continue, "how many people could you introduce me to, at your salon, who would admit to being degraded by my book?"

"I would not receive such people."

"And so you must know of some, in order not to receive them."

"Everyone knows such people."

"With the unique exception of myself," I say. "How curious!"

"You flatter yourself, Monsieur de Laclos."

"Rather that than flatter you, Madame."

I do not flinch from her baleful gaze. After skirmishes of that sort, gradually she is less often to be met in the public rooms, and I count myself the victor, particularly when the Prince asks me to spend more time at the palace.

"Your reports have been most enlightening," he says. "But someone else can do them now. I would like the benefit of your advice."

"On what question, Sire?"

"Oh, I don't know yet. Everything." Twitch, twitch. "Politics, money. I am surfeited with one and strapped for the other. Talk to Shee. He will indicate the matters on which your opinions will be useful."

"Very good, Sire. May I consider this an official appointment to your household staff?"

"No. Good gracious, no. How eager you are to acquire titles."

"It is the way of one who has suffered from the lack of them."

"And mine, I suppose, is that of one who has enough of

them to stuff his pillows. You do not look like a man who has suffered."

"I count upon it, Sire, that nothing in my appearance betrays my true self."

"That is truly spoken." The Prince chuckles. "It is remarkable, don't you think, how often our conversation turns upon that word, truth?"

"Turns, Sire, but does not dwell. I have always believed that truth is like a target. To hit it, one must never aim straight at it, or the ball will fall short."

"Quite. Quite." His eyes have become vacant. Then his lips twitch again. "The thing is this, Monsieur de Laclos. Continue to keep your association with me a secret, eh? That way, you will be able to perform services for me that would be misconstrued if you were known to be a member of my staff."

"Sire." I bow, and leave.

Shee seems surprised when I present myself in his office. "Yewer opinions, is it now? The Prince has said nothin' to me o' this." He is shaking his freckled pate bemusedly. "Well, d'yew have any knowledge o' financial administreetion?"

I reply that I have always been precise and methodical in mathematics.

Shee looks up at the ceiling, thrusting out his large lower lip and blowing across it. "That's something. If yew would care to busy yourself for an hour or two in the balancing o' that ledger there, we maight be eeble to have a discussion o' sorts on what it releetes to."

I am still busy with the ledger by the end of the afternoon, having detected anomalies in the current pages which lead to the unravelling of earlier errors, back through several years. It is not until late the following morning that I am able to present Shee with a meticulously balanced account of the Prince's revenues from certain tax fiefs in Normandy and Picardy since April 1784.

The Irishman studies my work for a few minutes, and congratulates me. Then he lowers his pince-nez, and asks me what my opinion is of the matters disclosed in the accounts.

Closing my eyes and pressing fingertips to my forehead, I answer that, now the figures have been corrected, everything seems largely in order, although it might be well if certain trimensual dues from the Bayeux region were to be aligned with the bimensual remittances commonly made by officers elsewhere. It is an easy opinion to offer, and that is why I offer it. I would not profit from any deeper analysis if I expressed it to Shee. He might appropriate it and use it to advance himself in the Prince's eyes. Even if he did not, I wish to establish a confidence between myself and the Prince alone. The considered opinions that I offer him will be political ones, not strictures of accountancy. I have formed the intention of supplanting Shee.

For the time being, it suits me that Shee invites me to scrutinise further ledgers. The more I know of the Prince's finances, the better placed I will be to determine the carry and angle in which I can advise him to direct his influence. Is he on the verge of bankruptcy, as most say, or is his fortune shrewdly hidden away, as a few such as Talleyrand allege? What is in no doubt is his popularity. I have stopped bothering to report to him on how often I hear the story that, when the King snubbed him by not inviting him to see the illuminations at the Trianon, he had simply gone along and stood among the common people. I ask Shee about that, one day, framing my question carefully. "Did the Prince not fear any taint of ignominy?"

"Ah," Shee replies. "I was after mentionin' that to him. But he answered me he wanted to see the fireworks and that was it, and his cousin be damned. And off he goes wi' Mademoiselle Agnès and some few bottles o' champeegne and the taime of his laife he has."

I nod, satisfied that the initiative had not been one to Shee's credit. The Prince's own generous if unruly nature is what makes him popular. But I doubt if Shee, still less the Prince, has given a moment's thought to the question of how popularity might be converted into power. I need a powerful prince. While continuing to tidy up one ledger after another, all of them disfigured by minor errors, I wait for my moment.

* * *

In late November, that year of 1788, a frost seized hold of France and did not let go for months. Icicles hung from every roof and branch, and in the streets people's breath made little mists in front of their faces, and the river froze down to Le Havre. Mornings and evenings, the pale sun turned the river into a dazzling street of light. Thousands of the poorer sort had no work. The price of bread doubled and tripled, and in the Palais-Royal gardens you heard jokes that the sacrament would be a sliver of turnip; but the orators howled that the Court at Versailles was refusing to make any economies at all, and bread was still baked there four times a day. Among the listening crowds, the women in particular shouted in their anger. I saw their faces, and their clenched, blue fists, and I advised the Prince to act at once. He should pay for charitable counters to be set up throughout Paris, and beyond the city if possible.

He did not take long to think about it. "I approve of your idea," he tells me. "Please tell Shee to make all the necessary arrangements."

Shee grumbles. "Haven't I already got my hands full? If it was yewer idea, why don't yew set about seein' to it?"

"The Prince specifically designated it as your responsibility. I have other duties to attend to for him."

"Hmm." Shee pulls his shaggy coat tighter around his shoulders. "Tell me, one of those duties now, would it be to whistle up the money we shall be needin' to feed the populace of Paris?"

I shrug. "The Prince was confident that you would know how to make all provisions."

Shee throws his head back, and stares at the ceiling. "Was he, now? Was he? Right." He stands up, blowing on his hands. "I think I'll be goin' along to enquire o' the Prince where I can

100

get hold of some o' that store o' confidence he has found. 'Tis a commodity we've been lackin'."

"The Prince has gone skating. But he did ask me to tell you that he counts on your making an immediate start to the arrangements."

I close the door of Shee's room behind me, and with a light step go down to the courtyard, where the Prince is waiting in his coach to take me skating with him. Not that I skate. I simply help him on with his skates, and then stand on the bank of the Seine and watch as, hands behind his back, he glides smilingly among skaters, and ragamuffins in wooden boots, and muffed women who nudge each other when they see who is skating among them.

Within the week, the first premise is ready, on the rue Saint-Antoine. When I advise the Prince that he should make an appearance to bless his own charitable work, he frowns. "I have arranged to spend the day with Mademoiselle de Buffon."

"It need not take longer than an hour, Sire. It does seem a pity, after so generous a conception on your part, if you deny the beneficiaries an opportunity to express their gratitude."

He sucks his teeth. "You are right. Go and fetch Shee. We will all go together."

"I believe that Shee will be too busy with his arrangements for the further premises that will open shortly."

"Tell him it need not take longer than an hour. I want him there, in case the thing needs improvement."

"Very good, Sire."

On the way, the Prince is testy again. "What the deuce do I *do*? Just beam upon my creation? Isn't it enough that I supply them with bread and fishes? Must I cavort for them as well?"

"Sire." I politely raise my hand. "If you will be advised by me, all that is required of you is that you should hand bread to three or four of the needy, and announce your sincere hope that His Majesty's government will shortly come to see it as their duty to follow your example, till the winter relents."

The Prince squints at me, as the carriage jolts over the

cobblestones of Saint-Antoine. "Tell me again, Laclos."

I repeat my advice. Across the carriage, Shee blinks and glares.

The Prince surpasses my expectations. Once he has descended from the carriage and entered the shop, a disused cobbler's, he is all graciousness. He faces the crowd, which has spilled beyond the doorway, and with a countenance as fresh as the smell of baked bread he tells them that their hunger and suffering are undeserved, the good people of Paris merit better treatment than he alone can provide, but if this small gesture were to alleviate their pangs even for one hour then he is grateful for the opportunity to be of comfort to them. And with that, he has his hands covered in flour as he reaches loaves down from the straw-lined shelves and donates them to women at the front of the crowd. With satisfaction, I note that two journalists I spoke to in the palace gardens earlier this morning are standing in the doorway, taking in the scene of benefaction.

Afterwards, the Prince is in high good humour. Again postponing his assignation with Mademoiselle de Buffon, he insists that Shee and I share two bottles of champagne with him. When Madame de Genlis is announced, and enters with some perfumed and tedious question to do with his children, he waves the matter aside and sends for another bottle, and some almond biscuits. Twitching his great red nose at me over his goblet, he says, "You must admit, Laclos, that the whole business came off devilish well."

I incline my head. "My opinion, Sire, is that it has proved the love and esteem in which you are held by the ordinary people."

When I raise my head again, Shee and la Genlis are watching me with faces of cold marble.

In the bitter heart of the winter, the country fell into the fitful dreaming of a man who is freezing to death. Travelling between Paris and Versailles, I seldom saw any living soul. Sometimes a muffled peasant might be tramping through the brittle ferns in search of dead birds, or gathering wood to burn or boil. From cottage chimneys, coils of smoke rose blue and vertical on the still air. The people were dreaming of bread. But in the Palais-Royal and in its gardens, the dreams were of different stuff. Every spouter or scribbler, every hanger-on in the Prince's drawing-room, had his utopian vision ready for you if you but caught his madly staring eye. And theirs were the dreams that started to be distilled when the King clucked his tongue and with a bad grace conceded to Necker that, oh very well, the numbers of the Third Estate could be equal to the nobility and the clergy together. Had the King walked in disguise through the Palais-Royal gardens that evening, he would have revoked his edict at daybreak. I never heard such a babbling, never saw so many arms waved, fists clenched, eyes rolling, so much spittle on the air.

I breathed contentedly, and almost smiled. It was possible, now, that the State might be saved, under a better régime. What was sure was that the aristocrats faced a bitter winter of their own. I enjoyed imagining their faces when they heard the news: Ségur, Florian, the Queen's crew, and all the predatory Mantises and Arachnidae of Grenoble.

By this time I was conducting the Prince's political correspondence for him. Shee had not the time for that any more since, on my recommendation, the Prince had asked him to be less slapdash in his accounting. There were many complicated ledgers, and I made it my habit to review them periodically, after Shee had balanced them. However, my chief duty was to read the Prince's mail, greatly swollen since the King's edict, and to draft replies where required. And so I was in touch with all the Prince's vast domains, and it was natural that he should turn to me for advice when the time came to invite every bailiwick in the land to submit its bill of grievances.

The royal council had absurdly ordained that the people should confer among themselves as to what needed to be redressed, and who should represent them when the Third Estate assembled. To everyone else, it was obvious that the people could not do what was asked of them without instruction. All the academies, clubs and lodges were bent on assisting the qualified populace to ensure its enfranchisement, and reminding it of what had for so many years ailed it, and what the cure would be. Our view, at the Palais-Royal, was that it would be irresponsible to fall silent at the very moment when every prating halfwit in France was having his say. The drawing-room of the palace, and the hustings in the gardens, had been the very vocal chords of protest in the first place. Now our slogans, heterodox though they were, had to triple in volume.

I never saw the Prince more gay. This great stirring-up was a capital sport. He was laying bets on the outcome of it all. The least thing it could achieve would be to annoy his cousin the King, and to distress the Queen. "Whatever happens, Laclos," he remarked, "that Austrian cow will know what it is to be milked by horny French hands." But a larger dream than that was preoccupying him, and made him giggle with excitement. Duport, Talleyrand, and the rest, even Shee, kept assuring him that he would achieve pre-eminence in the new state of affairs that the Estates-General would deliver. I see now, five years on, that he could never quite believe what they told him because he could never quite want it. But I believed in it then, along with the rest, even though I did not believe in yapping my strategy into every pink ear that passed.

At the Prince's behest, I draw up a draft list of grievances to be sent out to our bailiwicks. We are agreed on the main heads: taxing only by consent of the Estates-General; an end to arbitrary arrests; freedom of expression in print; confidentiality of the mails; property to be sacrosanct. I do not quibble at the Prince's insistence on freedom of movement, though I know it to be merely an obsession he has had since the King exiled him from Paris for a while after some unruliness. He, however, does fret at my own attachment to a right of divorce by joint consent, which I have held as a conviction since my essay on the enslavement of women. "The Church won't like it," he grumbles.

"The Church," I remind him, "won't like much else of what

104

we are demanding. The Church likes things just the way they always have been."

"Well ..." he drawls, not wishing to oppose me, nowadays, but reluctant to waste a point of view, "let us invite Bishop Talleyrand to arbitrate. What do you say?"

What I say to myself is that Talleyrand will instantly spot the chance to discredit my judgment, whatever opinion he might hold. "Talleyrand," I reply, "is at present pressed by so many matters that I doubt he would have the time to consult anyone else. May I respectfully propose that the Abbot Sieyès be asked instead? He is as true an atheist as Talleyrand, and will therefore be as impartial."

My master agrees to Sieyès, with whom I have been cordial since he told me that his ambition, from before his parents obliged him to take the cloth, has always been to fire cannons. His weatherworn gargoyle of a face, whose ruin has gained him a false reputation for piety, creases in a hundred lines as he adds, "Instead, I fire canons." I send for Sieyès, and hand him the draft of our manifesto, asking him to adjudicate on the phrasing of the point concerning divorce. He takes it away, and brings it back rewritten in its entirety. The whole document.

Together, we go in to see the Prince, each holding Sieyès's version by one corner. "I believe I have improved the persuasiveness of your proposals," the Abbot declares.

"I believe he has muffled our drum," I retort. "Let us be bold. That is what will stir the sleeping spirit of France."

The Prince reads Sieyès's paper, then he takes out his copy of mine and reads it over, nodding, and clearing his throat. Eventually, he leans forward and places both documents on his desk in front of me. His eyes wander about me as though I am too bright to be looked at, and he says, "Good. Here is my choice. We will have both the texts printed together. That will offer people the opportunity to make up their minds for themselves. Thank you, gentlemen, both."

As we walk away down the corridor, side by side, Sieyès and I say nothing to each other, and avoid catching the other's eye.

I took both manifestoes to a printing-house, and ordered a hundred thousand copies. Then I told Shee that the bill for the joint opinions would be larger than we had anticipated. He sighed, but I did not stay to discuss the matter. It was the Prince's decision.

The documents were sent out to the bailiwicks. When the bills of grievances started to come back to Versailles, I took advantage of connections among my circle there to get a sight of some of them. I read lamentations of a simplicity that would have made Rousseau weep: a yearning to be as we were in the golden age, cherished and protected by an infinitely benign king, who would ensure that all had daily bread to eat. Others, in contrast, probably dictated by bourgeois free-thinkers with knowledge of the American independencies, spoke of the imperative need to guarantee bread for all by policies that would produce work for all, through free trade. But the petitions that stopped my breath avowed that they had been "drawn up according to instructions received from the Duke of Orleans". Short of burgling the Palace of Versailles by night, I had no means of intercepting such inanities. However, quite a few bailiwicks nominated the Prince to represent them at the Estates-General. And in April, only a week before the Parlement met to prepare for the great assembly, the nobility of the Palais-Royal quarter elected the Prince to nominate their representatives in the First Estate, and requested him to choose someone else to assist him. "I told them you'll do it with me," he said.

"Sire." I bow. "Did you reflect that, in naming me, you discarded all vestiges of secrecy in my association with you?"

"Well, what of it? Everybody knew by now. Anyway, it's too late to matter. In a week or two we shall have what we wanted."

"Yes, Sire. What is it that we wanted, precisely?"

Twitch, twitch. "I have never been quite certain what it is that you want, de Laclos. For myself, I want something to change in this blasted country. I don't, frankly, much care what. Though I do not see how anything amusing could stick in place while my cousin and his cow rule the barnyard. That is why I'm willing to go along with what all of you have been telling me. We shall see, eh? It might be fun."

I decide not to tell him that I want to see the end of the aristocracy, though not of a modified class of nobility; that I want to see the fall of Louis XVI, though certainly not of the monarchy; or that he would suit me as the successor to the throne. Of all that I want in deadly earnest, I say only, "I will undertake to recommend to you noble representatives of the quarter, Sire. I propose, also, to speak with some members of the Third Estate, so that we may be fully apprised of their thinking."

"Good, good," he answers. "That sounds an excellent plan. I will see you tomorrow afternoon. In the morning, I must take the air."

9

I have realised what it is I most detest in this slavery Laclos puts me to. He trusts me.

What contempt that betrays. What a trespass upon my spiritual estate.

Let them come for me, take me in the tumbril, executioner at the prow, preceded by mounted gendarmes, us seated on boards, nodding all the way as though at the justice of it, gendarmes on foot following us, and to complete the procession the carriage packed with appointed bigots – still I will hold my head high, shirt ripped open, be seigneur of my self. Let them merely deny me my few miserable comforts in this place, let them starve me, sully me, I will not flinch. I will not allow them that satisfaction. They will not perforate my soul.

But this trust of his is a vile, oozing infringement. I must build monstrous walls to keep it out, seclude myself invulnerably behind fathomless ravines. It is like the horror of reading Rousseau. He played the same tricks, insinuated himself with such presumption, as though beguiling a cat from a chimney. Laclos must have shuddered at that, too, felt raped in the mind. Now he is using me to avenge himself for that horror, that guilt. Why otherwise all this suicidal maundering about monarchy, about his complicity with Orleans (though not a word yet about being the Prince's pretty boy, I notice, and perhaps that is what I can use to dam up his unction), all this sitting in the shade of apricot trees and droning on to me about what should be a shut book, shut, and his talking as though everybody else's behaviour has been merely evidence concerning a theory he is perfecting?

Is there something about a garden in springtime that deludes him? This garden is a deceit, one of Dante's visions. In the adjacent circle, citizen, a man with green spectacles still rules our roost, and we may be plucked and trussed tonight. I am tormented out here by the noise the birds make in the trees, those terrible primal cries which, to feel comfortable, men call singing.

He starts today with a string of disgusting excuses and threats.

* * *

Citizen Sade's kindness in assisting me with this memoir has whetted an unsuspected taste in me for setting down the exact part I played in the most momentous period of France's history. Should I be thought indiscreet to disclose the motive and method of certain initiatives I took, I will answer thus:

First, I have come to realise, shamefully long after being so moved by Rousseau's *Confessions*, that to unburden the soul is, truly, a potent cure. This past week I have slept better than for years, and my waking hours, moreover, have been almost free of the tedium that I dread more than death itself. I am sure it is waiting to greet me outside the Picpus gate, when I am released; the memory of this present refreshment may warm me then, as well as the company of my dear wife.

Second, I have nothing to be ashamed of! I may be accused of tactical error and I would not demur; but as to my intentions, nothing lies on my conscience for which I can reproach myself, or would expect reproach from the most extreme of revolutionaries. My adherence to monarchism was simply a perhaps old-fashioned form of the argument that the State must have a head, an argument still unresolved in the republic. My adherence to the Prince was congruent with that argument, though I have acknowledged that my judgment was faulty in believing him to be the sovereign France needed.

Third, the technical contribution I have made to the republic, and may still have to make, is recognised at the highest levels, even given Danton's demise. I allude chiefly to techniques I am still developing in explosives. My part in the triumph at Valmy is also known, as is my innocence of the reactionary tendencies later exhibited by some generals.

Fourth, leading members of the Committees are aware of certain information I have about them, and that it would not fall with my head into the basket, but on the contrary be released by such an event, through an agent I have appointed.

Why need I prevaricate since, last, Citizen Sade knows that the memoir is my property, that both his notes and transcript will be handed to me on his or my release from the Picpus, whichever shall occur first, and that any default therein, or interim disclosure, would be severely rebuked by – why not name him? – Citizen Robespierre? In years to come, the political temper may alter, and allow me to publish the memoir openly. Until then, Robespierre has a concern for me. Custody here is his device to shelter me from less well-informed members of the Committees, rather than a corrective sentence, still less a prelude to execution. (I trust, Citizen Sade, that as well as noting all that down you have also fully weighed its import.)

[I have not the remotest interest in disclosing this stuff. I shall accidentally burn the lot, once I have had my turn. Will that cost me my head, you complacent knob of snake turd? – L.S.]

§ **By the Fireside**

Many slanders have been aimed at me, and one of them I will rebut now. Talleyrand still lies that I inspired the riots when the Paris Parlement met. If he had the courage to return to France, I would face him down with the facts, which are as follows.

The Parlement meeting, as everyone knows, was a fiasco. Only ten minutes after Lamoignon started to speak, he had to shout in order to be heard above the King's snoring. Louis thought the chamber of justice meant a bedchamber, people said. But I wonder. The royal fool may have been sly enough to do it on purpose, so as to ridicule the occasion. He would have

111

done anything to achieve his single goal (his wife's single goal, that is), which was to have the Estates-General postponed, for ever if possible. When snoring will not avail, he tries his hand at despotism. "The assembly of the Estates-General summoned for the end of this week is postponed," he declares, and that is his edict, and it is a statute with instant effect.

"But you have not invited us to vote on it," Lamoignon quavers.

"There is no need for a vote," the King says. "I have promulgated the edict. You heard me."

The chamber is filled with open mouths, hardly daring to breathe. And then the silence of shock is followed by the silence of incredulity, at the sight of the Prince rising to speak. Of all people. A more inept orator even than his cousin. Both have tongues of clay. But what no one knows is that he and I have rehearsed him in a speech, over and over, with inflections and hot gestures, until he had it pat. This, of course, is not it, not the speech we have prepared, because this crisis has not been foreseen. However, our rehearsal has so fired him that he is prepared to stand up and speak impromptu.

"I beg Your Majesty to allow me to place at your feet and in the heart of this court the fact that I consider this edict illegal."

It is not well done, in any rhetorical manner, but the wonder to everyone is that it is done at all. And it works – I suppose because Louis must feel as though he has been savaged by the family's pet goldfish. All coherence deserts him.

"The edict is legal because ... because I have heard the opinions of everyone ... since no one has spoken ... Oh well, I don't care," he snapped. "You're the master. Of course." And he turns three-quarters away from the chamber in his feeble pique.

I wish I had a drawing of Marie-Antoinette's expression. It was a family quarrel, which you might argue decided the fate of France, though I think you would be wrong. The revolution was a sea that would find another open porthole if not this one.

Later, the Prince rather spoils the memory of that moment

when he rises to speak, in the Orleans tradition, against arbitrary taxation. This is the speech we have rehearsed, and it begins, "I beg Your Majesty to allow me to place at your feet and in the heart of this court ..." He brings it off well enough, and its substance, as we have planned, makes a hero of him for a time among the orators in the gardens, but it cannot stun the Parlement as his first intervention had.

That evening, by his fireside, the Prince and I discuss the need to consolidate the position thus established. It is good to have taken the King by the ears. But my conversations with elected members of the Third Estate have convinced me that we have to attack on another front.

The Prince's great popularity depended to a perilous extent upon an air of buffoonery he had. When people saw him, they smiled; they did not take him seriously. His reputation for liberal opinions was derived from his readiness to offend the King, as he had again proved today. But the view that one's royal cousin is stuffy, and his wife a cow, does not amount to a political programme. The bill of grievances we had drawn up for the bailiwicks was everyone's liberal charter, not just ours. An eclipse of the sun might be expected before he could impress an assembly again. Nor could any amount of handing out of charitable loaves make him seem a substantial figure of state. What people saw was a generous buffoon. It was already plain to me that the Third Estate was the constituency that had to be persuaded. I do not pretend, at that moment, to have foreseen the revolution. Who did? We could not even foresee what lay only days ahead, at the Estates-General. But I did not mistake the general drift of the smoke. Sober citizens were winning the field. Some of them were King's men or would be courted to be. The rest would be pleased by the Prince's forthright defence of their right to assemble this week, but would they take him seriously as a statesman, or smile at him as a royal horse-fly?

And so there we were, discussing how to advertise the Prince's fundamental gravity, when the answer found us.

Saint-Georges, his captain of guards, was requesting urgent admittance. His news was that some sort of riot was taking place in the streets. Émigré Talleyrand please note: a riot *was taking place*. It had something to do, Saint-Georges told us, with wages. Thousands were gathered outside the Town Hall, and sticks were out.

Shee, who had come in with Saint-Georges, says, "I'll be going along to faind out more."

"No," I tell him. "I'll go." I turn to the Prince. "Please will you wait here for me, Sire?"

"Oh, very well, if I must."

As I rush past Saint-Georges, he winks, and says, "Ohé!" I wish he wouldn't.

Among the angry crowd, plenty willingly give me their account, and I piece the story together. At an electoral meeting, manufacturers have said that wages have risen too high; soon the workers will be richer than the employers. One manufacturer, a M. Olivier, has been so disturbed by these intemperate remarks that he has reported them to the workers at his porcelain factory. In no time, the word is all over the city: the bourgeoisie are not only hoarding food, they intend to deny the workers any bread at all. A march in protest, headed by a drummer, has swollen to this tumult. Hundreds more arrive every minute. The crowd hold sticks aloft, and torches, and at the front, before the Town Hall, effigies of hanged manufacturers dangle from poles. A formation of armed soldiers is at the top of the steps, facing the crowd.

By the time I have heard the story, I am at the centre of a circle of men who are pleased to find someone who shows concern for their grievances. I choose the four quietest, and draw them aside. "What you will go on to do tonight," I say, "is already beyond anyone's bidding. Probably there will be shots fired. What will you have achieved? Will this display of anger, and a few martyred corpses, feed your children?"

They shake their heads.

"You will go home tonight, and what will you do tomorrow?

Will you find bread at four sous?"

Again, their heads are shaking. "Would you have us do nothing at all?" one asks. "Who are you, that you advise us to starve in silence? A priest?"

"Friends," I tell them, "I am *with* you. What has taken place here so far can only be approved, by any honest man. But I want to see you succeed. I want to see your grievances redressed, and your children fed." I pause. "And for that, you must go beyond sticks and shouting. You must direct your assault. And then sustain it to the point where the Third Estate, and eventually the King himself, are convinced that you will not go away. That your just anger must be accommodated within the new régime that we shall all enjoy shortly. You must be a force, not a rabble."

"What would you have us do?"

"You need tactics and a general," I answer. "I can show you a general, tomorrow. As for tactics, the Town Hall of Paris is a pointless objective. You must thrust at the true enemy, the bourgeoisie who steal your bread from you, the aristocrats who hold you in contempt. Who are they? Give me a name."

"Réveillon," one says.

"Who is he?"

"A manufacturer of wallpaper."

"Where?"

"There!" The man points to one of the dangling effigies, and the rest roar with laughter. "Réveillon is one of those who wants to cut our wages."

"Where is his factory?"

"In the Faubourg Saint-Antoine, rue de Montreuil."

"Very well," I say. "Let us start with Réveillon. Can you put the word about? We will gather outside his factory tomorrow at noon."

They look at each other doubtfully. "We shall be at work tomorrow," one says. "Today is Monday, but tomorrow is Tuesday."

I bring out my purse, with a few coins in it. "Here are your wages for tomorrow," I say. "Share them among you. Tomorrow I will have more for you. And also for, let us say, eight others, to be chosen by you, according to your judgment of who should join with you in spreading the word. Let it go out to as many factories as you can, and to the docks. Pass the word around your lodging-houses. Let tomorrow be another Monday, tell them, or we may soon have seven St Crispin's Mondays every week."

"Thank you, sir. Thank you."

I hurry back to the Palais-Royal full of misgivings. Who are the four men I have chosen at random? Will they be reliable? I don't mind that I might have wasted my money. All that matters is whether it buys what I want. If twenty people with two dogs are waiting for me tomorrow in the rue de Montreuil, my kindling will catch nothing.

Briefly, I tell the Prince what the riot was about. Then, with a deep breath of hope, I say, "I learned that the rioters plan to resume their protest tomorrow, in the Faubourg Saint-Antoine, outside the wallpaper factory of Réveillon, one of the manufacturers who has angered them. If it were possible for us to go there, Sire, at noon, you would have an opportunity to tell them, in a few words, which I will compose, that you are deeply concerned by the seriousness of their grievances, and will bring an equal seriousness to demanding their redress at the Estates-General."

"Ah." The Prince is scratching his ear with one hand, and stroking his cat with the other. "Yes. Yes, I see. But look here, Laclos. The thing has nothing to do with me. I don't even know what the price of wallpaper *is*."

"It is the price of bread that is in question, Sire."

"Well, I don't know that, either."

"Sire, with respect, I am not proposing that you direct the nation's economy. I am simply pointing to an extraordinary opening to effect what we were discussing earlier, you remember. The urgent need for you to manifest how gravely you regard the people's plight."

"Oh yes. Well, I can't do it tomorrow. I'm going to the races at Vincennes."

"Sire." I stroke my moist forehead with my fingers, which are shaking. "May I sit down?"

"Of course. Is there much more to say? It has been a long day, you know."

Vincennes! "Sire, to reach Vincennes, you will be travelling through the Faubourg Saint-Antoine."

"Will I? I suppose you're right."

"Could you arrange to do so at noon, Sire?"

"Hmm," he says. "Well, why not?"

"And on the way, I will suggest to you what few words you might think fit to say to the crowd."

"Oh, I can't take you with me, I'm afraid, de Laclos. I have arranged to go straight to the races with Mesdemoiselles de Buffon and Elliott, from their house. My wife is coming too, in her coach. So there you have it."

I nod. "If, then, I could simply write down a few words for you now, perhaps you would be kind enough to look them over at your leisure? I will meet you outside the factory of Réveillon."

"Very well. Minou, minou." He scratches the cat between its ears.

"At noon, Sire."

"Noon," he says. "Quite."

* * *

When I arrive at the rue de Montreuil I have to shove my way through the crowds in the narrow street. My four men have multiplied into thousands, like dragon's teeth. Last night's mob has been transported across Paris to continue the same performance. Again, a line of soldiers is drawn up facing the crowd, and I guess that reinforcements will not be far away. My four men see me arrive and, with a few companions, come to greet me. I slip them the money I promised them, and congratulate

117

them. "I chose you well."

"Thank you, sir," one says, "but the people were very ready to fall in with what we suggested. Anger is all they have in their bellies."

Another laughs. "Some weren't so keen, but this" – he brandishes a strong fist – "changed their minds for them."

I nod. "Very well. The general I promised you will be here shortly. Meanwhile, do what you can to prevent violence, or any outrage against the factory itself. We are here to bear witness to your grievances, remember, not to solve them for one day by robbery."

"Sir." They understand, and disperse.

That morning Shee, hearing of my arrangement with the Prince, had remarked that Réveillon was by no means an oppressive employer. On the contrary, he had some reputation for benevolence. I had shrugged. "Then it is his words, not his deeds, that have been inflammatory, and we will answer him in like coin."

But while I waited for the Prince I did have misgivings about the discipline of the crowd. I have been used to commanding trained men on the polygon. Here were thousands crammed together, some perched on window-sills, on the roofs even. Of course they had no order about them, nor any clear idea of what to do. A number were drunk. And so, yes, what might ensue did cause me some anxiety. But that is a thing entirely different from the slander that I inspired the affair. It had been ablaze the previous night before I ever heard about it, it would certainly erupt again with no fanning from me or anyone else, and all my responsibility is that I sought to guide it to more productive ends than a riotous affray. And, in spite of what happened, I do not reproach myself. Looking back, I believe it was the initiatory moment of the revolution itself, and even the likes of Talleyrand do not, I presume, deny the essential morality of our revolution, whatever its incidental damage. The Réveillon riot was the opening salvo of a campaign that would have broken out elsewhere if not there. I had, you may say, the honour of being first to command "Fire!"

I was looking at my watch and still the Prince was not there. Fortunately, a number of orators at the Palais-Royal had got wind of the business, and come out to address the crowd. Mirabeau is suddenly at my elbow. He leers at me with those big red cheeks of his. "I might have guessed I'd find you here."

"Why?" I ask, frigidly.

"Orleans told me he'd got to address a meeting down here. He'd need you to hold his hand. I expect you've told him what to say?"

"I am his private secretary, not his private thoughts."

Mirabeau roars. "That's a good one. Why don't you put it in the next speech you write for him?"

Whipped up by the orators, the crowd is chanting, "Liberty! Long live the Third Estate!"

"A good house, eh?" Mirabeau remarks. "I doubt if his nibs is counting on this many, even if he is top of the bill. I just wanted to see how they'd receive him after his performance yesterday. The King hasn't got over it yet. They've not seen him at Versailles all day. He hasn't got out of bed. I expect he's asleep and dreaming he's Louis Quatorze."

Watching the crowd, I too had found myself thinking of the Sun King, and of the rational order of his court, and could not suppress a momentary regret for that devotion to enlightenment. And yet, and yet. Is this hungry mob not a form, admittedly primitive, of the force of Nature, the storm, as it were, that will prove the gardens of Versailles a puny pretension?

The Prince gets there at ten past two. "Sorry," he says to me, leaning out of his coach window at the end of the street, "I couldn't remember the address of the riot."

Then he stands up at the window to speak to the crowd pressing up to him. "Come, friends, be calm. Peace." He raises one hand, holding on with the other. The people near him fall quiet, listening. "Tell me your grievances."

Cries of "Wages, wages, they want to lower our wages, they

want us to starve" swell in the multitude.

The Prince holds up his hand again, smiling. "We have happiness within our reach, friends." And with that, he repeatedly puts his hand behind him, bringing out bags of coins handed to him by mesdemoiselles de Buffon and Elliott. He flings the bags into the mob, who fight among themselves to pick them up.

Mirabeau has come up behind me. "The Duke is reviewing his troops," he says.

I hear the Prince order, "Drive on." As the coach pulls away he is looking back, waving and smiling through the open window.

I turn and watch the scene in the rue de Montreuil. Some are cheering and waving their hats to the departing Prince. Many are on the ground, struggling with each other. Those further away along the street press forward to see what is causing the fights. People are falling, being trampled, or pressed up against the walls, or knocked back by rifle butts. I turn again, and walk away alone.

What ensued is well known: Réveillon's house pillaged, his cellars ransacked, books and furniture hurled from the windows, all after the soldiers had shot many dead before being ordered to withdraw. And later still, some were hanged for their part in it. I have been told that the soldiers might have managed to keep the people back had they not been obliged to stand aside when the Duchess of Orleans insisted on taking the straightest route to Vincennes, along the rue de Montreuil, thus creating the breach through which the mob poured into the house and factory. I do not know if that is true, but suspect it to be one of the ten thousand myths that sprang, as though from the Hydra's head, out of the revolution. I have been assured that I myself stood there later that evening, in the rue de Montreuil, with flames flickering shadows over my face, even though I was by that time at home in Versailles, with Marie-Soulange and my children, beside my own fire.

10

Such a charming domestic scene, citizen. The Laclos family at their fireside, talking about Rousseau, after Papa's day's work has left a few hundred dead and maimed. I picture it painted mostly in hues of brown and dark green, with a few rosy highlights where the firelight catches the cherubic cheeks. And I was the one imprisoned as immoral, for nothing but a few harmless erotic games, and the vivid imagination I was born with. If I were to write a dictionary, I would define society as a machine invented for the production of madness.

No one was better at that than Mirabeau, which explains why he was accorded a state funeral and a place in the Pantheon. Telling Laclos to hold Orleans's hand, that's a joke. He was in Vincennes prison when I was there years ago, and I used to shout down at him in the exercise yard from my cell window, "I know about you, Count of Mirabeau. You are Commandant Rougemont's catamite, you are, and when I get at you I'm going to cut your ears off. Do you hear?" I loved to see how red his face would go. It was just mischief. One has to pass the time. It wouldn't pass, otherwise.

Rougemont himself was the best value, though. Where do they find these jokers to run our prisons? He was worth thirty sous for the performance he'd put on when I submitted one of my regular complaints. He'd arrive in my cell, gorged with food and his tongue dripping gobbets, and he belches them up and splutters, "Oh no, I'm telling you, you don't do me justice, sir. You believe that words are designed for mutual comprehension, which is far from being the case. You must not believe one word of what I am doing myself the honour of telling you, because words have no meaning, sir, none. Oh no ..." Then he is seized with a fit of the hiccoughs and can't go on. You must allow that it was saintly of me to refrain from driving this clown out with a boot in his belly.

De Launay was worse – a self-styled marquis, when we all knew his grandfather had been a valet. De Launay got his job, I suppose, from being born in the Bastille, where his father was governor before him. I cheered when I heard that that cook had jointed De Launay's head for him with a butcher's knife.

One thousand, nine hundred and eighty-one nights I spent in the Bastille. It was there I realised the power of numbers, if one learns how to interpret them. I used to calculate the date on which they would decide to let me out. They moved me to Charenton ten days before the Bastille was stormed, an event on which Laclos will hold forth shortly, and so I will steal his thunder by writing first about it here, since the letters I sent my wife about the place will not have been saved by her, who could not remember to save my masterpiece. Fifteen volumes of my works in manuscript, but above all the *120 Days of Sodom*, all marked up ready for the printer. And she was to have collected them for me, after I had been hustled off, but on the way she has to answer a call of fucking Nature, and then is distracted by the whim of going to the confessional, for God's sake – to confess what, a piss? – and after that, she says, she must have fallen asleep, and when she woke up it had slipped her mind what it was she had set out to do. Aah, those manuscripts for which I have since mourned in tears of blood every day of my life. The only comforts of my seclusion, the only joys I had to look forward to in my old age. She forgot. And then they tore the place down, and I dare say some stout hero of the revolution used them to wipe his leathery arse. The fourteenth of July 1789 is a date of horror to me; 14789, the most malign sequence in my numerology. Bugger the revolution, what about my manuscripts?

Laclos will peddle the line that a horde of grateful innocents streamed out when the place was stormed, but I was *there*, till the week before, and I can assure you, naïve posterity, nobody was left in there save half a dozen whey-faced old idiots and a delightful young Count whose name I will not publish. They moved me only because I had the wit to sense which way the wind was blowing, and the wisdom to call for the destruction of that monument of horror. I started it. I seized the brass funnel that served me for urinal, inverted it horn-fashion, and trumpeted down from the Liberty Tower to the people in the streets of Paris, "They're slaughtering us in here. Help! Come and save us! Raze the Bastille!" So they did, the next week. It was my doing. De Launay said so. He had me moved on account of my inflammatory behaviour, stating that he could no longer answer to the King for his fortress if I were allowed to remain in it. He was too late. People had listened to me, and they knew I was right. I wish I had been there to watch them finish the job. And to carry my manuscripts out with me.

I lost much else, of material account only. My camel-brown tailcoats, silk breeches, shirts, boots, shoes, dressing-gowns, hats, together with the mahogany wardrobe, a fine desk, fire-dogs and tongs, family portraits, tapestries, quilted velvet cushions, pillows, mattresses, eiderdowns, counterpanes, candles and lamps, a library of 133 volumes, including Fénélon, Hume, Fielding, Smollett, Homer, Captains Bougainville and Cook, and a number of scandalous chronicles, a collection of bespoke wooden dildos with which my wife had kept me supplied, distillations of three fragrances – orange-water, rose-water, and cologne water. I used to eat well in there, and enjoy a game of billiards or cards, and my wife visited me often, and so did the oculist until he offended me, and I applied a dildo to myself eight times every day at the prescribed hours, and I took walks in the garden, smelling earth as a change from stone, and sometimes would amuse myself and astound people in the streets by shouting witty suggestions down to them from the battlements.

It was a halcyon hell compared to this one. De Launay disgusted me, but Dupommier puts the fear of death in me, and I doubt very much if Laclos can afford his complacency, whatever protection he thinks he has. I have none. I am fresh

dog meat. I catch myself wondering if we have been allowed
the liberty of this garden in order that, when the time comes, it
will afford Dupommier an appetising chase before he thrusts
his slavering snout in where I have gone to earth.

As he starts to speak today, Laclos is smirking. He would be
better advised not to smirk. His features are too weak to carry it
off.

§ The King's Hat

I remember not a word of what was said in the first assembly of
the Estates-General, but none of us can forget the King's hat,
that ceremonial confection of beaver fur, white plumes, and
one enormous diamond. After his opening address, he went
through the routine, doffing it, waving it, and replacing it on his
wig, and there was a rustling as the nobility solemnly put their
hats on, in accordance with the custom. But then, another
rustling! The Third Estate were putting their hats on, too.
Having not met for two centuries, they didn't remember the
etiquette. Whispers, glares, one or two sharp injunctions from
the nobility and the clergy, and some of the Thirds were
snatching their hats off again, in confusion, and others were
looking askance at each other, and hats were rising and falling
everywhere you looked. At this point, Louis felt the best thing
was to doff his again. Fatal error! Now the noble hats and the
mitres were in confusion too, up and down, on and off. In spite
of my straight face, tears of mirth moistened my eyes, especially
when I saw that Marie-Antoinette had gone pale with rage.

It was soon apparent that it would all be a great preening of
feathers, nothing more. From the Third Estate, at least, we
looked for reasoned arguments about the plight of France, but
in vain. The best were bewildered by what was expected of
them. A few country priests testified to the misery of their
parishioners, but saw no recourse but to implore the King for
his benign intervention. In those first weeks, Louis must have

been relieved. He was still verbally anointed by all who spoke, because scarcely a soul in France had dared to imagine a country without a king. That dream had to be dreamed first by the King.

The radicals were asking, merely, *which* king? Their question was not voiced in the assembly. It was to be heard at the edge of the business, in the town of Versailles. I knew the corners in which to have a quiet talk with men worth talking quietly to, and soon I spent my time doing that, or watching to see which Third Estate renegades were talking with the Court party. It was a happy time for me. The May weather was fine, the air smelled of blossom, and the sense of contributing to form the nation's future made conversation agreeable.

Barnave introduced me to his colleague from Grenoble, Mounier, dedicated Rousseauists both of them.

Mounier says, "'The rights of man derive from Nature alone.'"

"Of course," I reply. "Why don't you cite that in the assembly?"

Barnave wipes his mouth. "The assembly, pah! I expect to see the assembly float up into the clouds like a balloon, such is the generation of hot air."

They were both in the riots from which Grenoble lays claim to be the cradle of the revolution. (And what part did my book play? Who *knows?*) Already they are averring that the moment when a royal soldier bayoneted a hatter was when the course of French history was altered. "I will not deny it," I reply, "but will add this. Many such determining moments have been proposed, and more will be, and if we assent to all of them, why, the course of our history will have been altered so often that no one can know whither we are sailing."

Mounier nods. "No one can," he says, "don't you think?" He sips his wine.

Now, I see that he was right. At the time I answered, of course, that the Duke of Orleans saw clearer to the horizon than anyone else.

"Then why doesn't he speak?" Barnave demands.

I shrug. Barnave was often in the drawing-room of the Palais-Royal. "You know him as well as I do."

"I wouldn't say that." Barnave grins. "But what I do know is this. Everybody is whispering about an Orleanist conspiracy. But has anyone thought to mention it to Orleans? Or did they, and has it slipped his mind?"

What Barnave said was true. The Palais-Royal was seen as a rival to Versailles, and the Prince as a pretender to the throne. His popularity had been gilded by his opposition to the King, and the affair at Réveillon's factory was interpreted as a gesture of revolt sponsored by the Prince. That was not quite what I had planned, but it would serve. And so when that question, *which* king?, was asked in the quiet coffee-houses of Versailles or the babbling gardens of the Palais-Royal, the Prince was the only alternative anyone considered. Even Mirabeau muttered to me, "If we need a puppet, that prick Orleans will do as well as any." I suspect that what Mirabeau really wanted was to keep Louis where he was, albeit a Louis whose tongue and limbs would be worked by cleverer men. But in all this ferment, the one man who said nothing was the Prince himself. That was the wiser course, I had decided. His silence was a vacuum that imagination filled with words far more eloquent than he could blather. When I was chid, as by Barnave, that instead of waxing hot in the assembly my master spent his days out riding with Mademoiselle Agnès, I pursed my lips and nodded my head wistfully, and inwardly thanked heaven.

Among the friends I met in Versailles was Alquier, now mayor of La Rochelle and representing the town in the Third Estate. He it was who introduced me to a deputy from Artois. Citizer Robespierre was sitting alone at a table in a garden, eating a neatly peeled and parted orange, and sipping a glass of water. When he rose to greet me, I saw him to be a short, wiry man, with clipped and powdered hair. His dark breeches and hose were of silk. I judged him to be of about my age, though I now know that he is fully seventeen years younger, like most of them at the Jacobins. My error owed something to the spareness of his body, and the dry rasp in his voice. It was impossible to imagine that he had ever been a red-cheeked, exuberant youth.

"I have heard of you, Monsieur de Laclos," he says. The green-tinted spectacles perched on his thin nose reflect the light. "You are a lover of Rousseau, I believe."

"Indeed," I say, leaving him to take the initiative.

But he sits very still and upright behind his spectacles, as I do behind my reserve, and it might be a mute meeting were Alquier not there to spur us on. "Monsieur de Laclos is also the lover and husband of La Rochelle's most beautiful daughter," he says gallantly.

"What has that to do with Rousseau?" Robespierre asks.

"We were talking of what Monsieur de Laclos loves," Alquier parries.

Robespierre turns to me. "When Rousseau enjoins us to entertain tender feelings for humanity, I do not suppose that he was speaking of the flesh. Do you?"

"He was recommending a fraternal care for each other," I tell him.

"Quite." Robespierre puts the last pig of orange in his mouth, takes out a handkerchief, and wipes his fingers, one by one. "I take his view to be that public administration ought to be governed by the same affections as are proper and normal within the family. So that politics may be called public morality. Would you agree, Monsieur de Laclos?"

"Yes," I say, "as we all should agree, don't you think?"

"Of course," he says crisply.

Very well, we have established where we both stand in the matter of Rousseau. But what of Orleans? Before I can frame a question, Alquier takes his leave of us, and in his turning his coat-tail brushes a piece of orange-peel from the table on to the earth. I lean down to pick it up, and find my fingers touching Robespierre's hand, already grasping the peel. I glance up at him. His thin nostrils twitch.

"Tell me, Monsieur Robespierre," I ask, "can you imagine a situation in which the King might abdicate his throne?"

"I can imagine it."

"With equanimity, or with horror?"

"With indifference. The man is of impure character."

"If a successor were required, would it be your opinion that the succession of blood should prevail?"

"Who would wish to see the succession of bad blood?" he answers. "And where could one with confidence look for better blood?"

"Many believe that the Duke of Orleans would be better."

"So I have heard. I have also heard that you are an exponent of that view. And that you would like to know how each of us in the Third Estate would incline if the choice were forced upon us." The light is glinting on his spectacles again.

"I do have a concern," I allow. "It is a concern for the French nation. You must know that I am incorruptible."

"I am glad to hear it," Robespierre says. "When I read your book, I thought it something ambiguous."

"I have a hatred for the privileged aristocracy. To express that was my whole intention."

He nods, sharply. "In that, I found that you succeeded."

"But you detected some further intention, in which I did not succeed?"

"I found the depiction of women and their fate excessively cruel."

"How else could I have dramatised my horror at the effects of libertinage?"

"By stating it clearly, Monsieur de Laclos, not by painting its consequences in lurid tears and blood."

"You mean I would have done better to write a treatise?"

"If you wished to be properly understood, yes. To luxuriate in carnal seduction is to pamper the appetite of the wicked, whatever your intention might have been."

"But I did not address myself to the wicked."

"The wicked is in everyone," he says, "give it but a little

crack."

I thank him for his critique and, seeing no turning back to the matter of Orleans, bid him good day.

It is no surprise to me that a man so firm and chaste in his opinions should later have played a prominent part in the painful birth of our republic. All of us should be grateful that Citizen Robespierre has contributed his mind to our debates.

I speak to as many as I can of the Third Estate deputies. I make lists to divide them into four categories: those for the King; those undecided; those who say they are for the Prince; and, of the last, those I believe. The support I trust is not a majority, if a head-count were introduced. To ensure the Prince decisive influence in a crisis, I debate as to the virtue of persuasion, threat, bribery, or

[Insertion by ZB. The translator notes that at this point there is a hiatus in the MS. Since Sade did not paginate, we cannot be sure whether pages he wrote up have been lost, or whether he simply got tired of scrivening and gave up for a time. The former is much more likely, for two reasons:

(1) Sade has already assured us that Laclos was by now insisting on scrutinising "our previous day's work together" (although the scrutineer will apparently relent at Chapters 12*ff*, no doubt because of the pressure of events just outside the Picpus).

(2) What I call in my colloquium paper (*q.v.*) Sade's "completion neurosis" would surely have compelled him to keep making notes.

Briefly, I surmise that the missing page(s) might be expected to deal with the Jeu de Paume episode, and we are infuriatingly left to conjecture whether Laclos had any personal connection with it. It was the point at which events took on a momentum of their own. The radical wing of the Third Estate lost patience after a month and a half of futile speeches, and declared themselves to represent a national assembly. Locked out then from the palace, on the first rainy day for weeks, they repaired (at Dr Guillotin's suggestion) to the shelter of the royal tennis court. And there the republicans found themselves in a void that Sartre would have recognised. How does a republican behave? What does one say, and do, which distinguishes one from the disaffected monarchist one was this morning? The only model of a republican they had was what they had studied at school. They imitated the Roman heroes. They took an Horatian oath to their republic, bending their limbs into indexical forms that paint and marble had prefigured for them.

Marie-Antoinette's characteristic response was to imitate the forms of melodrama. She had Necker dismissed, filled Versailles with armed soldiers, and sent to Prussia for more regiments. She missed her mark, of course. Melodrama always stirs up black laughter. Huge crowds, in a gay mood, invaded her palace at Versailles to demand Necker's recall, and when the Prince of Conti ordered "Fire!" the soldiers declined to shoot their own mothers and brothers.

The MS resumes.]

congregating day and night in the Palais-Royal gardens. They are not peaceful strollers any more. Orators and tracts are no longer a frivolous distraction. Now everyone wants to understand what is happening to them and be exhorted to do something about it. For the first time we see sober, well-to-do citizens in the gardens, lawyers and bankers and merchants, at last aware that something is coming to its term. They are galvanised by the slogans in favour of the Third Estate, standing shoulder to shoulder with market women and labourers, artisans, shopkeepers and soldiers. In the Faubourg Saint-Antoine, the Réveillon riot has never entirely abated. The district is dry tinder, spontaneously blazing up as often as it is damped down. The petty functionaries at the Town Hall still see the whole thing as a fit of bad temper and an impediment to trade, and are trying to raise a militia to keep control of the city, not only against rioters but also against Versailles's foreign troops. We already have military regiments in our pocket at the

Palais-Royal, by dint of distributing tracts among garrisons, and shrewd subventions. When Conti's rebellious guardsmen are thrown into the Abbaye prison, we soon have them out again.

The armies are in position. We have to judge the moment to take the offensive. I explain the tactical situation to the Prince. We could force the King to recognise the Third Estate Horatians as a national assembly if the Prince himself joined them and took with him enough members of the nobility to ensure a majority. How many of the First Estate would go over with him? And when would the move make the deepest impression? The Prince surprises me with his answer. "Wait for Mirabeau."

"Are you certain that Mirabeau wears our uniform?"

Twitch, twitch. But he says nothing, just twitches again, and I understand. I reflect that I need to have a word with Shee. There must be ledgers I have not yet reviewed.

Mirabeau acts the next day, after the King (buying time for his wife's Prussian mercenaries to crush the nation) has told the fractious assembly to disperse. I listen to Mirabeau speak: he is magnificent. When he sits down, it is Louis who has to disperse himself. Sooner than I had expected, I go to tell the Prince that nothing is to be gained by waiting now. With as many adherent gentlemen as he can muster, he must go over and join the citizens.

He does the next day, and forty-seven cross with him. The King gives in. He has no choice. Necker is retained, and the Third Estate is recognised as a National Assembly. A week later, the Prince is elected President of it.

I watch him stand up and say the words we have rehearsed, concerning the honour done to him and how onerous the position will be. Then he adds, "That is why I cannot accept this election. You must choose another President. Thank you." And he sits down.

He avoids me for four days. Not that I make much effort to see him. I spend most of the time at home, sitting by a window, admiring the beauties that grow from the earth, and closing my eyes every time I am made breathless again by black rage.

131

"He's a great singer, but he doesn't know any songs," Mirabeau tells me sympathetically. His tone alters. "I thought you were sharp enough to have worked that out for yourself."

* * *

[After reading the following section, Laclos demands that I rewrite it as he dictated it, not in the more amusing gavotte form in which I cast the notes I took. I am procrastinating, in the hope that he will forget about it. L.S.]

Having come so far, I would not be beaten.

"We shall go too far," says Sieyès. He sips his dark red wine. "If we could call a halt now, and give the Court time to draft and accept a constitution, enshrining the inalienable rights of the Third Estate to act as a restraint, then we would have come far. Far enough. But the thing is a cart rolling down a steep hill. We shall go too far."

"We shall go wrong," says Madame Pourrat. Deferential to our hostess, we allow her the time to breathe out and in again, thus swelling the ripe white curve above her bodice. "We shall continue to disregard the rights of women. Why should their voices not be equal to men's? Why is it that women are not elected, and neither do they elect? Why is the husband the head of the family? Why do we hear only the question "Which king?" Until we ask questions that reach further, we shall go wrong."

"France will go to hell," declares Gouverneur Morris. He stands stiffly on the lawn, knee-breeched legs apart, frequently wiping his nose, which is affected by our July blossom. "Paine is here. He is a dangerous radical. He will find the straw heads among you and set light to them. We know Tom Paine in Philadelphia, oh yes. I tell you, *mes amis*, just let him start to spit out democracy, and France will go to hell."

"The poor will go hungry," says Mademoiselle Vigée-Lebrun, shading her eyes with a parasol. "That is what haunts the Queen's dreams. All this constitutional strife, she says, but who spares a moment to think of what the poor will eat? That is why they have always loved us, she says, because we have cared for our people, the real people. While all these politicians fight for power, the labouring poor will go hungry."

"I shall go mad," says Chénier, one hand placed upon his heart. "In a society where reason grinds against reason, the poet is trapped between mill-stones. No space is left for the soul, and the heart has no room. Tell me, madame, when midnight comes, is it not the sanest recourse to go mad?"

"I shall go to England," says Madame de Staël, with a little flutter over her lorgnette for this week's young poet *à la mode*. "The weather there is abominable, yet their constitution is a model for us. It says much for their wit, which is to say the least."

I smile, and say nothing. Twenty thousand troops have arrived in Versailles and Paris, growling at each other in Marie-Antoinette's tongue. They are here, the Court says, to contain disorders. But they contain disorders in themselves. Hangdog and haggard they are, unruly, of doubtful loyalty, like ill-used dogs. Some have been put to massacring the rebellious workers in the Faubourg Saint-Antoine. But others have already come over to us, forming a rival militia to the Town Hall's armed grocers. And every day many of our own do the same. At the Palais-Royal last night I came across a detachment of my own regiment, eighty men of the Toul Artillery who had jumped barracks at the Invalides to join us. As their captain, I was obliged to remind them that the punishment for desertion, on first offence, is ten runs through a gauntlet of fifty men armed with ramrods. They laughed, brave fellows. I saluted them. Of course, I shall be accused of having incited them to it. A suspect man is suspected of everything. I have come too far to care.

I went this morning into the Palace of Versailles to see Lafayette. "Suppose," I said, "that the Duke of Orleans, in refusing the Presidency of the National Assembly, were reserving himself for an even more onerous office of state, would you think that admirable in him?"

One hand shot up to cover Lafayette's round mouth, which

had gasped, like the stuck-up little schoolboy he is. "How could you dare to think ..." he said, and could not find an end to his sentence, unless he were proposing a Cartesian dilemma to me, which was not, I think, the case.

And so, to refresh my spirit, I came here, to the Château de Voisins, on my way passing the Château de Louveciennes where the aged Madame du Barry still keeps her court, alas. "She was born in a pit," I whispered to myself. "Her titles are hollow ..." And I smiled to myself, as I smile now, but say nothing, because I have nothing to say, now. Yet.

The American stands so foursquare I do believe he has taken root in our earth, and will put forth branches and fruit, give him time. "What the Abbot tells you is the truth," he says. "This business is a herd of buffalo on an open prairie. You will not stop them till they have run themselves ragged, and trampled everything in their path."

Our hostess, so rich, and richly tempting, wonders how many deeds will match so many words. "I remember what Voltaire remarked to me, when I visited him at Ferney. "Incantations will destroy a flock of sheep if administered with a certain quantity of arsenic." That is what we need now, don't you believe, Monsieur de Laclos? A certain quantity of arsenic in our proceedings."

Chénier relieves me of the need to answer. "Not arsenic, Madame," he says, pouting, "but laudanum. What is it to die, if first we have not brilliantly imagined our death?"

Even Madame de Staël pretends not to have heard him. "Our best hope lies in what the feeling mind will hear when it listens to the reasoning heart. If Montesquieu could debate with Rousseau, all the propositions which matter to us would be tested."

Sieyès is shaking the decrepitude that serves him as a face. "We are dividing ourselves. What the Third Estate should represent is the honest nation against the handful of privileged thieves who call themselves aristocrats. But in Paris I hear it shouted up as a slogan of those who have nothing against those who have anything."

La Vigée-Lebrun is anxiously shaking her enlaced fingers which have so tenderly painted the portraits of the royal infants. "There you have it," she trills, "there you have it. The poor. What are we going to do about the poor? Something must be done."

But before we can settle the question of poverty, a messenger comes to tell Madame de Staël that her father, Necker, has been dismissed, again. He is making a career of it. I hasten back to the Palais-Royal.

To learn that the National Assembly has declared itself to be a constitutional branch of government, and the Court blames Necker for being soft.

The news spreads in the morning of 12th July, and by noon the crowds in the Palais-Royal gardens are pressing hip to hip. I watch from a window, and hear how silent thousands of people can be when all are of one mind and body. Camille Desmoulins speaks to them ringingly, about their oppressions, their reasonable initiatives, and the contempt and injustice with which they have been served by the Court. Even such words elicit only single cries of anger among the crowd, which is waiting for one word, to tell them what is to be done.

Then Desmoulins says it. *Aux armes!* And the cannon bellows.

Every boulevard is the conduit for a triumphal march, which will lead to Versailles. The crowds carry busts and placards of Necker and the Prince. They chant slogans and sing songs. Their feet stir dust from the cobblestones, and it makes a haze in the sunbeams and settles on the young leaves of the plane trees along the boulevards. All the church bells are ringing tocsins. The soldiers and the militia withdraw to the Champ de Mars, but some of them break ranks and join the processions.

At the Prince's palace, unlike the palace at Versailles, we have foreseen that the event might happen, and made our plans. Detachments of the crowd are encouraged to march on designated objectives. One is the Town Hall, whose inmates are still biting their fingernails. It is ransacked for arms and ammunition. If bread be found too, good luck to the hungry. Money is not to be stolen. An armed detachment is sent to take the Invalides, for its thirty thousand muskets. Cartloads of grain and flour are fetched from the Saint-Lazare Monastery. Most welcome of all to the crowds are the missions to destroy all customs houses, though we spare the two that belong to the Prince, thinking it hypocritical to disguise the people's loyalties. Many are crushed in the fury to tear down the iron railings and set fire to the tax registers, the hated instruments and symbols of privilege. The greatest and most sky-darkening symbol of all is left to a later phase of the conflict, though many cries of "To the Bastille!" can be heard on the boulevards, and we know that the fortress's cannons have been trained on the Faubourg Saint-Antoine.

All day and all night, the people of Paris claim back their dignity. At Versailles it is seen as an Orleanist plot. We knew it would be, but nevertheless the accusations are comic. As well might rotten apples blame the wind for their fall. By direction, we preserve Paris from looting, and save countless lives that would have perished in mere riot. That some do die is inevitable, in the vomiting of centuries of rage. A commander, however, is judged not by how many men he loses, but how few.

The commander-in-chief is not on the field of battle. The Prince spends that first day with Mesdemoiselles Agnès and Grace, fishing. I wonder at his taste in entertainment. As a formality in the constitutional crisis, we advise him the next day that he should go to Versailles to renew his oath of loyalty to the King. Having to alter his plans, and suspecting Mirabeau and myself of undisclosed motives, he goes with a bad grace, and is received with a worse. When he comes out from the chamber, his big face is pink. "Apparently," he mutters, "the kingdom's store of courtesy has been ransacked, too."

After the Bastille is stormed and its magazines of gunpowder taken, the city falls into a calm. At first it is the calm of exhaustion, but it turns to a superstitious brooding on what has been done. Soon, it is not a calm at all, but a silent, frozen hysteria, like that of Medea when she opened her eyes and saw her slaughtered children. Any event, now, might stir a fluttering of panic. Stories break out that Paris is being pillaged by marauding bands, of brigands, guttural soldiers, woodhouses, Jews. Scapegoats are required, as though the city has committed a sin, and the most frequently invoked one is Marie-Antoinette. She it was, straddling a broomstick, who had conjured up the inconceivable and now indecipherable behaviour of that Sabbath.

The position is unstable. Mirabeau and I agree that only the Prince has the authority to settle it. He will have to go back to Versailles. We have reservations. I am still tormented by his betrayal in declining the Presidency. I have said nothing to him on that score, reckoning that my silence will chasten him. Myself I have consoled with the reflection that I had let Lafayette glimpse: by dodging the Presidency, the Prince has kept himself available for the throne. I even wonder, indulgently, whether he has not made that calculation himself.

Mirabeau is more sceptical, although the process we now envisage suits his downright monarchism better than some presidential regency would. "We must get the stupid prick to see that this time he has no choice. None. It is no longer a question of what he wants. The very survival of the kingdom is at stake. Tomorrow morning he has got to go into the Assembly, first, and offer himself as the mediator between the King and the people of Paris. They will acclaim him for that. No other bugger wants to take it on. No one else could. They're all sitting there, in their noble Roman poses, wondering what the hell is supposed to happen next. We've run out of script. Then he goes in to see the King to explain that the game is up. There is no going back, nor any going forward with Louis Seize on the throne and Marie-Antoinette pulling the strings. The people will vomit them up again and again, if they try that. A graceful retirement is Louis's only option. Made smoother for him by his cousin's generous offer to take over as regent, for the time being. Later, we'll see. We tell Orleans that is *all* he has got to do. After that, he can piss off with his fishing-rod, and we'll do the rest. We'll pick up the strings. All right, Laclos? You know what we are going to tell him?"

I nod.

"And don't even listen to what he says," Mirabeau adds. "He is just going to do it."

"Well," the Prince answers when we tell him, "well, why not?"

He gets there too late. The Assembly has dispersed and the King retired to his chambers by the time the Prince's coach rolls into the palace yard at Versailles. Mirabeau and I have been waiting there for more than four hours, cursing ourselves. We should have manacled him in Paris, delivered him to the Assembly in chains, and frog-marched him in to claim the throne.

"Awfully sorry," the Prince says. "Something came up."

Mirabeau, with impressive obstinacy, seeks to redeem the farce. He speaks quickly and quietly with Breteuil, who has succeeded Necker, and comes to tell the Prince that the minister has agreed to take a note in for the King. "It's arse about face," he observes. "We should have got the Assembly's agreement first. But now we'll have to push it through this way." He stares balefully at the Prince, who has his head cocked to one side. "Will you write the note, Sire, or shall I, and you simply add your signature?"

"I will write the note," the Prince says.

He sits at a writing-table, and motions us to stop craning over his shoulder. It is soon done. He folds the paper and hands it to Breteuil, who bows, and takes it in for the King. The Prince is leaving. I run across to the balustrade and call down the staircase, "Will you not wait for the answer?" Is he really not interested in whether he is the King of France?

"It will be a courtesy to allow His Majesty time to consider," the Prince replies.

He leaves, and I rejoin Mirabeau. Almost at once, Breteuil comes out again, still holding the note. He hands it to Mirabeau.

"Will the King not accept the note?" I ask.

"His Majesty has read it, and written his reply upon it," Breteuil answers. "Would you be kind enough to deliver it to His Highness?"

Of course, we open it as soon as we are in our coach. The Prince has written: "Have I Your Majesty's gracious permission to go to England if things get quite out of hand?" The King has scribbled: "Granted".

* * *

It was a desultory summer. The panic abated, and resolved into another calm of sorts, baffled, sullen, like a fighting bull at bay. Necker was recalled within days. "Terribly sorry about that, Monsieur Necker, all a frightful mistake again, can't imagine what we were thinking of, of course you are the very man to supervise the national economy, no question of it." Talleyrand and Mirabeau sat beside him, and they contrived to keep the bailiffs from coming in to repossess the kingdom. There was an epidemic of patriotic charity. Even the whores were doing it for France, remitting part of their earnings to the Treasury. I saw the hunger of the poor, and circulated a subscription for their relief. The Prince was the first to sign it, for a hundred thousand écus. I did not dare ask Shee in which drawer he would look for it.

Of our pack of creditors, one, a certain Pinel, was found shot dead in the woods, and of course it was I who had executed this new way to settle old debts, everyone at Court knew that for a fact. Pinel had been denounced by the orators in the gardens as a notorious usurer; I had written their execrations. Just as it was I who had organised a troop of four horsemen to ride around the countryside stirring the people up against the King. To all who seemed to have any curiosity, I confessed, yes, that partial eclipse of the sun, I did it.

The Prince's income was bled whiter in August when feudal privileges were abolished, a proper decision by the National Assembly. The King refused his assent, but the Assembly sat and waited until everything would be conceded. The throne was collapsing, slowly, while the King still sat on it. Here a leg cocked askew, there the threadbare fabric gave and tore open. Had it not been piteous and terrible to watch, it would have been clownish.

I had to think of my own situation, with a growing family. The Bourbon horse I had ridden for nearly a year would go on refusing at every ditch. It was also dubious how much longer he would have the money to employ me, or anyone else. Accordingly, I prepared to resume my military career, if there were no alternative, and if any soldiers remained in the army after continual desertions. When I had left La Fère, it had been on paid leave, which I had extended into unpaid leave, on the understanding that I would return to the colours if offered command of a brigade. Nothing had been said in response, though Gribeauval had clutched his heart and dropped dead. Now I had the idea of requesting a further paid leave, this time in advance of another tour of duty.

I had an opportunity to raise the matter with the Minister of War, the Count of La Tour du Pin, when he invited me to dinner at Versailles. Seeing that my neighbour at the table was Citizen Robespierre, I understood the nature of the occasion. The Count was feasting his adversaries, if not to soften them, then to sound them. He got no change from Robespierre, who muttered to me, "This man is so weak, he will put out fires by squeezing oranges on them." When I put my modest request to the Minister, he said, "That sounds all right. Tell your employer, the Duke, to drop me a note about it."

Back at the Palais-Royal I wrote the note, the Prince signed it, and approval was received, though still with no mention of promotion for me. It is possible that the Prince read the note before signing it, because shortly afterwards I noticed that

Danton was spending time in his office, and I wondered if he were being coached as my successor. You will need Job's patience, Monsieur Danton, I thought to myself. Perhaps I was wrong. But my suspicion served a purpose. I told Shee that I required a regular note of funds disbursed to anyone not a member of the household staff, and such papers I kept safely at home. My motive was to protect my position, but later the papers protected my life.

The summer's heat lasted into September, and no one believed that the business started in July was finished yet. The popular mood was unquiet, people were jumpy, easily irritated, especially women, who had most complaint while the price of bread remained high. Bands of female brigands were raiding grain carts in the countryside. Armed guards stood outside the bakeries.

In the gardens, among the familiar slogans in favour of cheaper bread and the Third Estate, calls for "The King to Paris!" had started to appear. A new paper, in support of the poor, was circulating. It was written by Marat, who was kind enough to name me among the stoutest defenders of *la patrie*. But in the discussion clubs I frequented, the lodges, the salons, and in the Assembly itself, few spent much time lamenting the condition of the poor, or the growing mobs of unemployed men in Montmartre. There were some, indeed, who felt themselves threatened by the common people. At the Cordeliers I heard Lafayette, the Hero of Two Worlds and Commander of the National Guard, snap, "These people who are stealing bread need to be taught a lesson." The plumes in his hat quivered like a poodle's tail.

The Assembly sat and waited, waited for the aristocracy to crack into fragments with one terminal giggle, for the clergy to suffocate in incense fumes, and for the royal veto to veto itself out of existence. Everything that moved in that sour humidity would move in their direction, if they waited. But it was October before the thunder spoke again. Meanwhile, the Prince found himself at risk of being crowned by default. The sickly young Dauphin had died; his brother was an infant; the King's brother, the Count of Artois, had fled the country with his two sons; and that left only the Count of Provence in line to Louis's crumbling throne before my master, and everyone knew that Provence was impotent. When the Assembly discussed the matter they spent four days over it, and one deputy declared that in all this he detected the hand of "Laclos, that artillery officer." Was it now supposed that I had assassinated the Dauphin, castrated Provence, and driven Artois and his whelps to the border with a cracking whip? *Ohé!*

Mirabeau was to blame, I thought, with a speech that appalled many. The Assembly's view, he declared, should be that it would welcome the accession of the Duke of Orleans.

"Do you want to go through all that again?" I ask him, afterwards.

He grins at me. "Well, the great prick hasn't poked himself into England yet, has he?"

"He will *never* go through with it. You must know that by now."

"Then what are you waiting for?"

"What do you mean?"

"Your bull won't mount, you say. There's only the one cow, France, so you need to find yourself a keener bull."

I sigh. "There is no one else. Provence, puh, the people laugh at him. He'll go when Louis goes."

"So," Mirabeau says, "the next in line ..."

I shake my head in despair.

His voice loses its banter, his cheeks are bright pink. "There is nobody else, Laclos. You are right. I am not going to fuck around inviting the King of the Two Sicilies or the Ponce of the Nineteen Thessalies to come and squat on the French throne. It's there, it's his. He's got to sit on it and shit. I'll persuade him with a pistol to his head if I have to."

And in October the storm broke, again.

If it hadn't been this it would have been something else, but it was this: a merry banquet at Versailles at which the

Household Bodyguards trampled the national cockade, and licked the floor clean with their tongues when Marie-Antoinette made her entrance. Word of it got back to Paris. To the people, it seemed their faces were being used as a foot-up for the aristocrats to climb back into the saddle.

Desmoulins and Chamfort are in the Café Foy when I find them. "What are you going to do?" I ask.

"The King to Paris," Chamfort says.

"We've heard that for weeks," I say. "If the King won't come to Paris, we must fetch him. The people must go to Versailles and bring him back. 'To Versailles!' is what they want to hear."

Desmoulins strokes his chin. "Let's try it."

"It's a long way to Versailles," Chamfort says. "Four hours."

"They've been waiting four months," I observe.

"Come on," Desmoulins says, finishing his cognac. "To Versailles!"

On what a journey one step may lead us. "To Versailles!" It is as though my voice could be heard clear across the city. No sooner have the orators in the gardens declaimed it, the same cry is going up in the markets, and in the Faubourg Saint-Antoine. It is the women, again, the mothers of hungry children, who shout loudest. Meetings of women form themselves, and vow to march to Versailles with their demand for bread. Fishwives are side by side with ladies in feathered hats, and they urge or coerce the women they meet to fall into step with them. At the Cordeliers, I note that it is Danton who declares "To Versailles!" And I am more amused to note of whom he is making the demand. Lafayette! Danton is badgering the Commander of the National Guard and the tightest arse in town, as Mirabeau calls him, to lead a rebellious march with an ultimatum upon his sovereign. Poor Lafayette. He is the Hero in Two Minds now. He prevaricates for hours, saying anything to avert doing something.

Outside the club, the city whose peace Lafayette is charged to keep is at last in the ferment that has been dormant since

July. The tocsins are ringing. Word reaches us that women are leading an assault on the Town Hall, using arms snatched from the guards or cobblestones prised up with picks. We run over there to watch. The women are already inside the Town Hall. They have seized all the muskets, axes, pikes and scythes they could find, and stuffed what bread there is down their bodices. Then they start the march to Versailles, augmented by groups from all across Paris, over the Pont Neuf and through the Tuileries gardens.

When they reach Versailles, they swarm into the Assembly meeting, telling the startled deputies to budge up and make room. To the nobility and clergy they howl their want of bread, but are appeased by Citizen Robespierre, and charmed by Mirabeau. Back in Paris, Lafayette can think up no more words to blather. Some hours after the women, he is marched to Versailles, at the front of an army of soldiers, guardsmen and irregulars. Their confluence with the women produces a crowd at midnight in the Sun King's gardens so vast that I wonder if anyone is asleep in Paris.

They stay there all night, in chilly rain. Some inquisitively force their way into the royal apartments as far as the Queen's antechamber. One of the Household Bodyguard cracks with hatred, and squeezes his trigger. A young man in the crowd falls, shot through the heart. In reprisal, the crowd take off the heads of two guards, and hold them up on pikes. That is when the Prince arrives, in his grey tailcoat, mopping his brow. He takes one look at the piked heads and rushes in to see the King. To Mirabeau, standing next to me, I remark, "That's what it takes, then."

"One head might have done the trick," he answers, "but two heads are better than one."

A minute later, the Prince comes out again. "He won't see me. He holds me to blame for it all. It's too bad." And he leaves us, goes home to sob on Agnès's bosom.

What I have dictated to Citizen Sade is what I know. The following account also circulated: That Mirabeau and I had

144

been plotting to install the Duke of Orleans on the throne, by fomenting opposition to the King. (I will not call that an outright lie, but it does neglect the fact that most of the Third Estate were loudly and repeatedly asking for the same plot to be enacted, and were delighted when the march on Versailles dislodged the King from his aristocratic palace of air.) That the Prince had been at Versailles on that midnight, luxurious amid chants of "Our father is with us! Long live the King of Orleans!", had gaily led the masses up the grand staircase and conducted them around the royal apartments, before disappearing in a puff of smoke. That a bellicose assault on the Queen's bedchamber had been led by myself, disguised in a frock, bonnet, and dark grin.

The King bowed, and agreed to take up residence in the Tuileries immediately. The Paris Revolution was complete. Paradoxically, it did not throw out a king but brought him to his people, in the city. However, though the King lived, kingship was stabbed, mortally.

The Prince saw it as his cousinly duty to accompany the royal family's coach through the dark, cold and wet streets of Paris to their new palace. He took me with him on that sombre journey, and Barnave, representing the Assembly.

Later that day I returned to Versailles with a horse and cart to bring my family and belongings to Paris. The Prince wanted me by him all the time now, and allotted us an apartment in the Fountains Court of the Palais-Royal. Marie-Soulange was agitated by the turn of events, and wept most of the way. For myself, I had not felt so hopeful for many months. At last, it seemed, the great iron door that had defied me was swinging open. I was on the threshold. We all were, all the children of *la patrie*.

* * *

Mirabeau and I are with the Prince when word is brought in that Lafayette requires to be admitted at once. The Prince makes a face at us. "You'd better wait outside."

Lafayette is in the drawing-room, pacing rapidly up and down, the plumes in his hat wagging madly. When he sees us he draws himself up to attention, with a frigid glare. Then he strides in to see the Prince. In less than a minute he comes striding out again, and away, without a look in our direction. Mirabeau laughs loudly enough to be sure that the Hero of Two Worlds will hear. Then he mutters to me, "A brief painful interview with the headmaster."

The Prince looks up at us with his great vague eyes when we enter again. The smile on his face is bemused.

"What was it?" Mirabeau asks. "Did he come to explain that what happened at Versailles was not at all his fault, Sire, oh no, the Commander of the National Guard cannot be held responsible for guarding the national sovereign?"

The Prince shakes his head, and is quiet for a moment. Then he clears his throat, and tells us, "All he said was: 'Get out of the kingdom, or be arrested.' That was all."

"I hope your considered reply," Mirabeau says, "was: 'Kindly go and do your farting in somebody else's office.'"

"Oh no."

"Well, what did you say?" Mirabeau asks impatiently.

"I said I'd go to London."

Neither of us speaks.

Twitch, twitch. "Tomorrow," the Prince adds, and smiles again.

We plead with him. The crown is his to pluck now, as if from a hatstand. As king he will be even freer than he is now to enjoy every pleasure, since he will be a constitutional monarch only, ratifying the Assembly's decrees. Eventually Mirabeau loses his temper and, more vehement than I have ever heard him, barks, "They are just clearing you out of the way. Can't you see that? Can't you see it?"

But I have surrendered. I watch the Prince, his face averted from Mirabeau, and see how happy the man is to be running away from responsibility, politics, creditors, family worries, and running away, moreover, to England. Lafayette has brought

146

him delightful news.

Mirabeau gives up too, in the end. Without a goodbye, he turns and stamps out of the room. We hear him bellowing at someone, Shee perhaps, or Danton, "He's a useless bugger, a eunuch who can't wank. Don't let me hear his name again. Never!"

The Prince looks up, and quietly asks, "Will you come with me, Laclos?"

"Yes." Later, I wondered why I knew the answer at once. I was surely not touched by the oaf's helplessness. I think I must have reckoned, instantly, that my only alternative would be La Fère.

We left the Palais-Royal at five in the morning on October 14th. Many tears were wiped away in my apartment. We would all miss each other dreadfully, but I could not take a wife and two small children with me to the end of the earth.

11

If Laclos were to be believed – I trust my subjunctive makes it clear that he isn't – he, with Mirabeau's fatuous collusion, was the Samson who tore down the old régime. That will certainly look well in the eyes of the present wardens of our fate when he is called to account, which is no doubt his real motive for putting me to this drudgery. I am the clerk for the defence counsel at his tribunal.

Very well. As a conscientious clerk, I cannot conceal from the court that others made some auxiliary contribution to the revolution. I myself, as I have hinted, caused the Bastille to fall. I am glad Citizen Laclos has not annexed that honour. I was driven to it because, of all the victims of the tyranny of kings, I was and am the wretchedest. What has been visited upon me will one day be seen as the most spectacular of injustices. It should be recorded, too, that a few people beyond Paris and Versailles did get wind of what was happening and acted in emulation. Marseilles was a theatre of horror where savages performed melodramas in the English style which made one's hair stand on end. Ah, long ago I said to myself that this fine and gentle nation which ate the Marshal d'Ancre's buttocks from a grill only awaited a galvanic occasion to prove that, poised always between cruelty and fanaticism, it would revert to its natural tone on demand.

But how, the court asks, can you know of such matters, clerical Citizen Sade, you who were sequestered like a satanic bishop, unable even to defend your poor wife from such vexations as fishwives who, meeting her when she was about her witless daily business near the Pont Neuf, swore with sticks and oaths that she must join them to march upon her sovereign at Versailles?

The answer is this. On Good Friday in 1790 (2-4-90, N.B.) I was in conversation with a charming young monk, one of the order who governed the sanatorium at Charenton, and from him learned that my confinement there was not ordered by law. I had been referred from the Bastille on the grounds that my soul was in need of nurture. Those idlers had kept me there because they wanted my rent. Imperiously, I told them I would leave now. They opened the gate and showed me out.

Out I came. And found myself treated in Paris with something approaching respect. Approaching it, not quite there yet. Nothing could have nurtured my soul better. One set of laws had been overthrown, the next set had not yet been invented. It was a time when all the power and pleasure that should rightly belong to man and not to God, that creation of original sin, did.

But soft, here he comes, his glass of water ready to irrigate his sanctimonious throat. Preen yourself, quill.

§ Waiting for the Tide

At Boulogne, we have to wait for the tide. The Prince's coach, outside the Golden Lion, attracts attention. When I tell the people who is inside the inn, and why, a gratifying clamour arises, fetching more citizens to join the crowd. They start to chant, with all their hearts, "They're sending our Prince into exile. Don't go, Your Majesty. Don't go. We need you in France." The demonstration becomes so excited that the authorities of the city are alerted, and eventually the Mayor of Boulogne is there, demanding to be told what has caused this disturbance in his streets. When I tell him, he is incredulous. "The Duke of Orleans is sent into exile?" he exclaims. "That can't be right."

"It is not right," I agree, "but it is the case."

"Whose case?" he asks. "Who is responsible for this? As Mayor of Boulogne, I cannot permit such an untoward egress until I have been shown evidence that it has been authorised by

150

the highest power. I cannot believe it. The Duke of Orleans? No. I require evidence, sir."

Finally, the Prince himself is sent for. He nods solemnly. "Yes," he tells the Mayor, "it is as Monsieur de Laclos has told you."

"Sire!" The Mayor is flabbergasted. "How can this be?"

The Prince, always ready to please, shrugs his shoulders and smiles wanly, as though to say, well, there you have it, who can account for the actions of the fools in Paris? But he has misjudged his effect.

With a bow, the Mayor announces, "On behalf of the City of Boulogne, I humbly offer Your Highness our civic hospitality until this matter has been elaborated. I will send a messenger to Paris at once, with instructions to ask our deputies in the Third Estate to raise the matter in the National Assembly."

"No, no," the Prince says quickly. "Really, Your Worship is too kind. I am afraid there is no gainsaying the decree."

The Mayor shakes his head, and smiles at the touching humility of the Duke. "Sire, permit me to do what I can. I will at least have written evidence before I consider concurrence with so grievous a thing." And, with a loyally raised hand, he forbids the Prince further protest.

"Dammit," the Prince mutters to me, "we'll have to send to Lafayette for official permission to be booted out."

He assures the Mayor that it will be most expedient if one of his own staff is sent back to Paris to see those responsible. Clarke, the administrative secretary with us (Shee is staying in Paris to look after the ledgers) is put on a horse. It takes him three days. Lafayette, he tells me, was reluctant to put his name to the paper, but saw no alternative in the end.

While the Mayor is scrutinising Lafayette's command, the Prince goes through a repertoire of gestures and grimaces to indicate, "There you have it." I hear him sigh quietly with relief when His Worship mumbles, "It is so, Your Highness. May God bless you, and bring you safely back to us in no time at all."

The dock is lined with fluttering handkerchiefs as, for the first time, I set sail on the Atlantic, an embarkation I might have made years earlier. That, too, would have been under the command of Lafayette. I lean on the rail, watching our bow cut through the dark green water, and cannot but reflect that Lafayette is young enough to be my son.

*　*　*

The Prince's mansion in London has been sold to pay off creditors, so we rent a house in Chapel Street, near the gardens of Buckingham Palace. The ground and first floors are furnished for the Prince and Mademoiselle Agnès. Clarke and I, and the physician Seiffert, live at the top of the stairs, beneath the servants' quarters. It is cold, dark, and the wallpaper smells of old damp, but rain does from time to time not fall.

We soon have a visitor, an old man called Sir Horace Walpole. He speaks French with an execrable accent, but that he can speak it at all singles him out among his compatriots. I ask him where he learned his French. Sir Walpole replies, "From the letters of Madame de Sévigné, Monsieur."

"How curious," I say. "You have not then read Rousseau, Voltaire, Montesquieu, Boileau, Marivaux, Beaumarchais, or any of our great classical dramatists?"

"I did, once, when I thought myself an author. Racine, sir, I found very tedious. The whole first act he spends in telling you what has happened already. Rousseau I thought sociable."

"Sociable."

"Quite. But the manners of the golden age of Louis Quatorze are what give me most delight. Madame de Sévigné's letters are all I need. Letters are what I write myself."

"I see," I lie.

"That is why I can truthfully call myself a man of letters." He laughs, I am not sure why.

So do I, guardedly. Then I think I understand him. "Oh, you employ the epistolary form."

152

"No, sir. I write letters."

"Ah."

"In your country, to call oneself a man of letters is to assert that one will behave like a brutal puppy. But the saving grace is that no one will take any notice of one, which is much the same as here. Well, sir, I trust you enjoy your sojourn in London, and have not come here to burn it to ashes." He laughs again – I am learning that laughter is intrinsic to English grammar – and we part with deep bows.

When I ask what the purpose of Sir Walpole's visit was, the Prince pulls a face and shakes his head. "None, as far as I can tell. The English are very hospitable, you know. He just wants to make sure that we don't feel neglected."

"Could he be spying on us?" I ask.

"What could there be here for the English to spy out?"

"You have charged me to make certain enquiries, Sire."

"Yes, but they don't know that."

"If they did know, they wouldn't need to spy on us."

The enquiries to which I refer were communicated to the Prince, soon after our arrival, by the French ambassador, Monsieur de la Luzerne. This mediocrity, speaking on behalf of the mediocre Minister Montmorin, asked the Prince to advise him if he heard anything that suggested the English King might be seeking to aggravate the difficulties in France, or even to be planning a war on us. It is plain to me that Lafayette is behind it. He is manufacturing an excuse to the French people if they call him to account for exiling their beloved Duke. What else has our ambassador got to do other than make such enquiries himself? Luzerne has also asked the Prince to keep an eye on the situation in the Netherlands, where English designs are suspected. "There was a hint," the Prince tells me, "that I might be offered the crown of Belgium."

You rejected the crown of France, I think to myself, yet you can be tempted by *Belgium*? All this great ninny desires is a toy.

To me falls the work of actually making the enquiries. I start at our own embassy, where I request an interview with the

153

ambassador's secretary, deeming him more likely than the ambassador to know what was known. I find myself ushered in to meet Chénier. "You," I say. "The private secretary?"

"Oh yes," he answers. "I was always destined for a diplomatic career."

"You do not feel yourself ground between mill-stones?" I ask. "As it were?"

"Life is very pleasant here." He smiles, very pleasantly. "Now, how can I help you?"

"Tell me your opinion of the English King's French policy."

Chénier thinks. "I don't believe he has one. I think he's waiting to see."

"So are we all."

"Yes, but he's prepared to wait longer than some of us have been."

Chénier's sarcasm tells me all that I will derive from the interview. I am a suspect man here as much as in Paris, and can look for no help from the embassy. I did not expect better. Lafayette has done his work. I bow curtly to the posturing boy behind his ormolu desk, and go to look for more profitable ways to waste my time in purgatory.

Some part of each day I consume by writing to my wife, in her lonely apartment at the Palais-Royal. I console both of us by recalling in detail the happier passages of our life together. I refresh the advice I have given her concerning the economies of the household in my absence, and ask her to let me know if anything wayward should appear in the behaviour of our children, so that I can do my duty in recommending how it should be corrected. I seldom omit a tender reference to the project we have shared for some years, without the time to practise it, that of cultivating a garden. That desire sprang of course from our reading of Rousseau, but it is also, we have agreed, an apt remembrance of the place and moment of our first meeting, when she had been cradling the squirrel's body.

I teach myself some serviceable English. My enquiries, even if they are not merely Lafayette's fig-leaf, are otiose while I have so few acquaintances. I might increase them if I could converse in English. And at least the exercise will ward off the shadow of tedium. Every day I pine for the excitement I knew in Paris, the joy I took in contributing to crush the arrogance of the aristocracy. Our sources there keep us informed of what is happening, which is not a great deal. Or so it seems, though I have no doubt that letters sent to us are known to be scrutinised by Lafayette, hence written with caution.

At last, Talleyrand comes, and everything changes. He is now the President of the National Assembly, and has to pay a visit first to the embassy, but from there he comes to Chapel Street, brushing the rainwater from his shoulders. The royalists, he tells me, have been jubilant at our exile, and identify me as Lafayette's true target. "There was a pamphlet," Talleyrand says, seating himself with one leg stretched straight out. "They crowed, 'It was needful for Laclos to stir the Duke from his usual apathy, but nothing was impossible for Tourvel's seducer. One breath from Lafayette blew Laclos clean out of France.'"

"The truth," I remark, "is that I chose to accompany the Prince."

"I know that. But you should hear the rant, now they think Lafayette has cleansed the temple. Tilly, of all debauchees, goes around giggling that the only political programme on which everyone at the Palais-Royal was ever agreed was the absolute necessity of a good dinner." He chuckles, and rubs his hands. "So let's have one, hm? If such a thing is possible in this country."

"We have engaged a Burgundian family to supervise the kitchen," I tell him. "If you will excuse me, I will tell the Prince that you are here."

"His nibs is at home, is he? That surprises me."

"I took it that it was him you came to see."

"I don't mind. But it's you I want to talk to."

"I am flattered."

"No you're not. I want something done. It's quicker to tell the jockey than the horse."

When the Prince joins us, Talleyrand unfolds an idea that he and Mirabeau have planned. England, they are sure, is going to war with Spain. Instead of the reflexive Bourbon-Habsburg alliance, we should support England, and get Prussia to do likewise. "It's time to tear up all the old maps," Talleyrand says, "and draw new ones. Whatever people feel about Louis, there's not a thinking Frenchman who doesn't despise the Queen's Holy Roman crew. We can crush Austria and Spain. The Netherlands would be freed. And in return the English would be obliged to renegotiate this damned trade treaty that is bankrupting us."

As the Prince looks vacant, I ask Talleyrand, "Why would the English agree?"

"They wouldn't. Not yet. That's what we want you to do."

"How? I know few people here."

"Talk to the Whigs. Talk to Fox, if you can. He'll listen. No one else in London is talking French to him. Pitt just wants us to stop all our nonsense and go back to the old régime. He's afraid that the revolutionary disease will cross the Channel in a bale of skins. That's why they won't talk to you. They think you've come here to incite the English to storm the Tower of London. The Whigs, that's who you must talk to, Laclos. Sound them out. I'll tell you now what their price will be. The Prince of Wales at the Tuileries. Well, Sire" – he leers at the Prince, who wakes up – "that's a price you'd be glad to pay, hm? What horse-races there would be then. And people would stop trying to cram the crown on your head."

"Well," the Prince says, "well, why not?"

"Your job, Sire," Talleyrand goes on, "would be simply to represent a Bourbon wing that loathes the Habsburgs. You wouldn't find that a difficult part to play, would you? Enter left, one who detests Marie-Antoinette?"

"I think I have already learned the part," the Prince replies.

"And yours," Talleyrand says to me, "is to pass the idea under the Whigs' noses and see if they sniff the bouquet. We need people in Berlin, as well. That would be easier done from here. Mirabeau and I doubt if all the birds could be bagged without Prussian guns."

"I admire their military traditions," I say. "But won't they side with the Austrians, again? We've already seen them in Paris this year."

"Yes," Talleyrand answers. "They didn't look enthusiastic, did they? Things are changing, Laclos. You have got to wipe the slate clean and do new sums. That is the advantage we have. We know Lafayette's sums. He doesn't know what ours will look like."

When Talleyrand is leaving, I go with him to the front door, and he nods for me to step outside with him. "Has he got anything left in his pocket?" he asks me, as a mist of rain moistens our faces.

"I can't say. However scrupulously I see to the ledgers, I know he has other investments, undisclosed to me. Whether they represent credit or debt would require a regiment of book-keepers to assess."

Talleyrand nods. "The best guess Mirabeau and I can make is that the game is close to up. He's been smuggling money over here. There can't be much left. We've been glad to serve his cause, but these are days, as you and I know, when one needs to be versatile, hm? Get him to help you in this, and the National Assembly will not discard him. It may be his last chance. What a waste." He hops into his coach, still shaking his head.

Now I have a strategy. I write to Whigs, asking for an appointment at their house or club, never at Chapel Street; I know from my acquaintance among the embassy staff that Luzerne has planted spies in our household. One Whig leads to another, and further introductions are arranged for me by Clarke, who has formed an attachment to an English woman whose uncle is close to Fox. When I sound these men on their feelings toward France, I cannot show them the cards in my hand, but I do let fall the name of Talleyrand, as evidence that we are discussing policy, not gossiping. They know I am an emissary of the Duke of Orleans, and that he is spending his days with the Prince of Wales. I keep up a correspondence, also, with military acquaintances in Berlin, asking for some assessment of the temper there. I have further letters to write to Montmorin in Paris, disdaining to address them via the embassy; in these, I maintain the semblance of reconnoitring English interest in our private quarrels, while at the same time hinting that we might stand to gain from an alliance.

I know that Luzerne has reported to Montmorin that I do nothing but write and receive letters all day. The fact is that for my office I have appropriated a room with a landing behind it which leads to a servants' staircase and the rear door of the house, and thus I go to my meetings unobserved. It does occur to me to wear a frock and bonnet for disguise, but it would be to amuse myself only. Luzerne's spies are too stupid to need deceiving.

The letters to Paris have of course to be copied out by the prince in his own hand. That is his "work", when he is not gambling or debauching himself. He comes back from a day of horse-races at Newmarket still drunkenly chuckling at a thing told him by the Prince of Wales. "He says that the whole of London is scandalised that I keep Agnès here with me. I said, 'You have mistresses, everyone knows that.' 'Yes,' Prinny came back, 'but everyone knows I pretend I don't. There's the difference, d'you see? Keeping her openly in your house, that's not how it's done, old boy.'"

It might be useful were the Prince to sound his royal friend on Talleyrand's plan, but I do not suggest it. Every rascal on Newmarket Heath would be prattling about it. The Prince would take odds against the Habsburgs.

I cannot find a way to Fox himself. I get Clarke to marry his English woman, but then find that her uncle has left on the Grand Tour (and besides, she soon takes to spending her nights in the bed of a young English cavalry officer). It would be futile to ask the Prince to speak to Fox. For myself, I have no standing to request an interview. I have asked Montmorin to appoint me to an official position. My master, after all, is still third in line to the throne, and our exile has never been promulgated. I propose the title of special attaché, and assure the Minister of my qualifications. My rule for assessing negotiations, I tell him, is to estimate the probity of the person with whom I am dealing, and how much interest he can be expected to have in delivering all that he promises. No reply is received.

Sooner or later, the Prince has to pay his respects to King George the Third. He leaves the house with a scowl, and returns with it intact. I expected nothing useful from the meeting, but ask if he has assessed His Majesty's attitude to France?

"I didn't have to. The first thing he told me was that no people on earth love their king more than the French do, and what has been done to Louis is a disgrace."

"And does he seek to stir our pot of troubles, do you think?"

"Oh, my dear Laclos, you have no idea what a penance it is to spend one minute in that man's company. Once he had got that off his chest, he wouldn't hear the name of France again. That was the sum of his opinions. I learned a great deal more than I wish to know about sheep-farming in the Cotswolds. You can imagine how droll the repartee was. I wondered if he mightn't be turning into a sheep himself. He does tedious often make a *baa-aah* sort of noise, don't you know?"

"And later you lunched with Her Majesty?"

"Yes, but I met some friends in the Court and was an hour late for her. She was so cross she couldn't raise a simper. The silence was colder than the collation. To drink, water was served, would you believe? I'm afraid I haven't been much of a spy for you today. *Baa-aah.*"

No matter, alas. Events are already rolling to crush the fragile flower Talleyrand and I have planted. First, the newspapers announce an alliance between England, Prussia, and the Netherlands. I write to Montmorin at once, enlarging my previous hints into a statement that France should be party to it. But even while the letter is on its way to Paris, the Austrian army sets out for Brussels.

Before the final curtain, there is time for a burlesque interlude or two. Of all people, old Montalembert comes a-calling. At the age of seventy-seven, he is divorcing his wife, a blameless woman as I know, and on his return to Paris will embrace the revolution and an apothecary's daughter. That boast delivered, he tells me that in Paris the royalist tongues are wagging about my plot, in collusion with the English, to install the Prince, Talleyrand and Mirabeau as masters of France. It was to that end that the Prince had financed the revolution. I answer that it might be possible to finance a modest riot, but hardly a revolution. "Well, well," Montalembert says, "I just thought you should know." I smile, and say nothing, wondering where the slander has trickled from. The embassy, or a perfidious Whig? Talleyrand, even? He is clever enough to play each side against the other.

More poisonous slander is circulating in London, where Madame de Genlis has published a tissue of clumsily forged correspondence allegedly between the Prince and me (as though we need to write letters to each other), which purports to expose the demonic dominion in which I hold my feckless master. She does not let the opportunity pass to spit out that the Duchess has become the mistress of, God help us all, old Ségur. I feel like the dying Brutus, reviewing the ghosts of all his past adversaries. The truth is that la Genlis, eaten up with spite, is taking revenge on all of us, including that true innocent, the Duchess of Orleans, who has no wish left in her life but to have her children restored to her from la Genlis's thrall.

Never two without three, as one says, and here comes the third, Chénier, at the double, to gasp out that Luzerne, the master spy, has without our help succeeded in identifying England's chief agent in Paris, the man who has spent a treasury of English sovereigns to stir up the French against their doe-eyed King. "That man," Chénier declares, pointing his finger at the ceiling in feeble imitation of some atrocious melodrama he is no doubt writing, "that man, Messieurs, is – Danton!"

"Oh really?" I reply. "Well I never, how extraordinary! Would you stay for a cup of tea, I expect you are too busy, good-bye."

Then England declares war on Spain, Paris allies itself with the Habsburgs, and the curtain is down. We have nothing more to do in London.

I write a letter to Lafayette in which the Prince tells him we will soon be home. His reply asks us not to return: we will threaten the tranquillity of France by reviving old animosity. I write again, saying we will be in Paris by early July. He replies, "I have evidence that will destroy you." I don't deign to answer. Instead, I write and have published, in Paris, a *Brief Description of the Exemplary Conduct of the Duke of Orleans in the Revolution of France*. I will not cite it here, Sade, the gist is in what you already have there. The only fault to be found in it is that, by the time it was printed, my master was no longer the Duke of Orleans. The Assembly had abolished the nobility, and he was "Monsieur Philippe of Orleans. Occupation: Prince".

The letter in which Lafayette threatened us was missing from my dossier when I looked for it again later, in Paris. I had left it with the Prince, and he must have stuffed it, along with a number of losing wager slips, ladies' garters, corks and invitation cards, at the back of a drawer in his desk in the house in Chapel Street, off Grosvenor Place.

* * *

A few days before we leave London, Sir Walpole sends us a letter inviting us to lunch at his house by the Thames, at Twickenham. Having little else to do, we accept, but when the day comes the Prince tells me to go alone. He has pressing business at Epsom.

Descending from the coach, I behold the most bizarre house I expect ever to see. Some bilious architect has brought up a grotesque vomit of turrets and battlements, cloisters, belfries, gargoyles and spires. It is a thing of horror that Chénier might dream after taking a strong draft of laudanum while watching a gothic revenge drama. In doubt, not to say alarm, I am on the point of riding off again, thinking to have misconstrued Sir Walpole's directions, when he sets my mind if not my eyes at rest by coming out at a hobbling sprint to greet me. "Monsieur de Laclos, Monsieur de Laclos, I am charmed to welcome you. Is the Duke with you?"

I apologise for my master's unavoidable absence, with one foot still on the step by way of offering to withdraw if Sir Walpole will not entertain less than a duke. But he very courteously leads the way into his pile, which is as choice within as without, a bricolage of curios, knick-knacks, *objets trouvés* and *objets* that had been better not *trouvés*. Some smell of cheese is pervasive. My host is already nattering away, hoping that my journey has been a pleasant one.

"In France, of course, everyone travels by balloon now. Your roads are under the plough, they tell me. Soon we may expect to see warfare carried on by means of bows and arrows among the clouds." He titters. "Forgive my fooleries. All that truly pains me in French customs is that habit you have of adopting from us only our own most egregious follies, of which the flower is horse-racing. I have heard that the Duke is devoted to it?"

"Ah, Sir Walpole," I smile, "I do believe that you have been spying on us."

"Oh, no need, no need." He flaps his fingers at a footman to serve the soup. "The Duke's foibles have been the talk of London. I am sorry that I have no other guests for your company, but – well, to be candid, one never knows what to expect of the Duke of Orleans. When I visited you at Chapel Street, I confess that I *was* spying. I wanted to see what buttons the Duke is wearing nowadays."

I cough politely. "Buttons, Sir Walpole?"

"Yes. Don't you know? At Lady Duncannon's soirée some years ago the Duke appeared in a frock-coat that was somewhat soiled, but rendered quite filthy by the buttons on it." His lips are writhing, and I see the soup tremble in his spoon. "The buttons, Monsieur de Laclos, had designs enamelled upon them. One represented a stallion covering a mare, and another two dogs equally conjugal. Such vulgar indelicacy to Lady Duncannon. As George Selwyn remarked – I still have a very good memory for what people say, you know – George observed that such buttoning was worse than unbuttoning, since there could be some excuse for the one but none for the other." He swallows his spoonful at last, puts a finger on one nostril, rolls his eyes up, and sniffs violently. "So you see," he continues, "anxious though I have been to entertain the Duke, one cannot invite him without taking certain precautions, such as inviting nobody else. And now, apparently, even he cannot tolerate his own company. It is a shame. I wanted to hear what attitude he takes to the sacrilege that your philosophers, geometricians and other reformers have committed upon that saintly and gentle cousin of his."

"I could perhaps ..." I begin, but Sir Walpole's spate is as strong as that of the river, which we can see through the window. Does deafness explain the eccentricity of his conversation, or has he quite blocked up his ears with the sniffing?

"I know of the Duke's liberal leaning, of course, but who could countenance liberty arrived at by massacre? Why is it that in any commotion your countrymen are always so barbaric? Mark my words, all they will achieve is to replace what they call despotism with a thing far worse, namely, atheism. From such savage behaviour, how can order and justice be expected to arise? I heard Pitt remark that such an ocean of questions as your country has embarked upon will take a century to discuss. One achieves a sound constitution by systematic reform, not by plunging blindly into the chaos."

Since I cannot make myself heard, I use my mouth on the food, which is passable, and let him continue his jabbering. I have a mind to leave after the meal, but he insists that I walk through a park with him to see Hampton Court.

On the way, we pass a small house in which, he tells me, a

gamekeeper has recently killed himself. Perhaps the fresh air has opened his ears, because he hears me when I return the story of the Duperrés' cook. "Tish," he says testily. "It is very provoking that people must always be hanging or drowning themselves, or going mad. Now, tell me what you think." He gestures at the grounds of Hampton Court, through the gates of which we have just walked. "Parts of it, as you see, are of course imitated after Versailles. Ah, Versailles – to walk in those gardens conversing with Madame de Sévigné, that is a day-dream I have indulged often. These will bear a degree of comparison, I think, in that our lawns will always be finer than yours, which lack for water. You cannot have such beautiful landscapes as ours till you have as bad a climate. Don't you agree?"

I see his gesticulating reflection beside mine as I lean on a parapet and gaze down at the sour Thames. Later, in my coach back to London, after Sir Walpole has bidden me farewell and promised to send me letters, I think back on the image I have seen of my face, never still, never resolved, jigging and fractur-ing itself on the surface of the deep and dark water.

12

As I lie on my bed this morning, exercising my hand, my poor hand, in readiness for yet another day of devilling for Laclos, and in the evening creating exalted scenes in my own manuscript, I am alerted by voices laughing and oathing outside my window. I stand up and look out, expecting it to be an unruly group of inmates, probably with a purchased woman or two. No. It is another gang of labourers, with spades and picks. Governor Coignard is there, with not Dupommier, thank God, but three other well-dressed men. They are all standing just outside the hedge that embraces our garden, so that they are in the adjacent field. Although the gate to the Picpus also serves that field, none of us ever goes over there, because it is rough ground, with tall grass, probably an abandoned vegetable garden. Are they going to open a passage to it, through the hedge? Is there no limit to the luxury of verdure to which we have to submit? Could that grey building I thought a derelict barn, on the further side of the field, be another nunnery that we are to expropriate? This time, let there be nuns, young, fresh nuns, their vows still moist on their lips, like morning dew upon ripe quinces.

Later, I look out again. There are many diggers, nearly three dozen of them, and they seem not to be opening the hedge but clearing the field, excavating pits. And some of them are working on the wall beside the gate, apparently knocking it down. If Coignard were not there, I would assume it was nothing to do with us, some building works, perhaps. But he is there, and I am here, legally confined, and the cold hand of fear twists my gut again. I cannot find concierge Blanchard. I will ask Laclos about it. I don't care what indignities it may lead to, how many cockroaches come scuttling past my nose, just so long as I know what is going on. What I hate is to be the object of other people's verbs. In the present state of things, I am willing to overlook that I am Lord of the Manor of Saumane and of La Coste, and co-Lord of Mazan. But surely, even in a republic, one may still say aloud that one is lord of oneself? And claim the right to be told about anything that may affect one's own well-being? That is not a feudal right, is it? I can tolerate, though I scorn, decrees such as the one that we are all to ride on the right-hand side of our roads now. A truly revolutionary decision, citizens. What if we do have to brandish our sabres left-handed? That is little enough to pay for the evidence of our thoroughgoing commitment to turning the world upside-down. (As long as you have remembered to tell everyone, so that our carriages are not to be always crashing into each other.) I do not feel my autonomy infringed. You can invent ever more rational weights and measures every week for all I care, and subdivide France into twenty thousand departments – nay, twenty million, to every Frenchman his own department: how may we in all democratic logic stop short of that? Cry havoc, and let Reason off the leash. But when you send a crowd of malingerers to dig up an inoffensive field outside my window, I need to know why. I will not be kept in the dark, unable to defend myself against nameless threats. Especially not on 15-6-94, a malign combination if ever I saw one. Though if I knew what numbers they have ascribed to their very revolutionary new months, it is possible that 27-prairial-1 might be more reassuring. Probably they will change all the numbers soon, and the alphabet. There is an infamous stink of the old régime in ABC and 123.

And now that it is time to present myself, clerically modest with paper and pen, for Laclos's use of me, he says No, we will not go into his beloved garden today, but remain, as we used to, in his room. Why? "Because," he says, "haven't you heard? – Governor Coignard has advised us all to remain indoors for the time being."

Why?

He doesn't know, but Coignard has promised to give us

more information.

Why? Why, citizen? What is going on? I tell him about the diggers. He didn't know about them, since his window is on a different wall from mine. There may be some connection, he allows. I want to know.

"Yes," he says, "I sympathise, but for the present there is nothing we can do about it, so let us distract our misgivings by the means we have found so efficacious."

§ The Man in Black

"I am back in Paris, almost to the day twelve months after we stormed the Bastille."

We, citizen? Your first-person plural is unusually comprehensive today.

"All right, after the Bastille stormed itself. It is of no significance here, merely a date. And the Prince goes straight into the Assembly, where his entry is applauded by all the radicals. We have come so far, I think to myself, and got nowhere, yet still he is a figure to them. As he is to the King. When the Prince goes to the Tuileries, simply to pay his humble respects, Louis takes one look and turns his back. Such vulgarity. As for Lafayette, he is nowhere to be seen with his evidence that will destroy us, his one breath that would blow me out of France again.

"I detect that bad breath, though, issuing from the throats of others. I find myself called a traitor to my class. All my life I have been penalised for lacking one quarter of nobility, now I am vilified for betraying the three I have got. Rivarol reviews me as one of the Great Men of the Revolution. (Poor Rivarol, always reaching for irony and grasping only a handful of spite.) 'Laclos,' he wrote, 'the confidant, counsellor, and friend, perhaps, of the Duke of Orleans. He it is who tells the Duke what he feels, what his plans will be, and wipes away his fears for him; in a word, he who briefly made the Duke the idol and hope of the people. To what realms of glory might he have spurred that potent prince, could he but have encouraged him without frightening him? But one can nourish any moral quality save only courage, and poor Laclos could not lend his own to his pupil. So he remains uselessly tethered to fate.' Others of Lafayette's dummies are less generous than Rivarol. I am everyone's Man in Black, the diabolical conspirator, a Valmont of politics, using the naïve Prince's fortune to manoeuvre him to the centre of the stage, and then calling out his lines to him. As if he could have spoken them right, even then. He went on going to the Assembly, but seldom said anything, which was just as well since he had nothing to say.

"They are building stands in the Champ de Mars, and making banners and firework displays, and putting out baskets of flowers and rehearsing balloon flights, all for the Fête de la Fédération on July 14th. Such a pity it rains all day. The military bands squelch past, and the petals thrown down upon them stick to their uniforms. The big brass horns sound like pigs drowning. Talleyrand keeps his mitre dry, of course, under the awning of the saluting stand. If he die before I do, I shall see to it that they inscribe on his tomb, 'He kept his mitre dry.' Waiting to celebrate Mass, he is impatient. A place is being kept for him at the card table. The soldiers are late because of the rain, and the leaders of the Assembly are following the soldiers, and Talleyrand cannot hold up his chalice and intone his Latin pieties until all the host are there. He stares at the vast crowd below him, with dripping banners that read TREMBLE, ARISTO-CRATS, WE ARE THE BUTCHER BOYS and suchlike, and I am close enough to hear the Bishop mutter, 'Why can't those buggers hurry up?' Later, after he limped off through the puddles, he won all night. Magnificent salvoes of artillery punctuate speeches in which politicians assure the people that something has been completed. Perhaps they are right. But it is nothing compared to what is only just beginning. How could any of us know that, then? Twelve months later, at the same place, we would be wiser."

Wiser? A curious choice of word, citizen. Do not forget that I am now

170

a free spirit in the world you describe. I heard from witnesses exactly what Lafayette did the following July, and would not call it wisdom.

"Not him. If he live another fifty years, he will still be a stupid, spoiled child. *We* would be wiser, I said, Sade. Through suffering. Is that always the price of wisdom? Did Plato suffer, and Aristotle, and Euclid, do you think?"

How much sadder to pay the price and yet be cheated of the commodity.

"Some are," Laclos grunts.

I have heard, I say daintily, *that you had some connection yourself with what would happen the following July.*

He gazes out of the window, where thin streaks of cloud chalk the deep blue slate of the sky. "If what you have heard is what actually took place, I shall be astonished." He turns to me. "Yes, I did have some connection with it. And when we come to it I will be plain. But now I am restored to the loving arms of my family, at the Palais-Royal. I take little Cathérine on my knee, while my son stands at my shoulder, and Marie-Soulange is seated facing us. They are intrigued by the tales I bring them from a strange country. 'Papa,' Étienne-Fargeau asks me, 'is it true that in England they killed their king?' 'A long time ago,' I told him. 'Why? What had he done?' 'He was a bad king.' 'They didn't have to kill him though, did they? Why couldn't they just make someone else king, instead?' I tried to explain the divinity of kings to a six-year-old child. He did not understand. Nor, as I continued, did I. A fable by La Fontaine would have been more credible.

"Surprisingly soon, the pleasure of being home again fell away. I had moods of despair. Fifty years of frustration stretched behind me like a snail's track. Never an assault or a siege, a book that everyone misunderstands, a political coup that captured only ridicule. Again, it seemed I had to invent the rest of my life. The private happiness of a family home would go stale without some public cause for me to serve, especially at a moment when France, too, was on the point of inventing itself afresh. I was haunted by that coinciding crisis in the country and in myself, and couldn't shake off the idea that both

171

might find the same resolution. I was dark with passion, but had no object. I was – I almost wept with bitterness at the ironic recognition of it – I was a primed cannon with no target. I do not know if you have ever experienced such a condition, Sade. Only from habit does one get out of bed in the morning, since the new day brings no purpose. I would catch myself staring at the hands of my watch. I longed for the next meal-time. It was in such a state that I started to go every evening to the Jacobins club. I had never pictured myself as an orator. It was something to do. And – who knew? – it might throw up some way for me to follow.

"It was not an arbitrary choice, of course. The Prince still employed me. I had lost any illusion that he would ever condescend to occupy a great office of state, but I owed him my loyalty, which entailed informing myself about political developments, and the Jacobins was the best place for that. Also, I was being prudent. Lafayette's bullying threat to destroy us had turned into a judicial hearing. The charge was that my master and Mirabeau were leaders of the invasion of Versailles. I was not accused, but would surely be punished if they were found guilty. The case was abject, of course. Lafayette was peevishly kicking a donkey. Mirabeau had gone over to the King's party by now, and who in the land could seriously suspect the Prince of political designs? Nevertheless, many new judges had been appointed, and a good number of them were Jacobins, so it seemed wise to go there and acquaint myself with them.

"You will remember the absurd uproar when the charges were dismissed. All Lafayette's puppets were squeaking 'Scandal!' Paris was littered with forged letters in which the Prince was supposed to reproach me for duping him into vain ambition. What a misfortune to have known me, that sort of rubbish. And more loathsome lies about our relations. I have attracted much of that and never been touched by it. Some would feign to laugh it off. I can't be bothered to do even that.

"At that time, the Jacobins met in the Dominicans' old

library. It is a dark place. The light of smoky oil lamps flickers on hundreds of serious faces, under wigs, or tall, round hats, and throws large shadows across the walls. The members sit around three sides of the chamber, on tiers of benches. A speaker at the tribune can be heard clearly by all, perhaps because of the book-lined walls or the great vaulted ceiling, but certainly because of the attentiveness of the audience. Sincerity is the only style of oratory. Mirabeau is hotly sincere, Barnave crisply sincere, Duport and the Lameths passionately sincere, Danton sincerely sensible, and Robespierre is sincerely quiet, logical, impeccable in his attachment to constitutional virtue and in his readiness to pledge his life for freedom. Because here, unlike in the Assembly, these men are not debating topics or measures, they are seeking principles. Above all, the one principle: how shall we live together as a nation?

"In that odour of burning oil and soap, the sober discourses contend, evening after evening, as though a process of abrasion might bring us to one irreducible principle upon which the constitution can rest. Because that is the avowed aim of all. We are the Society of the Friends of the Constitution. But there is no constitution! We have asked the question of history, 'Why are things as they are?', and the question has sounded back through time and found no echoing answer. And so we are in a worse case than Pascal's gulf. We have nothing at all to gamble our faith on. We have to construct something in the void.

"There are some at the Jacobins – Lafayette is one, of course – who urge us to cling to what we have, the established monarchy. But King Louis is a man descending a staircase in darkness, believing every step down must be the bottom one. Were we to put one straw of faith upon him, he would tumble into the void. Shall we find a better king? Do we need a king? If there is no head, will the body politic not collapse into lawlessness, since no one will be answerable for what is done? How could any man put his hand on his spade and say, 'This spade is mine', when he would have no reply to the question, Why is it yours? Property, marriage, one's very life, all would be vulnerable to that question, Why? Now you may see the reason that many at the Jacobins, when they spoke, adopted a pose that referred to the Romans as painted by David (who often sat amongst us). If these intransigent and terrifying questions cannot be answered, at least one can embody a way to behave in such a predicament. If Danton, with his great forehead and shaggy head, can present himself as one who will never infringe another man's freedom, then I will reciprocate. If Barnave goes to the tribune and, by modelling himself upon Brutus or Cato, reminds us that a Stoic hero may not have long to live, thus are we all confirmed in our resolve to die rather than abandon our questions."

I put my pen down, stretch my hand, and then clap it twice on my other. *Bravo, citizen*, I say. *Spoken like one who expects this memoir to save his skin when the democratic inquisition comes sniffing for you. But, lest you misread my tone as sardonic, let me answer you in equally noble anguish. Was it not Rousseau himself who wrote that the general will – call it sovereignty – cannot be incarnated? Ha! Did you ever put that to The Roman?*

Laclos frowns, at my interruption of his train of what he'd call thought, but what anyone with an ounce of sense would recognise as futile hand-wringing.

"Robespierre and I often discussed Rousseau, to see what aid he could offer to our reasoning." He pauses, and at this moment we are interrupted by a din of shouts, and saucepans beaten with spoons. I run into the corridor, and am told that Governor Coignard wishes to address us all, at once, in the common room, *née* salon.

Why? I ask Laclos. *This has never happened before. What is going on?*

"It is very provoking," Laclos says. "I am anxious to keep up the good work we are doing. However, I suppose we must go and see what the matter is."

A noxious crew we are, standing in groups waiting for Coignard. A rank smell accompanies a crowd of men who live enclosed lives. The smell becomes viler when we hear what the

Governor has to tell us. "I want you to know about a development that affects every one of us in this house, and I entreat you to follow the advice I shall give you." He coughs on to his fist, and draws a breath. The men are quiet. "The adjacent field, beyond the hedge, has been adopted by the Committee for Public Safety for use as a cemetery. You may have seen workmen in the field today. They are digging mortuary pits. They are also widening the gateway." He pauses, and when he speaks again it is more slowly. "The reason for widening the gateway is that space is needed for the tumbrils to enter. The tumbrils will be bringing bodies here to bury because it is convenient to what has been designated as a new site for the guillotine, just up the road, at La Place du Trône."

Coignard goes on speaking, with the intention of quelling the horror he knows his announcement will have caused, but it is no good. From every throat in the room, I think, certainly from mine, possibly not from Laclos's, a growl rasps, on a rising tone. Coignard has to wait, and repeat what was drowned. "For the safety of all of you, I implore you from now on to live in this house as quietly as you can. Do nothing to attract the attention of anyone outside. Let this house have the appearance of being deserted. With these precautions," Coignard continues, with something near a sob in his voice, "we may all hope to go on living undisturbed. That is my most earnest wish."

A voice calls out, "Why are they moving it here?"

Coignard waits for the shouts in support of the question to subside. "All I can tell you is all that I know myself. The citizens who live in the Place de la Révolution have been complaining that they wanted the guillotine moved away from their homes. I cannot tell you why the Committee has chosen to move it here. What I am certain of is that their choice of site has nothing at all to do with the Picpus. It is merely a coincidence, a most unfortunate one for us. I will not conceal from you, since most of you know it already, that I have always done my utmost to discourage the authorities from even thinking about the Picpus when they are discussing prisons. The Picpus is not a prison. It is a house of recuperation. A sanatorium, loosely speaking. I have always regarded all of you as in my care rather than my custody. Your detention here is on grounds of health, not of criminal conviction. However, let us not beat about the bush. You all know that many among you were confined here for reasons of *political* health, so to speak ..." Coignard halts, shaking his head.

Laclos, next to me, asks, "Governor, may I have your permission to address the meeting?"

Coignard nods. I do not think he would have nodded to me.

"The point I believe Governor Coignard finds a painful one to make," Laclos says in the level voice he must have used to cadets for thirty years, "is this. Only five days ago, the Law of the 22nd of prairial authorised the Committee for Public Safety to arraign whomsoever it saw fit. The position, friends, is that the State has once again filled its prisons full, and will be seeking to clear space to accommodate fresh prisoners." He pauses, but the room is silent. "The advice that the Governor has given us is correct, and it is vital that we follow it every minute of the day. Our status here is a nicety that will be overlooked if a committee starts to think of the Picpus as a prison where space might be cleared. And the risk of that is evidently much greater with the tumbrils visiting us. Thank you, Governor."

"Thank you, Citizen Laclos," Coignard says.

I have no recollection at all of walking back to Laclos's room. I am near to vomiting with terror. I sit on the edge of his bed, and wish he would put his arm around my shoulders. Every footstep in the corridor is Dupommier's. I will be the first space to be cleared. *Is that all I am?* I hear myself say aloud.

"What?" Laclos is watching out of the window.

A space. To be cleared.

"Where were we? Could you read back the last few sentences to me?"

Good God, I say, looking at the door, not at him. *We have a few hours to live at best, and you suppose that ...*

"Stop that. They will not be taking people from here. I have told you that before, and this development does not alter the position."

That is not what you told the meeting just now.

"I merely wished to endorse Coignard's sensible advice. There is no point in taking foolish risks."

So there is a risk.

"As long as we breathe we are at risk of death. There is only one way to avoid that. But they have never taken anyone from here yet, and my information is that the new law will not alter that. The Abbaye, the Luxembourg, prisons like those are where they will clear spaces."

Those bastards in the Place de la Révolution, I am muttering. Their prim nostrils and gentle eyes are offended by the evidence of what they themselves vociferously approve. So they have it moved away, as though they can't bear to watch the pig slaughtered that they will dine on this evening. Under our windows, Laclos. It is too horrible.

"I am sure, in spite of your incessant complaining, that you have found our work together an effective means of distracting our minds from sombre brooding. So let us resume."

I have an insight. Laclos is just as frightened as I am, and perhaps has been all along. These bracing injunctions to me have been addressed to himself, this distraction is his distraction. And yet, sentimental fool that I am, I experience a twinge of gratitude. What he says is true, this toil has numbed my fears. It is the nearest that cold Northern herring could come to putting a comforting arm around me. How glad I am to have grown up in Provence, where we do not live in dark, cold rooms and go mad in winter with the ideas locked inside our solitary heads, but instead go out into the warm nights and sunny days and share our insanities with each other. Whoops, I have missed the start of his next homily. I will make it up, later. He cannot sustain his intention to scrutinise my transcripts when we are working under the very wheels of the tumbril.

"No one objected to my admission to the Jacobins – not even Lafayette, interestingly. Perhaps he wanted to keep his eye on me.

"Danton became a friend. We would walk together over to the Palais-Royal for our weekly meeting with the Prince. On the Prince's behalf I sometimes went to hear the wilder notions that hotheads in other clubs were puffing. The Social Circle was notorious. They were for Rousseau's idea, which he had not examined properly, that the land should be shared among the poorer people. The same crew wanted all women to be commonly available, without any sanction of marriage. I mounted the tribune to denounce people like that, who were as depraved as the aristocrats they pretended to scorn. The Cordeliers were almost as intemperate. Their subscription was only two sous a month, which meant that many of them were from the most desperate class of society. They debated whether to admit women as members. In the rue St-Honoré, anybody was welcome to listen, but constitutionally we stayed within the boundaries that the Assembly defined. The truth was that we dominated the Assembly. For example, primed by a discussion at the Jacobins, Bishop Talleyrand could go over there and propose the expropriation of the Church, to reduce the national debt."

From the example the Jacobins had set in expropriating the Dominican house for your premises?

"We paid them rent. Some of them joined us."

They changed their habits.

"Quite. But our thinking was always in advance of the Assembly, where the threnody was that the King, once the sovereign of twenty-seven million subjects, was likely to find himself the only subject of twenty-seven million sovereigns. We tried to alert the Assembly to the risk of mob rule if the franchise were not extended.

"I was appointed to the Correspondence Committee. We had hundreds of Jacobin branches throughout France, because we wanted the nation to join our discourse. Many letters came every day. We selected passages and read them to the chamber.

"I found that I enjoyed speaking at the tribune, and considered whether it might be a way forward for me. I would have preferred the artillery. With a new constitution, my military career might at last be unimpeded by old fools like Ségur. For the time being I did not want to return to the polygon, with no prospect of action in the field, and so I applied for another term of leave, with an accompanying letter in which the Prince avowed that he still had need of me. As fortune had it the Minister, La Tour du Pin, resigned at that point, after Danton had denounced him in the Assembly, and almost at once I received a note extending my leave for six more months.

"The Prince's affairs needed all the help he could afford. I had the dust blown off the ledgers, and an audit disclosed that his creditors numbered three thousand or so. To pay off the most demanding ones, before they had him gaoled, we had to sell many of his estates. My thanks was that la Elliott spent her time telling the Prince he should be rid of me. I was to blame for all the offences to the spotless King that the Orleans party was supposed to have committed. The Duke was my dupe, all that poodle-yapping, yet again. Meanwhile, the Prince was sobbing to her that he would gladly give up everything if only he could have a little squire's estate for himself by the River Thames. I walked to the heights of Montmartre to cool my rage when I was told all that. It served. I saw the hordes of workless labourers dragging their feet through the dust of the cobbles. I looked down and saw Paris in the autumn sunshine, and thought that nothing could be more fair. And I resolved that labourers and city would find their harmony again under any constitution I could help to create.

"The Prince's seventeen-year-old son, Louis-Philippe, had expressed a wish to join the Jacobins, and I was pleased to propose his admission. The boy might – who knew? – develop the sense of duty of which just one grain in his father would have changed everything. He had already shown some independence. An arrangement that he should dine with his mother three nights a week he had amended to two. True, that may have expressed only the malign influence upon all those children of their witch of a governess, la Genlis. Her husband,

Sillery, rushed to embrace the boy upon his entrance to the Jacobins. But I found him a job to do, helping me with the correspondence, and very keen he proved himself.

"Whenever I spoke at the tribune, I was libelled within hours. You will remember the outcry against the nobility who were emigrating."

Oh, I remember it well, citizen.

"There was a risk they would form an external threat to the peace of France. All the same, I could see no purpose in forbidding two of the King's elderly aunts from leaving the country, and said so. In return, I am called an odious hypocrite. My true intention, I am told, is that no one should ever leave France, or indeed their native parishes, and all who disagree with me, including the royal family, are to have their throats slit while a red flag is run up above the Assembly. Though of course my dear pupil and respected master, the Prince, will be excepted. All I suggested in fact was a small tax on those who emigrated, in recompense for what France had given them all their lives. Mirabeau spoke against me, saying that any such restriction was a barbarous precedent. I answered him, how can any law, if it be justly introduced, be barbarous?

"Robespierre proposed to restrict the liberty of the press. I disagreed with him. I spoke in favour of protecting provincial dialects. I supported the exclusion from the franchise of women, Jews, and colonial natives, on the grounds that a vote represents a property right. I defended the slave trade, seeing the great harm that would be done to our perilous economy if it were abolished. I supported the freedom to stick up posters, providing one did not disfigure people's houses. And my every opinion is gnawed by the royalist jackals the next day: I have seized the helm of the Jacobins, I am having a street named for me, I have told Barnave that I expect to stand in the shadows behind the throne manipulating King Philippe the Red, I bellyache that the King is appointing ministers who are not Jacobins, I am the leader of a cabal sworn to destroy the throne unless the Prince sits on it, and those under my sinister thrall include – judge the ignorance of it – Talleyrand, Mirabeau, and Lafayette. When I said that the National Guard should serve as the citizenry's defence against servile obedience, it was reported as: the martial law is not to my taste, so why should I obey it?

"But the best of all, howled by Tilly, is saved for the occasion when I question the propriety of a Te Deum to celebrate the King's recovery from illness. 'The Lord Laclos vomited a gutful of bile against the King at the Jacobins' Sabbath. The delicate, candid author of *Les Liaisons Dangereuses*, the guiding spirit of the mighty Philippe, demanded, by all the devils, why must we endure this medical bulletin? The thing is this, the King has not died, not yet. This time he insists on returning to us. And may we all enjoy health as good as his. But in some I detect the wish for an ostentatious celebration of this resurrection, to give thanks to God, as in the times of despotism.' (Cries of 'Long live His Majesty!' from those who, unlike me and my crew, do not detest the tenderest of royal fathers and the most honest man in the kingdom.) 'Messieurs,' my script continues, 'let us not sully our principles with royalism. But, if you wish at present to disguise our true feelings, here is my proposal. Instead of a Te Deum, let us fuck four nubile virgins. It would be appropriate to select four from the Faubourg Saint-Antoine who were made orphans at the Bastille.' Hardly have I finished making my virtuous proposal when – what is this Tilly hears? 'Is it an angry sea? A flock of crows cawing across the fields? No. It is a great roar of approval, showing that the Jacobins club is now the unique shrine of good taste.' The ensuing debate concerns which members shall be chosen to deflower the virgins. By our choice, we shall express our views on the propagation of the human race. The name of Desmoulins is acclaimed, and of Mirabeau, Sieyès; the name of Robespierre ...

"It was immediately after that phantasmagoria that Mirabeau's heart stopped. You remember how all Paris followed the catafalque to the Pantheon. I walked along wondering if he had choked to death with laughing at what was being said about the Jacobins. I would like to think I still saw a smile on those red cheeks."

13

Itry to stop myself, but it is no good. At dusk I am drawn to the window, and soon enough here it comes, this evening's macabre pageant. You see the lights first, a few dim lamps on poles coming along the road. And then, in through the gate, the tumbril, loaded, its cargo pale in the lamplight. Along behind the hedge they go, and halt. Some fifteen or twenty minutes it takes them. The aura of lamplight behind the hedge is a false dawn. They are stripping the clothes off, and pocketing anything of value. Then, like a cloud of ghastly will-o'-the-wisps, the pale light moves back again, to the gate, where they run with the empty tumbril, thinking only of getting to the tavern. The stench is already dreadful, in this summer heat. Do they cover the contents of the pit, once they have tipped their load in? Do they use lime? I shall most certainly not go and see for myself. The fear of death perturbs me, the smell of it disgusts me. I could not bear the sight of it.

Laclos, too, is subdued, and talks slowly, with pauses for reflection. On what, I wonder. I feel something in me that is astonishing, a small, frail, fleeting bond with him, and I believe he reciprocates it. He would term it fraternity, in the impossible event that either of us alluded to it. It is not a thing I have felt before. And to feel it with *him*, of all people. I am fraternal with a North Sea herring.

§ Falling Apart

"In that springtime, only three years ago ..." He shakes his head and sucks his teeth, which are in remarkably good condition for a man of his age. "Many things were falling apart. It was the time when the Assembly voted to resign *en bloc*, in the touching belief that a fresh collection of heads might see a way through the thickets. I wondered if it wasn't an acknowledgment that the Assembly had become merely an administrative office. All the vital arguments took place at the Jacobins. Well, with hindsight I suppose one should add that they took place in the streets, too. Every day there was a new disturbance, about some old grievance – bread, wages, the King, representation, taxes, the weather, nothing had been resolved. All our thunderstorms had not cleared the air.

"A sight that still saddens me, in memory, was the falling apart at the Palais-Royal. The Prince had been ordered by the Assembly to get rid of his Cabinet, all the advisers, hangers-on and cronies he kept about him. Not me. I was his private secretary. But the rest had to be shovelled out into the gardens. He was given no choice. It was his own fault, as usual. He had proudly rejected the Assembly's first offer, to bail him out of his debts. So they said, *Very well, sink.* And that mighty galleon, leaking at every board, went down with its sails still proud. But more poignant was the fact that the Duchess decided she could no longer stay on board. Had the man allowed himself to enjoy the contentment of family life, how different the history of France might have been. There was a sour argument over the settlement. Worst of all was the children's refusal to go with their mother. Our true mother is Madame de Genlis, they said. We want to stay with her. That witch had enchanted them. I had published an anonymous squib about the small brain that produced her witless novels, but my God, it knew how to bind those children to her with iron hoops. The Prince tried to run away from it all and join the army – or the navy would do – but the King wouldn't let him.

"Probably the King was right. The army was in a bad enough state as it was. Not the artillery (which had proved itself to be both accomplished and civically minded) but the infantry. And your cavalry, Sade, oh. We had a debate at the Jacobins about it. They would have voted to elect a new army. That fool

Anthoine made no fine distinctions, just insulted the civic instincts of everyone who wore an officer's uniform. People like him did not take the army seriously. But they would have to soon enough. The strategy that Talleyrand and I had planned in London, entailing a Prussian alliance, was now in general favour at the club. Our distaste for Frederick the Great's nephew, who was as obnoxious an aristocrat as his uncle, was overridden by the need to oppose Marie-Antoinette. I need scarcely add that she was the source of tittle-tattle that we were in Prussia's pay.

"Everywhere, one could not fail to see evidence that the fabric of society was threadbare, and likely to rip. I had merely to walk from the Jacobins along to the Palais-Royal. Behind me, I left a chamber in which every man had soaped and bathed himself that morning, and might do so again before retiring to a well-laundered bed, no matter what price the water-carrier charged. It was the outward show of inward virtue. A scrubbed and modestly attired body betokened a civic spirit, a respect for other citizens' bodies, their most private property. Or perhaps there was something in it of self-mastery. I wash, therefore I am indivisible. I will not sully myself with compromise. To dismiss my ideas, you must kill me. God knows if it contributed to old Mirabeau's demise. With his belches and farts and harlots and cussing, he must have felt himself adrift. As an artillery officer, I had always had a daily ablution, and so the new custom required no change in my habits. I wonder how people like you got on? Were you shamed?"

I have never been a bourgeois beast. You must know that. Have you truly read nothing I have written?

He infuriates me by merely chuckling in reply. Is that the review my few surviving writings have deserved, a cosmic chuckle?

"But as I turn off the rue St-Honoré into the gardens of the Palais-Royal, or rather the Maison d'Égalité as we must now call it, what a rip in the fabric. The Wild Man is openly copulating with the girl who assists him. First she comes on to the platform, pale, with long hair, and takes her clothes off as

185

though she were going to bathe. When she is nude, she walks around with one finger in her rosy lips, turning her young body for all to desire. The Wild Man enters with a roar, already naked, his dark body gleaming with grease, his long hair matted. She shrieks, and feigns to look for escape. He seizes her about the waist, then drags her down upon a table-top, her legs dangling. With his arms behind her, he pulls her down by her shoulders upon himself. He bellows, she shudders. They perform nineteen times a day, until enough coins are in the hat to pay for their supper. The stew of whores promote them, perhaps, because the trade in prostitution has never been so seething. I talk to one or two of these women occasionally, because I feel pity for them. Gamblers, money-lenders, hawkers, actors and charlatans swarm in the gardens. As I leave, and enter the quiet of Fountains Court, I think to myself that those are children of *la patrie* second, still children of Rabelais first of all.

"How could we mend the fabric? I had the idea of a national petition to the Assembly. It would join together millions of our voices in asking for a proper constitution. But also, a petition might help to repair the damage, by allowing everyone in the country to feel that their individual voice was respected, down to ordinary soldiers and servants.

"Citizen Robespierre opposed my idea. By now we had moved downstairs to the old chapel, with room on the terraced benches for hundreds more. Robespierre grated out his objections not just to my proposal but to my influence in the Correspondence Committee. 'We should change the committee completely,' he said quietly. 'Every committee should be renewed as often as is practicable, to extirpate bad habits. This one has aroused, I will not say complaints but fears of a sort of moderatism, a coolness that sits ill with our fierce patriotism.'

"Barnave answered him. 'We must be brothers here, not slanderers of each other. But, very well, let the whole committee be renewed, if it is felt that a fresh ardour is wanted. We will all resign.'

"So we did. An election was held, and the old committee was re-elected in its entirety. Robespierre accepted that, of course, but asked us to co-opt him as an extra member, which we did.

"Afterwards, I stood with Barnave in the courtyard outside, off the rue St-Honoré, next to the liberty tree which had been planted, and he asked me if Robespierre might not find the committee's work humdrum, from time to time. 'He is,' Barnave sighed, 'a man of such moral passion, so chastely logical in detecting a want of virtue in others, that he might find some of the questions with which we deal to be, let us say, provincial.' Barnave coughed gently. 'I mean, who could imagine Citizen Robespierre doing something normal and domestic, like keeping chickens? Or fishing?'

"And then the royal family ran away. In our constitutional debates, the image had arisen of a head of state who would embody the civic virtue that every citizen should feel. I had drawn the distinction between that and the old notion of royal grace, which I called a monstrous superstition. If there is such a thing as grace, I said, it resides in the Assembly. No event could have more dramatically made the point for me than the graceless flight of the royal family, to be caught like truants at Varennes. In Paris, royal effigies were torn down, and royalist posters were defaced by smoking them over with burning oily rags.

"While the carriage was on its way to Varennes, the throne was empty. To go and sit upon it was incumbent upon the first gentleman of France, and that was now the Prince."

14

They came and took one of us yesterday. An old man, I didn't know his name, his offence not known to me, nor to him probably. Some of us watched him go. So they do know we're here, a ripe and almost unplucked orchard, how could anyone resist us? At fifty a day, it won't be long now. Fifty, I'd say, from the look of the tumbril in the pale lamplight. He went so calmly, as though he'd been told his lunch was ready. I was terrified at how calm he was. He didn't look at us, or at any of the guards who came for him, he didn't say anything, or weep, just walked with them along the corridor, his head slightly forward, but it would be, at eighty. His hands were clenched, that was all. Their footsteps died away. He came back in the evening, the other side of the hedge. His name was published this morning, that's how we knew, but I've already forgotten it.

He was about eighty years old, Laclos. You can see how menaced the republic must have felt by his existence.

Laclos put in a lot of brow-kneading before he answered. "What do we know? He may have been a special case, someone they already knew about, and all along intended to deal with, when it was time."

Time, I remark, *there's an interesting word.*

"Yes." Nothing more.

Citizen Laclos, I say, *I hope you're smeared with your own shit when you go. You have deceived me. They've never taken anyone from* here, *oh no. We've been preserved by a mystical protection that was too ineffable for you ever to condescend to explain it to a poor empty detachable head like mine.* I pause, to prevent myself from sobbing. *Well, now the Almighty has winked, hasn't he? Nudged the angel next door in the ribs and done a little fart in pleasure at the divine joke he's played upon us.* Now I can't control my sobs. With my hand covering my eyes,

I weep, loudly, until I recover my composure, breathe deeply, wipe my eyes. *Well*, I say, *shall we continue?*

Laclos sits sideways to me and dictates in a flat voice.

§ An Accident of Birth

"The Prince should go straight into the Tuileries and proclaim himself lieutenant-general of the State. That is his duty. But he gets as far as the Carrousel courtyard, and sits there, facing the Tuileries. We wait. Then he stands up and walks away again. We don't bother to follow him. What's the point? The man is broken. Danton and I look at each other, and say not a word. The only words we might say are 'civil war', and they are better not said.

"Later, we hear that the Prince called for his open carriage and rode in it all over Paris for two hours, looking left and right for someone to wave at, hoping that the citizens would rise up in acclamation of him. They didn't. They knew about him. I think they must have been embarrassed by him, that's all.

"The Assembly meets. People make speeches and say nothing. No one can look into the void. No one can find words to describe what has happened, still less to state what should happen next.

"At the Jacobins, the speeches do have a discernible content. Mostly, it is fear. Not just of what is to come, but fear of their own responsibility for what has happened. The loudest applause is for St-Just, when he goes into his Brutus pose, one arm raised, one leg forward, and declares that the club will defend itself against any aggressors. It is not clear which aggressors he has in mind, though the cellars are searched, just in case. The royalists are in no mood for aggression. They are as frightened as the rest. Lafayette has the gall to attend the Jacobins that evening. I suppose it is the only place where anyone might be saying anything to the point. Danton rushes to the tribune, his hair like bushes in a gale, and he points at

Lafayette, who has just sat down. 'To appear in this assembly!' Danton roars. 'You, who only yesterday pledged your head against the King's! You are incapable of leading us.' Lafayette sits there with set lips, staring ahead at nothing. He must be wishing himself back in Pennsylvania.

"Danton and I talk together half the night. The situation has become so dangerous, since human nature abhors a vacuum, that we agree we have to take an initiative the next day: a constitutionally correct initiative, but one in which we have scarce faith.

"We catch the Prince in his dressing-room, before he can run away for the day. 'Whatever may have happened in the past,' I tell him, 'should now be forgotten. There is no precedent for the crisis that France faces this morning. You must, Sire, you must do what Mirabeau used to urge you to. Put aside all your personal predilections, all your doubts. Just this once, please, put your country first.'

"The Prince is staring at the space of air between Danton and me.

"I continue, 'No one will blame you, or think you vain and ambitious. On the contrary, Sire, every French man and woman will forever be grateful to you for rescuing us from the horror that will otherwise engulf us. It need not be any permanent commitment of yourself. It may be only for a matter of weeks. But we entreat you, today, save the *patrie*.'

"From the Prince there comes a squeak. Then he nods. 'What would you have me do?' His voice is almost a treble.

"We explain. He must assume the regency, at which he has always baulked. 'But with this provision and promise, Sire.' I speak quickly and firmly. 'That Louis-Philippe be proclaimed King Louis the Seventeenth, as soon as it can be done. So that all your responsibility, after that, will be to take care of your own son.'

"'I don't know where he is,' the Prince says.

"'We will find him, Sire. I believe he is in Anjou with Madame de Genlis.'

191

"We ask the Prince to come to the Jacobins and request immediate membership. He does. One or two grumblers remind us of the rule book, which requires a waiting period, but the majority recognise the unique moment, and he is admitted.

"Danton and I have agreed that we will not thrust our initiative upon the Jacobins. In their present mood, it would panic them, as one more act for which they might be blamed. Instead we will hold open the gate and let them find their own way through it. Danton goes to the tribune. He says, 'The person who calls himself the King of France, and swore to maintain the constitution, ran away. And I sit here and listen to people arguing that the crown should remain on his head! The least we can do is to declare the man an imbecile. But then, in whose hands (let us not yet say, on whose head) shall we place the crown for safe-keeping?' He spreads his hands wide, lets his eyes travel slowly across the width of the packed chamber, and leaves it at that. I have kept one eye on Robespierre. He is listening intently, but he does not speak.

"Meanwhile, Barnave has gone to Varennes, and is accompanying that sad procession home to the Tuileries, like a magistrate. When they get back, the Prince goes to meet them.

"I was writing an article, arguing that the Capetian dynasty had committed suicide, but that young Louis-Philippe of Orleans could represent the fresh start for which all Frenchmen now yearned. That would close the constitutional void. In the interim, let the Prince his father, as regent, hold the crown. As for government, let us appoint ministers responsible to the Assembly. When the young king was crowned, the ministers would retain real power. Surely, I urged, this was what most of us now wanted, a constitutional monarchy. Only a king could defend us against usurping Caesars; could ensure the continuity of France, as against tyrannical rule from Paris; could symbolise all the empire, which might otherwise break up into dissident fractions. I signed the article 'P. Choderlos', to distinguish my argument from the maligned author of my novel.

"Barnave comes back from the Tuileries with a wet

handkerchief, and urges the Jacobins to be reconciled with Louis. He is howled and laughed off the tribune. I am appalled. His sudden conversion to sentimentality will damage the credibility of myself, as his colleague, and merely raise emotions, when cool reason is our only refuge. I see the Prince sitting there with closed eyes, and I sigh. That is the moment at which I know our initiative will fail. I go on trying. I picture my mighty galleon, scuttled but still afloat, being washed into harbour by the tide. The Assembly is still hesitant. No one save a few royalist simpletons even hints at pardoning the royal family. Slowly, the discussion comes round on to the wind that Danton and I have started. The Prince is stigmatised by his loose life, his financial incorrectness, and the proof he has frequently given that he has no taste for the job. Nevertheless, it is the constitutional answer. Someone proposes that he be invited to assume the regency immediately. No one names the next king. The vote is carried.

"Twitch, twitch. 'I have repeatedly vowed to serve my country in every way that the public good might require, but I must renounce my constitutional right to the regency. Having made many sacrifices in the interests of the people and of liberty, I cannot quit the rank of simple citizen.' He sits down.

"For him, it is a long speech, and coherently delivered. I wonder who has coached him, and decide it must have been la Genlis. She is keeping Louis-Philippe away from it all too, I suspect. I see a letter that the Prince has put out to be taken to his son. 'Everything's fine here,' it says. 'Not much news.' When I go to see him, those vague eyes avoid mine, but he tries to offer me an apology of sorts by letting me know I am not the only one he has disappointed. 'Agnès,' he guffaws, 'oh dear. She will not stop needling me. When those feeble creatures get ideas of grandeur into their head, they're more ambitious than we men are, Laclos.'

"'If you will have it so, Sire.' What am I expected to say?

"At the Jacobins, no one takes any notice of the Prince's renunciation. Robespierre keeps everyone concentrated on what the constitutionally logical procedure is, and the answer is Citizen Égalité, and that's that. I say nothing against it, of course, because it is what I believe, too. But I know our breath would be better used in cooling our broth. Unless, I reflect, the King were not simply in disgrace, but deposed. The Prince would still not want the job. But were we to remove his cousin, there would at least be no barrier of social embarrassment.

"Although it puts me athwart Robespierre, I have not abandoned my idea of circulating a petition throughout France. We need the strength of popular opinion to carry us through the crisis. The problem is that no precise proposal has been made that could be circulated. I am turning it over in my mind when, for the first time, the word 'republic' is said out loud at the Jacobins, by Citizen Billaud-Varenne. In the stir this causes, Robespierre's expression tells us nothing. The same day, the Assembly arrives to find a poster affixed to the chamber door. 'Royalty is finished,' it says. 'What is it but an office open to an accident of birth, as likely as not filled by an idiot?' It is the Englishman Paine who has written it, but many take the question seriously.

"I cannot remain silent. The King is beyond recall – I speak in favour of uncrowning him and putting him on trial – but the question of monarchy is still unresolved. I send a letter to all our provincial branches, asking them to let us know what view the people are taking of the King's flight and arrest, and how they would regard a prosecution of him, leading to deposition. I urge them, if necessary, to make people recognise the impossibility of leaving such an animal on the throne, led on a ring through his nose by a wife who is a born enemy of France, a traitress and adulteress. I ask for opinions on a regency, without naming a regent or an heir presumptive.

"On 14th July we had a banquet and ball in the courtyard around the liberty tree. It was a fine evening. On the tables were vases of red roses, and their scent hung on the warm summer air. I danced with Marie-Soulange, and perhaps drank more wine than usual, because I remember I felt quite cheerful going to bed.

"Barnave tells the Assembly the next day, 'We have gone far enough. Any continuation of the revolution is a disaster. One step more and we will fatally, culpably, destroy royalty, and with it all property.' They all nod sagely, as though that answers any of the questions. No one mentions the King.

"I walk back to the Palais-Royal with Danton and Desmoulins. We are full of misgivings. Barnave's wet handkerchief cannot wipe out what two years have inscribed. There is no question of stopping now. Desmoulins agrees with us that a petition is the next step, in favour of deposing the King and installing a regent.

"The Cordeliers have already voted to depose Louis. That night at the Jacobins we are to debate a motion that we follow their lead. I am President of the chamber at this time, and so can speak when I choose. The debate goes as I expect. Many are for the motion. 'No,' Robespierre warns us. 'We are sworn Friends of the Constitution. We cannot go further than the Assembly goes. And the Assembly, today, did not even refer to the King. If we vote here to depose him, we vote for armed insurrection. I would give my life rather than incite that. It is not the way to do it. The way to do it is by an elected convention to discuss the constitution.' Heads nod, and there is no vote.

"I see my opportunity. If there were to be a convention, I say, how much stronger it would feel if it had heard the voice of the nation. And so I propose my petition. I suggest that all citizens, and women and grown children too, be invited to sign it. I avow that ten million would assent to a regency. The Assembly could not disregard it. Danton supports me, and I sense we will win a majority, even though Robespierre is preparing to speak against it, when our proceedings are interrupted. An usher calls out that an enormous crowd of people are descending the rue St-Honoré, and demanding to hear our debate. I ask for a vote on whether they should be allowed in. It is in favour. It would look churlish to reject them.

"It seems that the whole of the Palais-Royal gardens is decanting itself into our chamber. They cram themselves on to the benches, stand in the aisles and jam the doorways. They are in gay mood. They want to support our deliberations, their spokesmen say, but they also have a request. Would the club be kind enough to arrange a petition for them all to sign?

"When I can make myself heard, I tell them that their arrival is opportune, since a petition is the very subject of our debate. It will be circulated throughout France as soon as possible, if the club's vote, which has yet to be taken, is in approval.

"They protest, 'No, no, we want a petition now. We don't want to wait weeks. Give us something now.'

"I catch Danton's eye. He frowns, shrugs, and nods. The crowd are silent, eagerly waiting. I am, to be honest, disconcerted. It is not what I wanted. But people are shouting, 'It's our revolution. We started it, us Parisians. Give us a petition now to get rid of the King. Let us finish the job.' I see no alternative but to put their request to the vote. The tellers have a difficult job in distinguishing the members from our visitors, but the result is conclusively in favour. Five members, and myself as President, are deputed to draft the petition and present it to the club the next morning.

"We retire to the correspondence office. I excuse myself from actually writing the text. I had not slept well the previous night, and my evening as President has taxed me. I will not be able to concentrate. Brissot, a republican, is persuaded to draft the petition. I tell him to keep it simple. The crucial phrase should be, 'that the Assembly should consider the King as abdicated, and replace him with a regent.'

"Brissot will not have it. 'Robespierre will not stop talking until he has got that changed. The people said nothing about a regent, only to get rid of the King.' I say it would be irresponsible to propose that the throne be vacated until further notice. It is our duty to put forward some thought of what happens next. Brissot scratches his nose. Danton says, 'Brissot is right. All we can say is, *replace him by constitutional means.*' 'Oh, very well,' I say.

'Make it, *by* all *constitutional means*.' 'How many are there?' Brissot asks. 'I don't know,' I reply. 'No one knows. That's the trouble.'

"The next morning, the chamber is packed again, with members and the crowd from the Palais-Royal. I read out the text, and a vote approves it. Then I propose that the petition, with papers for people to sign, be taken to the Champ de Mars. It is the only space in Paris big enough to accommodate the crowds we can anticipate. Again, approval is given. Robespierre has not spoken.

"Someone must run across to the Cordeliers, because by the time we have all thronged over the Louis Seize bridge and through the Faubourg St-Germain and reached the Champ de Mars with our petition, the Cordeliers are already there with one of their own. It simply asks for the abrogation of monarchy. When we read ours out, the Cordeliers raise a riot over the phrase 'all constitutional means'. They shout to the crowd, 'What does that mean? There is no constitution. All it means is Citizen Égalité. It means, let us depose one clown to make room for another.'

"It is an impossible situation. We cannot invite the people to choose between rival petitions then and there. We march back to the Jacobins. Sillery and his crowd are waiting for us: la Genlis has to have her hand in this business, of course. They tell us the Assembly is in a rage. They believe the Jacobins club has been stormed by the Orleans gang, led by myself, and supported by the foot infantry of the Palais-Royal gardens. Sillery leads his lot off elsewhere, claiming that they are the senior members of the Jacobins, and they need a quiet place to discuss how to rescue the club. The truth is that they will discuss how to rescue the old régime. The Prince is with them. As they are leaving, he murmurs to me, 'Sorry I wasn't here last night, Laclos. I didn't hear about it until too late. I was having a quiet supper with Grace.'

"Those left, still surrounded by the mob, want to debate what 'all constitutional means' meant. I point out that loyal friends of the constitution have no alternative but to support its

197

means. There is agreement. Then Robespierre advances to the tribune. As President, I acknowledge him, assuming he can do no more than support the logic of what I have just said. Instead, with a tic in his cheek and a more scuffed voice than ever, he declares, 'I do not care about my own fate. If I perish, so be it. It will not be as Brutus or Cato did, to save a dying liberty. It will be, quite simply, to identify myself, to the last drop of passion in my heart, with the good of a sensitive people, the people of France, the generous and amiable citizens of this country of ours.' He is still at the tribune when another message from the Assembly is brought in. There, they have voted to prepare a new constitution and to invite the King to sign it. That will end the crisis.

"I cannot control the chamber's shouts of anger. 'So we are to forget the King's little holiday in Varennes!' 'The royalists take us for fools!' 'Sillery is behind this!'

Eventually, Robespierre makes himself heard again. 'We cannot disregard the Assembly's vote. We are sworn to respect the National Assembly, even when we disagree with it. We cannot go faster than it goes. We must withdraw our petition.' Renewed uproar, especially among the Palais-Royal crowd. 'We will have a petition,' they chant.

"Then word reaches us that the Cordeliers have called for a demonstration against the Assembly the following morning at the Champ de Mars. The mob cheers. Danton moves that we go to the demonstration, to explain our position. Robespierre speaks against. The vote is against.

"Most of us go anyway. I walk with Danton, among the crowds on the boulevards. I am marching to defeat on the Champ de Mars. Were you there?"

No, of course not. I detest crowds.

"You must have been lonely, then, wherever you were. Most of Paris was there. That huge area was packed like a slave-ship. Danton and I manage to get through to the platform, but we never have the chance to speak. The Cordeliers are still calling for the King to be put on trial when Lafayette arrives.

"The whole air of the place is already eerie, on account of two corpses hanged above the crowd, from a window. Two men, with their eyes bulging, their tongues out, and their fingers spread. I took one look and assumed that royalists were being strung up. But I learn that they had been caught hiding beneath the platform. Their intentions had probably been no more subversive than to peep between the planks up women's skirts. But the crowd, in its fever, has summarily convicted them as undesirables and executed them. I think the sight must have sobered everyone for a time, because they are strangely quiet while the Cordeliers are addressing them.

"Then Lafayette arrives. Mayor Bailly, one of Sillery's lot, has been persuaded that the demonstration represents such a threat that he should declare martial law. He clambers on to the platform, and interrupts the speaker to tell everyone to go back home at once. The gathering is unlawful. His speech has the effect he has calculated. The calm explodes into fury. Lafayette is ready, just off stage with companies of guardsmen. He points his sword and in they march, at the port-arms. The people throw stones. Lafayette turns, marches back to the rear rank, turns again, orders 'Aim!', raises his sword, and commands 'Fire!' After the first volley, through the blue smoke I see dozens lying on the ground. 'Fire!' again. And again.

"That evening, Robespierre is in spate against my petition. 'There is published in my name a seditious discourse of which not a word has ever passed my lips. To all of you, members of this club, are attributed the abominable events we have witnessed today. If I were ...' He never finishes that sentence. The door is flung open, and Lafayette stands there in full fig, plumes a-wagging. 'This gathering is unlawful,' he advises his fellow members, and his rhetoric is a platoon with fixed bayonets drawn up behind him. We flee, for the second time that day.

"But we meet again the next day. We have to discuss the survival of the Jacobins club. I take a motion that Sillery's lot, as the founders, should morally be allowed to take away all our archives, those being the club's only property and title. That seems to me indisputably in order, and I say so, before inviting speakers. Most in the chamber are instantly on their feet, reviling me. Citizen Billaud-Varenne is shouting, 'It is disgraceful that Monsieur Laclos, the prime mover of the petition that caused this division, should be among the first to propose a retreat, in the guise of proper order, which would befit wretched slaves rather than free men.' When the hubbub abates, Robespierre is at the tribune. He says, 'Those who did not abandon this chamber are its proper inheritors.' He stares at me, across the floor, through his green spectacles. 'Thank you,' he says, and returns to his seat.

"I ask for the chamber's permission to retire, and walk slowly home, alone. I had thought Danton or Desmoulins might come with me. Only Clarke is in the Prince's apartments. He tells me the Prince was asked at the Assembly for a statement on his relations with his private secretary. 'Monsieur Laclos is no longer in my service,' the Prince had replied, and sat down again.

"I hardly sleep that night, such is the anger seething in my head. My restlessness keeps waking Marie-Soulange, and eventually I go to my bureau, in my night-shirt. I have to cool myself by writing something on paper. What I write is a letter to a journal, in which I give as full an account as I can of the petition business. I sign it 'P. Choderlos, formerly Laclos'.

"After my letter is published, Brissot accosts me. 'I see you are claiming now that you did not write the petition,' he says. 'That is strictly true,' I answer. 'I tried to tell the strict truth in my letter.' He replies, 'Ah. When I took down your dictation, I did not know I was playing out a scene from *Les Liaisons Dangereuses.*'"

Laclos has fallen silent. *Is that it?* I ask curtly.

"Just one thing more, Sade. When you are next overcome by fear, please do not express it by mouthing obscenities and blasphemies at me. Remember that we are both military officers. Do try to discipline yourself. It is your best hope for survival."

15

They came for Laclos today. I was awed. I spent yesterday evening in my room cursing him, writing down his name and across it the most malevolent numerological combinations, and then burning the papers while performing an invocatory dance of my own devising, and *this morning* he was sent for, to the governor's office. He came back an hour later, but with narrowed nostrils. I do not know when I shall find the time to perform my ceremony 665 times and one time more, which is what it would take. But this was pleasing. The Committee for Public Safety are making an inventory of the prisoners they have. He was interrogated by people sent from his own section, and then had to wait while they entered him in their inventory, read their report back to him and made him sign it as accurate and true. So he was required to put his signature to a description of himself as "clever and cold". They are shrewder than I supposed, these municipals. It defined him as the author of his book, and an orator, but one whom true republicans had suspected as "not sufficiently committed to fighting our enemies".

Touché!

And they must know he stage-managed the massacre in the Faubourg Saint-Antoine, and another on the Champ de Mars, and split the Jacobins, and everybody knows he was Orleans's *agent provocateur* and pretty boy, and his pal Danton has gone – yes, he looks like a suitable space to be cleared. Many have gone for much, much less.

He was certainly gnawing a lip, and not bragging any more about using blackmail to save his skin. How shameless that brag was, how undignified. I was embarrassed that he should watch me write it down. As he came back just now, I heard the men taunting him. "You're top of the list now, Monsieur Choderlos-delosdelosclos," they were chortling. "You've written a book about fallen women, why don't you go down the corridor and ask the whores to protect you?"

He tries to put a brave face on it, with me. "They'll lose the papers," he says. "The Mountain they sit on is a mountain of paper. They intend to interrogate every detainee in Paris. Your turn will come. It is absurd, all these committees. There have been disturbances in prisons since they started clearing space in them. And so the committees have become more alarmed, and are trying to empty the prisons even faster, so that they can replenish them with more satisfactory prisoners. That is the reason for these interrogations. I am not disturbed. It was just a formality. But, to be doubly sure, I would like you, please, to leave my memoir in here with me, in future. I have told nothing but the truth in it, but the truth, as we know, is a flame in times like these. It can burn the one who lights it. The observations I have dictated on certain citizens could easily be turned against me by my enemies."

I object. *If I leave my notes in here with you, I cannot make a fair copy of them. And you would assuredly be unable to decipher them. They would be worthless.*

"You could make your fair copy in here. It might help you to concentrate. There are many pages of notes you have not yet copied."

You cannot expect me to spend my evenings in here, too. I must have some time alone each day. I would go mad without it.

"All I am asking is that you deliver the copy book to me, after your copying, together of course with the notes."

Can you not trust me? I would destroy everything on the instant that I heard you had been taken away. Indeed, the memoir is surely much safer with me, since you, if you had the misfortune to be summarily haled before the tribune, would not be allowed the time to destroy it. If you tried, it would look damnably suspicious.

"But what if you were taken first?"

Then you would swiftly ask Blanchard for the key to my room, and retrieve the memoir. And if we were taken at the same time, what matter where the papers are?

He has no answer to that, just asks me to be sure to keep all the papers carefully hidden. As a matter of fact, I keep them on a shelf, with a note on top commending them to the attention of Citizen Robespierre.

After his nasty shock, Laclos is clipped and offhand in his narrative today, in some cases merely giving me brief notes to be expanded. I am tempted to parrot back one of his own sanctimonies, that by attending to "our work together" we would most effectively distract our minds from more ominous matters, but I do not wish to give myself needless labour. I confess I am torn about his impending doom, eager to celebrate it with cognac, but rather hoping that his doom impend long enough for him to be my scrivener, even though it would have to impend for years before all I have to say were chronicled.

§ A Leaf in a Whirlpool

He continued to go to the Jacobins occasionally, until a few months after his downfall they voted to cancel his membership. (I expect he claimed back the balance of his subscription.) His mood was disgust, scorn, disappointment, weariness. He had organised the Jacobins like a good regiment, with all appropriate officers (including spies). Now, the benefit would be enjoyed by Field-Marshal Robespierre. (The metaphor will not carry, but *Archbishop* Robespierre would be apter. No, Archangel Robespierre.) Talleyrand was in London, talking to the Whigs and whispering to Berlin, also cropping a field Laclos had ploughed. Himself was sucked into tedium again, the horror: talk, talk, inaction, papers on a desk, and dreaming of the clarity, the order, act and certitude of command, on a fine morning, under a great general. That would not be the King, or Robespierre, or God. Oh, he sighs, the ache for absolutes. For just one absolute. (Failing that, for absolution. A solution, even.) He asks me if I have ever seen a leaf in a whirlpool.

This is a man in trouble, citizens. Your interrogation this morning has unbalanced him into poetic images. Incidentally, I hear they have got little Chénier locked up somewhere. Good. Come on, citizens, do your duty, pitch all our heads into the basket, anybody who has ever strung together two words worth reading. Cleanse the State of literature. Do it in the name of Plato. He was right, we're all liars, every one of us. Nothing any of us writes could match the veracity of the square on the hypotenuse. Next time you come across a square on a hypotenuse, respect it for the profound and witty insight into human nature it is offering you.

The King swears to the Constitution, at which the Assembly sighs with relief and declares the revolution accomplished. Thank you very much, messieurs the buffalo, you can stop stampeding now. We are officially ushered into the most charming garden, in which nobody ever dreams of insurrection, the Jacobins and Cordeliers politely question an occasional administrative anomaly, all military officers are seasoned professionals, and those who own no property do not presume to have any voice in the governance of affairs, nor any care about the price of bread. Barnave painted that water-colour for Marie-Antoinette. She scoffed at it, thus finding herself strangely allied with Robespierre. What they had in common was that, now and then, they had glimpsed the real world, albeit not the same real world. Robespierre said that the arguments were not over yet: in the Republic of Virtues, the King should not have his veto, the State should not have its scaffold, the price of bread, and sugar, and probably oranges, should be controlled, and for all this, and more, the Incorruptible would choose to die, rather than compromise.

I, too, saw the real world at this time. It was when my drama was being whistled off stage by ill-favoured men in red bonnets with the point turned forward. I ordered the curtain down at once.

Nor was Laclos deceived, he says. The curtain came down

on his major work too, when he received his formal discharge from the army. They allowed him a pension, and the Prince, after denying that Laclos was in his service, went on paying him and letting him live in the Palais-Royal, which was characteristically generous, since the man was still at bay before his creditors. He had gone to the Tuileries to try to patch up his quarrels with his royal cousin, but Marie-Antoinette's foaming courtiers had ejected him as soon as he showed his face in the royal apartments. She was now in a towering pique with anything French, and it did not take the perspicacity of a Talleyrand to spot whose idea it had been when the Austrian army formed up and started to march upon revolutionary France. To hear Laclos tell it, you would think that the whole known world had devised a scenario to oppress him: they take his uniform away, then start the first decent war since he was a cadet. I love to watch how he lacerates the palm of his left hand with the nail of his right hand's little finger when he dictates such passages of frustration. If, just once in his life, he would get drunk for a week, and fornicate, throw stones at windows, throttle cats, anything, he would find the rest of his life so much more agreeable. I would not urge him to engage in criminal activity on a satanic scale, which is my own resource. A few peccadillos to relax the rectum is all he needs. I do not offer him this wise diagnosis, naturally. One of my own small comforts here is to watch him rush to apoplexy.

It was not as though we had many officers to fight the war. Most of them had emigrated, and were probably coming back in grey uniforms. The Prince, an honorary admiral, asked the Marine Ministry if he could have a boat to command, but Marie-Antoinette, speaking through their salty mouths, told him to bugger off. He tried again, this time begging to enlist as a simple soldier, and the King muttered, "Oh, let him go where he chooses." Off to the North he dashes, just when the Austrians are coming across the Scheldt and the Prussians are joining in. To celebrate our defeats on all fronts we make the ritual sacrifice of the Minister of War, Servan, a cold and slippery fish if ever I hooked one. The new man, that chancer Dumouriez, orders an immediate invasion of the Netherlands. He is at once deeply suspect, apparently having a plan of campaign, and three days later they re-appoint Servan.

The real front of this war is of course the façade of the Tuileries Palace. Lafayette has it covered, no problems there. Well, just a sneaky enfilade of people from the Faubourg St-Antoine, who find a side door left open and make a bridgehead of it. Laclos tells me I know what happened next. I do. Of all the sights our revolution offered and I did not see, that is the one I most regret, Louis Seize obliged to sit there in his apartments for hours with a red bonnet nodding on his silly head, while an endless line of people file past him, taking the time to make their speeches to him, teaching him their slogans, warning him that his wife's compatriots are about to turn France into a Viennese colony. "Naturally," Laclos remarks acerbically, "the royal household staff later swore that they had recognised the Prince, Danton, Desmoulins and myself there, behind false moustaches, and that we were directing the operation with the eventual aim of slitting the royal throats and putting the Prince on the throne. No less naturally, Lafayette, having once more proved his incompetence by exposing his sovereign to ridicule, blamed it all on the Jacobins, and asked the Assembly to arrest the whole club. Marie-Antoinette vetoed that, not I think because it was a fatuous idea but because it was a French idea. So Lafayette busied his mind instead with foreign quarrels, and dashed off to command the army in Alsace. But when he got there, he decided he was too far away from whatever might be happening in Paris, so he proposed to Lückner, who was in Flanders, that they should swap positions. Lückner said *Oui*, about the only word of French he could manage, and then found that what Lafayette had in mind was not an exchange of commands but that their two armies should swap positions. And they did, many thousands of men solemnly marching past each other for days. I imagine the Austrians were terrified by the brilliance of a manoeuvre about which no military instructor had ever warned them."

Oh, the agony for Laclos, to hear the cannon on the hour warn Paris that the *patrie* was in danger, to see civilians enlisting but himself, decommissioned, not called upon. The rich irony of it, that even the Prince was sniffing gunsmoke. Though not for long. After a week or two in the ranks, Citizen Égalité felt he had earned his épaulettes, came back to Paris to ask for them, and was told to go home and stay there. So he sat down at a chart table with Laclos, and together they plotted a daring campaign by which the Prince might evade the regiment of creditors besieging him.

And then the King fell, and Laclos missed that one, too. "Although it was a shock, after eight centuries of the Capets," Laclos observes, "it was hardly a surprise. That rickety throne had been threatening to collapse in a cloud of sawdust and mildew for so long that one's first response was almost of *déjà vu*. What caused it finally to give way was war, always the great engine of history. Many battalions from the provinces had come to Paris. Things had seemed clearer to them, watching from afar, than to us in the centre of it all. They heard the Austrians trying to bully us, saying that if we did not forget all this revolutionary nonsense they would come to Paris and knock our heads together for us. Massed along our borders they saw seventy thousand ruthless Prussian troops. And what was the King of France doing? He was out hunting deer, while his witch wife stirred the broth. The men from Marseilles, in particular, fraternised with the National Guard, who had had to be augmented, for the defence of Paris, with many who were not Lafayette's hand-picked royalists. Most of the guardsmen listened and agreed with what the Marseillais were saying, and Robespierre's people nodded, and everyone said the time had come. They marched on the Tuileries.

"When the King heard them coming, he ran over to the Assembly for shelter. The guardsmen outside the Tuileries did an about-turn and stood with their comrades. That left a thousand Swiss guards, hopelessly outnumbered. The citizens walked up to them, to discuss the situation, and the Switzers pulled their triggers. Before they could fire again, they were killed on the spot, or taken off to be executed later. The King was thrown into the Temple Prison. Barnave was thought to have come out of it all rather badly, and he was arrested, too. When Lafayette heard the news, he simply jumped across the border and put on an Austrian uniform. I heard, later, that he took one book to read, mine. So that was that. Our task was no longer to correct the manners of the old régime, but to invent a new state. All we had were the people."

At once, Laclos shot to glittering prominence, as Vice-President of his local municipal section, the Butte-des-Moulins, and even that only over the protests of the Paris Commune, who did not trust him. They were told to shut up by Danton, who was now Minister of Justice, and was anxious to see his associate stir himself again in these stirring times. But within days the hawking Prussians trudged into France, to hang the Jacobins they said, and Danton had to invent the republican way of fighting a war. He picked commissars to liaise between the generals and Paris. Laclos got the summons to see Servan, who sent him to the eastern front, attached to Marshal of France Lückner. "I was exalted," Laclos breathes. "I could not abide my stagnation, just watching, contemplating. I had to commit myself, to action." And at the thrill of the memory he pirouettes on his narrow constipated arse, which has only days to live.

He'd known Lückner at the Jacobins, a doddering old soak, with a red eye, a huge conk, and an accent as thick as a Bavarian sausage. Nobody understood a word he said, and it was no better when he scrawled his orders down on paper, so his commanders just did what they thought best. From Laclos's contemptuous account, Lückner was clearly intimidated by the new-born Man in Black, with his tricolour cravat and neat, powdered wig, whose first action was to present the Marshal of France with Servan's order removing him from the battlefront, and whose second was to relieve him of the red ribbon of

St-Louis, a military distinction now suppressed by our democratic government. It will be conceded that Lückner was doing
less than well in the war. Verdun had just fallen to the
Prussians, and the Austrians were marching south. Kellermann
replaced Lückner, whose job now was to organise the rabble of
volunteers being sent to the east. "It was my responsibility,"
Laclos says delicately, "to assist him. The camp was designed to
accommodate twelve thousand men. Forty thousand volunteers
were already there, and every day another two thousand arrived,
together with their squadrons of camp followers. They had no
food, no weapons, no uniforms, no training, no discipline, and
no leaders. They had been told to elect their own officers, on
the basis of civic virtue."

Laclos shuts his eyes for a second, trapped between horrors:
the military mystique of the old régime, and one suicidal word
in doubt of the new order, which holds as an article of faith that
the people will always defeat a mercenary invader, however
formidable he is in arms. God knew what those volunteers
would do to the Prussians. They had certainly inflicted heavy
casualties on the French. In their march eastwards, they left a
path of rapine, smouldering cinders of châteaux, gentry with
their throats slit, their wives and daughters violated. I had
thanked heaven when I heard that the Provençal levies had not
marched through my manors.

"Nothing could be done until these men were armed,"
Laclos continued. "Our only resource was pikes. Every commune was told to cease all other work and spend their days
making pikes, the people's weapon, the patriot's defence."

Ah, pikes, yes. We saw plenty of those in Paris, after the
King had been shackled. Robespierre didn't like the war, but
there was nothing he could do to stop it. So his Jacobins turned
their attention to the enemy within, and washed their supper
down with goblets of blood drawn from the prisons. It was
self-evident that the gaols of Paris were pullulating with traitors,
waiting to cheer the Austrian troops as they marched along the
boulevards. The prisoners, in a planned and concerted

operation, were going to throw open their cell doors and swarm out to kill us all. It was only prudent to go in and kill them first. Those who behaved like lunatics were laughed at for their performance, and run through with a pike. So were those traitors who pretended that their only crime was prostitution or forging or preaching or pilfering. One thrust of a pike confirmed each of them as a citizen lacking in patriotism. Who could ever tell the difference between a whore and a traitor? Both offer passion to rent.

After that spectacle, less than two years ago, does Laclos really wonder that I shudder every morning when I awake and find myself, still, in prison? It is the most dangerous dwelling in France, particularly now that we have a guillotine handy, just up the road. It was a miracle that I was not in prison then, for once. Oh, I boil. Murder in the guise of legal justice is monstrous. That is why I resigned the magistracy of my section. It is why I did not denounce my mother-in-law. I would be happy, no, transported with bliss, to skewer her and roast her over a slow fire, sending her black soul back to God as a warning of what I would do to Him, if I could. But cold justice in a wig, or executed by a mindless mob, revolts me, and I will have no part in it. There is nothing evil in it, nothing so noble.

Laclos is maundering that it takes him merely a week to sort matters out at Soissons and Reims, and then down to Châlons he goes. One glance tells him that Berthier is an inept commander, and that Augean stall is cleansed with a note sent back to Servan. Beurnonville and Dumouriez are left, with Kellermann at Metz. He will give them their chance to prove themselves worthy generals of the republic. (I suppress my smile at what contempt such heroes must have felt for Danton's spies.) Laclos announces their strategy. They will keep their three armies separate. Two will defend the Marne, one will harass. If forced to retreat, the pioneers are to leave nothing behind them intact. Stores, roads, wells, all are to be razed. Dumouriez takes him aside and, as one Jacobin to another, persuades him that all three armies should be brought together to defend Châlons.

Laclos is doubtful, but agrees to give the plan a try. Fifty thousand troops, though exhausted and frightened, execute the regrouping superbly. Now the campaign requires a central directive.

Choderlos de Laclos commits the most grievous tactical error of his life. He rides back to Paris. He is going to see Minister Servan, to assure himself of the honour of having planned and supervised the whole thing. As he leaves, Saint-Georges arrives, colonel of a colonial legion. With him from the Palais-Royal have come a troupe of actors, dancers and musicians. "Even *they* were there," Laclos says. His voice, controlled since his scare this morning, throbs with passion. When the great Gribeauval cannons, just perfected, spoke in battle for the first time, and at Valmy the fate of France was decided, Laclos was taking a coach-ride to Paris.

How gay Paris was. Soon after the prisons had been purified, I was sitting with a lady friend at a café table, near the Tuileries. Outside the window, a chanting procession came along the street. "Oh, look who's going past," I said. "Isn't that the Princesse de Lamballe?" My friend glanced through the window and fainted off her chair. They had the Princess's curly blonde head high up on a pike. Blood had trickled down the pole on to the man's hands. They paraded her past us. People in the café had crowded the doorway, to watch. They carried the Princess's head past the first-floor windows of the Tuileries, so that her friend Marie-Antoinette could see her looking in. Later, they broiled her heart and ate it.

It took Laclos and Servan a while to appreciate what had happened at Valmy. But the Duke of Brunswick had heard enough of Dumouriez's cannons, and was for leaving Marie-Antoinette and the rest of France to stew. Just as the revolution began with the diamond necklace affair, so the negotiations for Brunswick's withdrawal were settled with the gift to him of that enormous diamond the King used to wear in his ceremonial hat. He took it back home with him through the rain, smiling at it, as though it were all he had come for, really.

16

Sade did not come to work with me today. When I went to knock at his door, there was no answer. Blanchard told me that they came early this morning with a list of twenty-eight people to be tried, and Sade was one of them. So that is that. Well, the worst is over for him. It must have been almost a relief.

I borrowed the key to his room, but could not find my memoir anywhere. I looked through all the cupboards, wardrobes, drawers, shelves, and cabinets, even under the bedclothes, but he had hidden it too cleverly. I cannot believe he had time to destroy it. I am anxious. They could have found it when they were arresting him, and taken it. Yet other manuscripts of his were left behind. Such as I could decipher were vilely depraved. They would surely have taken those if they were collecting evidence. I destroyed them for him, just in case they send back for further material. It is disquieting. I will discreetly make enquiries to find out if perhaps he asked someone else to hide it. For the present, I can think of nothing to do but to continue the work myself. The discipline has served me well, and so I will go on, even if these pages turn out to be orphans.

§ Picaresque

For me, the period after Valmy was one of appointments and disappointments. I was restored to the army, with the rank of Field-Marshal, but in the line regiments, the artillery being not ready to accept newly promoted officers. I was given command of an army for the Pyrenees, but was told there were no soldiers for it. Danton had left the War Council, and soon Servan quit the Ministry, saying that he was not well. Those whom the newly elected Convention put in charge of military matters were fervid patriots, to be sure, but arguably to a fault. As with the others grouped around Robespierre, it was their habit to suspect negligence or treachery when anything went wrong, rather than to accept that the republic would necessarily need experience and sound strategies to build a new France from the ruins Louis left. Many of us were uneasy that policies were being advanced by withering speeches denouncing dead monarchy, instead of through the painstaking arguments of councils. "Liberation by deliberation" was a slogan I attempted to circulate, but it was never taken up. It was as though no one could trust any rhetoric save the style that had brought us so far, that of the orators in the gardens, and subsequently at the Jacobins. It seemed to me that that style was one of opposition, not of reconstruction. I write these comments in the knowledge that many will think they prove me pusillanimous. I think the reverse, with respect.

My family travelled with me to Toulouse. It took us a week. Waiting for me were a few companies of untrained men, lacking equipment and provisions. When I applied for funds at least to see them fed, I was told that none were yet available. I set to instructing one company in artillery practice, although we had no cannons. Orders came from Minister Pache that we should move to Perpignan, since an invasion of Spain was contemplated. I pointed out that it would be better strategy to remain in Toulouse, giving us more choice of where to cross the Pyrenees and the enemy no signal of our intentions. Pache replied that the Pyrenees could be crossed only at the eastern or western seaboard. I respectfully advised him that the case was otherwise, and I would remain in Toulouse pending further orders. They never came. The War Council must have been preoccupied with our active campaigns elsewhere.

In Nice, Frankfurt, the Savoy, and Belgium, our armies were winning every battle. For my part, I was called upon to lead a company as far as a square in Toulouse, where I had to attack a liberty tree with tricolour ribbons. I suppose my wife and children could feel some pride at the ceremony as they watched me in my dress uniform of blue trimmed with gold, white breeches, and on my head the revolutionary cone with ribbons, and they enjoyed the fireworks and farandols. If Sade were here, I would ask him why the Midi always smells of putrid fruit. And why it takes so long for the simplest tasks to be accomplished. The heat will not do as an explanation. It was November when I arrived. There is something in the temperament of the people that disinclines them to enthusiasm. Even their cries of *Vive la république, ça ira!* around the beribboned poplar tree were uttered with a palpable edge of mockery. It cannot be thus in Marseilles, to judge from their patriotic fervour when they came to Paris.

It was disheartening how little support I got from Paris. In spite of all obstacles, I had begun to train the men properly, and had plotted in detail alternative strategies for our Spanish campaign. I wasted my time. Nothing had been decided when I was recalled to Paris, just before Christmas. Fortunately, I had something else to exercise my mind. I had received another appointment, to be activated when propitious, as Governor-General of French possessions east of the Cape of Good Hope. Effectively, it meant I had command in India. The Sultan of Mysore was our loyal ally. He had even founded a Jacobin club in Seringapatam, and planted a liberty tree. From the old régime, he had been sent no aid for his war against the English. Now, he hoped for better help from the Convention. I calculated that with fifteen warships, each carrying a thousand men, we could seize Ceylon and descend upon Bengal.

When I left Toulouse, there was a farewell banquet for me. I had to stop Étienne-Fargeau from eating the brandied cherries, or he would have made himself drunk. Afterwards, we were sent on our way with a patriotic ballet at the theatre. There was an absurd song:

215

He's going bravely overseas,
The Indians will lift their knees
To the boom of the cannon,
Boom-boom, boom-boom

Back in Paris, I had to sort out the estate of my mother, who had just died. I was still lodged at the Palais-Royal. Citizen Égalité seemed to be enjoying the Convention, and gave the appearance of having discovered a Jacobin enthusiasm in himself. He sat up on those tiers they call the Mountain, with the keenest of them. I knew from a letter he had sent his son, who was at Valmy, that he expected the new assembly to be "great fun". Now, he told me, "It is all going excellently."

"Our military victories are wonderful", I said, "but do you not fear that a disillusion might set in as to the economic difficulties the republic inherited?"

"Come, come, Laclos," he rallied me. "There are problems, of course. But the watchword is: 'Optimism'."

"Everything is for the best," I murmured.

"Quite, quite," he agreed, missing my allusion. "That's the spirit one needs now."

I addressed the General Committee of Defence with a precise exposition of my Indian strategy. I was incredulous to see old Montalembert sitting there, nearly eighty now, and presumably still living with the apothecary's daughter. The committee appreciated what I proposed, but pointed out that it would entail declaring war on England. "Quite," I said. They adjourned further action.

On 1st February we declared war on England, and with a pounding heart I went straight back to the committee, but they were in the process of sacking Pache. When Beurnonville took over as Minister, I presented my plan again. This time it was approved, and I was handed sealed orders, to be opened when I was on the Indian Ocean. But they said I could not take up my command yet, not until we had finished the war in Spain, which had just started.

I have always scorned the picaresque novel, just one thing after another. Unfortunately, it had become the form of my inconsequential life.

Having nothing else to occupy me, I turned back to an old interest, my invention of explosive shells for marine warfare. With Montalembert's support, I was given permission to conduct experiments, and so, for good reason, broke my vow never to return to La Fère. To advise me, they appointed Berthollet, the scientist who invented Javel water. As we rode to La Fère, I told him I did not envisage bleaching the enemy's ships. He is a good fellow, and laughed. The other with us, an artillery officer named Fabre, did not. Officially he was to assist me, but I knew that his true function was to be a spy, keeping an eye on me for the Convention. We started with large shells, but their trajectory was unreliable. We had begun to make some of smaller bore when word was sent that the experiments were to be abandoned. I had to comply, but I would not relinquish my commitment to the project. And I am glad that I did not.

When the King was put on trial, I had to reflect once more on the Prince's optimism. Libels were flying all over Paris again: if the King were not condemned to death, the Prince and I, and all the old Palais-Royal Orleanists, would seize Louis and slit his throat ourselves. Lord, I thought, can those jackdaws not learn any new songs? Then the Prince voted for executing his cousin, and I realised how frightened the man was of the foremost exponents of our new morality.

* * *

Laclos complains that he could not find this memoir in my room. Oh dear, what a vexing day he must have had. I, in contrast, have merely been carted off with a tumbrilful of common criminals, as so many cattle to the knacker. The stink of fear will never be purged from my nostrils, however refined the orange-water. The tribunal disposed of twenty-seven lives as casually as my gardener would sweep up a few leaves. By now they will be along the street, at La Place du Trône, waiting for the banality of the falling blade. Down, up, down, up, the executioner can do it with one hand, in his sleep (if he sleeps). To kill somebody takes such a little movement. Even to kill the last King of the French, it is all one, down, up. What an efficient machine it is, how full of virtue. It will not wait for your fine farewell speech. There was time for that when we were burned, or impaled, or broken, when it was our right as noblemen to demand the axe, until they botched Lally-Tollendal and he danced around for half a minute trying to hold his head on, there was always time to ennoble one's inexpressible rage at being cut short, through a few words tossed back at those who would unforgivably go on living. Perhaps that is why, so they say, the heads talk afterwards now. "Et tu," said Louis's. Even the spectators don't like it. It's too abrupt, too high up, uniforms always get in the way. There was a call for provision to be made for the people to be able to dance and sing, otherwise how is an aristocrat to see what happiness his death brings them? Not that my family were ever aristocrats. I told them that, looking straight into their eyes, the eyes of those who boast they are the sons of Saturn. Is it their father they eat? I could hardly suppress the impish proposal that they eat a wafer in remembrance of me, instead. The joke would have gone too deep for them. Nothing is holy. We live in a stew, stirred and forked by the State. When the body politic has no head, it has no reason, and gives none. It cannot speak. And so all we see, sitting up at that bench, are dismembered limbs, preening themselves on their sensitive virtuousness. I was led in, quivering, to face that row of arms and legs gouting blood. I was number 11 of 28. Truly, number 11, I will sing hosannas to thee every day of my life, which may not be many days, but at least I am not yet delivered, hands bound behind me, coatless, head shaven, shirt ripped open, and then trundled by pale lamplight behind the hedge. My politics have always been what circumstance demands, and now the demand was the most sacred of all lusts, that of preserving my own bodily self at no matter what expense. They looked at Citizen Sade, but what looked back at them was the only thing that is wholly my possession.

I had thought to take with me the memoir of Citizen Laclos, with many allusions to Citizen Robespierre and other famously virtuous men, all of them bigger prizes than I could ever be. Alas, they found much of it illegible, since it is written in my code, but what they could read interested them. "Give me time," I said, "and I can transcribe it all for you. I can add to it. Give me time." I played the Scheherazade of the Picpus, and they gave me time. "A few days only," they said. Oh God, I can hardly breathe even now, my heart is racing, I want to weep and weep. Those severed arms and thighs were spurting like crimson fountains behind their baize-covered table, but they let me come back. I do not know how soon they will come for Laclos, but I think it may be tomorrow. There is no time to waste. I must collect every drop I can of his heart's blood, act the clerk again, having told him that it was all a mistake, nothing to worry about, let us pursue our work together. *Why, thank you, citizen, for these sheets in your own hand, yes, of course I will gladly add them to the memoir. You could not find it? No, I was most careful to hide it, as I always promised you I would be. Not even to you will I disclose where it was, ha-ha. Now, do continue. Your story grows more engrossing with every day we spend together.*

"Needless to say, the Prince and I were represented as celebrating the King's death with an orgiastic feast. But real events were threatening us more seriously. When Dumouriez handed an officer over to the Austrians, and then danced over to them himself with the fool Sillery and Louis-Philippe, who was too young to know better, those of us left at the Palais-Royal were dangerously implicated.

"Everyone was denying that they had ever had any connection with Citizen Égalité. He even denied it himself. He stood up at the Jacobins, twitching that big Bourbon nose, and said, 'I am not the son of the Duke of Orleans. My father was the Duke's coachman.' Then he cast his vote for a revolutionary tribunal which, once appointed, promptly came to the Palais-Royal and arrested us both. I ducked my head to enter that filthy hole the Abbaye. It was half empty, after the massacre. Danton got me out two days later, but each committee thought itself superior to the rest, and I was back in again within the week. I had sealed orders to conquer India, and was in a grimy prison cell. You believe I never laugh. I did then, alone.

"They kept me in for five weeks. I heard what was going on outside, the Convention purging itself, the Central Committee rooting out people like me, for at best lacking in patriotism, at worst conspiring to reverse the revolution. It was springtime, quite warm, and every day I watched a patch of barred sunshine move down one wall, creep diagonally across the floor, and just touch the corner of my cell. I used a loose stone to scratch marks logging its progress each day, and saw how each successive arc was fractionally closer to the wall in which the window was set.

"Marie-Soulange came to see me every morning, and we did what we could to secure my release. I wrote to everyone who might help me. My section testified to the Central Committee that I had been zealous for the municipality. All it availed me was a promise that I would not be brought to trial without a written accusation. Citizen Égalité was in the Abbaye, too. That suited his creditors, they knew where to find him. He received them in a daily audience, until he was transferred to Marseilles. I have never known who it was who finally authorised my release, but it may have been Alquier. He was on the Committee for Public Safety, and Marie-Soulange went personally to entreat his intervention.

"Back at the Palais-Royal, I was still under house arrest, in the custody of our neighbour in the Fountains Court, Dreys. The first thing I did was send my wife and children, with the chambermaid and most of our household effects, back to Versailles. It was simply for their safety: in Paris, there was continual rioting over the price of food, and it was only a matter of time before Citizen Robespierre would invite the people, together with the National Guard, to complete the purgation of the Convention. Dreys became very anxious when he saw me left alone, with a servant and a cook whom I lodged in the adjoining apartment. He went to the section and asked how he could be held responsible for the custody of a man with two doors. The section referred Dreys's dilemma to the Committee for Public Safety, who fortunately took the view that I was not the chief secret agent of the Orleanists, of the reactionaries, the hostile powers of Europe, the Man in the Moon, and every other party opposed to the general will. They restored me to liberty, on condition that I report to the section regularly. At the same time, someone saw fit to send me papers terminating my military service again.

"That summer now seems ten years ago, not one. What we have lived through, Sade! The suspicions that Dumouriez had aroused, with his desertion, took their toll. Servan was implicated and imprisoned as a traitor. Then Danton was denounced, and stripped of all his offices. Scarcely had I digested that when Marat was murdered. I always thought his journal extravagantly emotional. The reaction to his death was in keeping."

I sense that Laclos's flow is dwindling. *I do agree with you, citizen,* I say eagerly. *I spoke at Marat's funeral, you know, beside the corpse that David designed. He conceived Marat with an arm raised and a pen placed in the hand. Unfortunately, rigor mortis was a faster sculptor. The arm resisted David's vision. First it kept dropping the pen, then under David's manipulation the whole arm came off. It had to be replaced with one borrowed from another corpse, the join disguised with a robe.*

"And to complete the gothic horror," Laclos adds, "they suspend his heart from the roof of the Pantheon!"

What of Corday?

"I always assumed she did it from her own royalist convictions. But women are not supposed to have convictions, only feelings, so her lover was held to blame, just as I have been blamed for what others did. The horror Corday aroused fed, I am sure, on the hatred people felt for Marie-Antoinette. In the Roman pageant we are acting out, the only rôles for women are

221

those of female vice: Cleopatra, Messalina." Laclos pauses.

Do say more on that theme, I encourage him.

"Why?"

Because you have many times told me how deeply you feel on the subject of women's education, as I do myself. Laclos is looking me full in the face. Could he suspect anything? I smile pleasantly, and wave my quill in waggish imitation of a whip.

"There are educated women who are stupid," he says slowly. "I would not put myself out to defend someone like Vigée-Lebrun, who cast herself in the rôle of the voluptuous virgin as set forth in the works of la Genlis, la Riccoboni, and their like. The point I was making is the restriction of women in public life by men passionate for democracy. They mean demidemocracy. I remember that Olympe de Gouges asked them, 'If a woman has the right to mount the scaffold, has she not the right to mount the platform?'"

And what was Citizen Robespierre's answer to that?

"Robespierre? I don't know. Why?"

He is looking very sharply at me. He suspects something. I decide to let him go on betraying himself slowly, without my urging. I have surely got enough already. This blister on the middle finger of my right hand is the most civically virtuous part of my body.

"Robespierre approved when divorce was instituted, I remember that. But in his general attitude to women, I have the impression that he, too, fears their carnality might distract men. He has always seemed a complex man to me." Laclos is back in his steepled-finger position, so efficacious for his dictation, and I breathe more easily. "He has a deep love for the French people, but is distant with persons. I know him to have been sickened by the massacres, especially those in which his associates connived. He said they dishonoured the revolution. Yet his unsleeping pursuit of the incorrect has certainly sent some to an undeserved fate. When he was authorised to order the arrest of anyone he suspected, in that time of purgation, there was a moment when the logic dictated that he would be the only man left alive in France, because the only one utterly beyond his suspicion. I think he finds the world an uncomfortable place, yet he it was, just last month, who gave the people back something of the God they said they missed with his Festival of the Supreme Being. I have heard he spends more time at home now, exhausted. But tell me, why are you so interested in what I might have to say about him? Are you being inquisitive?"

Really, citizen, my question was idler than you suppose. It is merely that Citizen Robespierre was a member of Les Piques section when I had the honour to be secretary of it, and so I have a natural fraternity for him.

"Very well. I will mention in passing that his concern for me is entirely to do with technical expertise I have been able to offer the republic. The note I gave you about personal dealings by certain members of the committees, which would be made public in the event of my execution, in no way related to Citizen Robespierre."

I understand, I say, chewing my pen. *Do proceed.*

"Why do you say you understand, when you cannot? I have said almost nothing about my explosives, nor shall I say much. The information is sensitive. And there is work to do yet. I was allowed to resume the experiments only last autumn, and they were still in progress when I was clapped in here, for my own protection. Berthollet and I had found a better site, nearer Paris, yet, more importantly, remote from prying eyes. It was the old château at Meudon. During the revolution it was sacked. That left it fit for our experiments. And it stands beside the river, so we were able to test certain nautical devices. Once we had established our operation, with secret funds approved by Citizen Robespierre, the place was used for related experiments, in metals particularly, and other military applications of science. Rumours of course leaked out, and some local residents spoke in horror of the château. A tanning process, which emitted a dreadful smell, gave rise to stories that human skin was being cured to make breeches for the leaders of the Convention. I did nothing to dispel such beliefs. That the place should be thought

223

a satanic factory secured our secrecy.

"With much to supervise, I had an apartment in the château furnished for me, and spent most of my nights there. I am extremely anxious to resume the work, when it is safe for me to be released again. Meanwhile, I have been preparing certain data while confined here, and conveying it to the Committee for General Security. That little spy Fabre has been trying to claim the credit for our research, but Robespierre is not deceived. There, now you understand, even though you know nothing. You do seem feverish today, Sade. Are you sure you want to go on working? What happened to you this morning must have alarmed you very much. I had given you up for dead."

I do believe there is the wintry ghost of a smile near his lips. He meant it as a joke. The only subject he has found amusing, in all these months together, is my immolation.

"I am sure you would have borne yourself with joyful gravity, as the motto is. Well, the motto for the male bourgeoisie. I am not sure if you class yourself among them. You have no profession or trade, after all, have you?'"

This man's sense of humour is barbaric. I am headily tempted to tear off my veils and sibilantly tell him that the blade is whispering ever closer to his neck, inching up with every word he says. But instead, I clear my throat and smile, pen eagerly poised.

"Joyful gravity, that's the thing now, I hear. When they throw you in a cell, you don't wait to be demeaned by the guillotine, or run the risk that your head will have time to contemplate the atrocity done to you. And you cannot tolerate what you and I have suffered in here, the ribald mockery of common men whose only care is to stay alive, and the devil take dignity. So you gather your family and friends around you, and with a bare bodkin end it. That is the Stoical script, they tell me. If the body be frozen by terror, take care that it is in a noble pose. I am confident you would have found in yourself the resources for that, at the end. You were a marquis, and a count.

How could your bearing be less than noble? How could you be found wanting in sincerity, which is the only political virtue in demand? Be inspired by the examples around us. Why do you suppose St-Just achieved his heart's desire, and sits next to Robespierre? Was it not his response when he was at first rejected? 'Dear God! Must Brutus languish far from Rome? My decision is already taken: if Brutus cannot kill others, he will kill himself.' Those words won St-Just many admirers. He has developed the part. When he demanded the Prince's expulsion from the Convention, he put one leg forward, one arm up, and cried, 'It is not I who demand this, but the father of Roman liberty, Brutus.' I heard someone say that it is difficult to see him nowadays. One is told that Monsieur St-Just is in rehearsal."

Laclos stands up. I say, *We cannot finish there.*

"Why not? It is a decent day's work."

But it is so fascinating, citizen. You have so much to tell, and such wise observations to make. And besides, it would be a true kindness to me to go on. More than ever, I appreciate the distraction today.

"It will not be long before we catch up with ourselves. I have been detained since November, and there is little to say about that. We will save it for another day."

Oh citizen, who knows if there will be another day? I do beg you to continue.

He sits down again, thinks for a time, and then grunts. "I was talking about St-Just. When Robespierre formed him and the others into the Committee for General Security, there was a sense of order. Only for a little while. They saved France from our enemies by recruiting all the young men, and arming them with munitions made from every scrap of metal the country could yield. Someone came to empty the Prince's kitchen. Everywhere you went you saw forges in the streets, and circles of women sewing uniforms and tents. You must have seen them yourself. That was why anyone with scientific knowledge was in demand. Were you, with your skills in geometry, not requisitioned?"

I was indisposed at that time.

"A pity. The army won more victories, and the revolts in the provinces were put down. For a while, the price of food was restrained. There was, I found, a true thanksgiving in that ceremony that David designed, to celebrate the overthrow of Louis. We moved around the stations of the revolution, and finally congregated at the flames of liberty, where three thousand doves were released.

"It couldn't last. What does, apart from one's family? The people said, What good were victories when eggs cost a hundred sous? Robespierre was too moderate. The other committees at the Convention said, What health could the republic enjoy while traitors were left unpunished? Robespierre was too arrogant. Wages were cut, and that led to bitter strikes, and now Robespierre was a dictator or a threat to private property, according to how much you had on your pantry shelves. Someone fired a shot at him. And so the sacrificial victims were led to the altar, in propitiation of everyone else. The Law of Suspects could be invoked with impunity. Any hint of sympathy for tyranny, or faintness of virtue, would serve.

"Lückner and Kellermann are among the first to be arrested. Marie-Antoinette is taken to the guillotine. *Ohé!* Sillery and his lot soon follow her. They bring Citizen Égalité back to Paris, and then it is my turn again. I am 'a very suspect man, still at large in Paris, who can only disturb public order.' Into La Force I go, this time. I had played outside the walls as a child. From the rue St-Antoine they lead me down a reeking alley, past the boundary stone on which la Lamballe's curly head was removed. The next day, Citizen Égalité faces the tribunal. Danton watched, and told me my poor master was haughtier than he'd ever seen him, and quite offhand. The President remarked, 'Servan was only nominally the Minister of War. The one who ran the show was your henchman, Laclos.' I wondered if I was being given my medal for Valmy, albeit nigh posthumously. They took Citizen Égalité's head off that evening. *Well, why not?*

"I prepare myself. But the days go by. They decide Bailly's

last sight should be of the Champ de Mars. They take him on foot, through rain, wind and mud, and then find there is no scaffold for him. So he has to wait for three hours, watching it built. 'You're trembling, Bailly,' one of the scaffolders jeers, 'Yes, with the cold,' he says. He was an old man. Barnave went. Madame du Barry, what a standing offence to the republic she represented, at her age. Old Ségur came hurtling into the cell next to mine."

I keep nodding eagerly. If none of it is news to anybody, the general tone is, surely, rich evidence of a very suspect man indeed. In the pauses, I rehearse my presentation of the material to the tribunal. It could last me many days, if not a thousand and one.

"Since Danton has gone now, too, I can say that he kept me informed about all of that, and, more vitally, about my own situation. Robespierre had not wished to oppose the rest of his committee on my arrest, but he contrived to have my tribunal postponed because of the experiments at Meudon. Danton wanted to see me moved here, out of harm's way, or so it seemed then, but he dared not draw attention to me by openly suggesting it. And besides, Robespierre hated him, and would have been offended. 'I will do what I can,' Danton assured me. 'You will write about me, when I am gone, won't you?' It was Robespierre's signature on the order to bring me here from La Force, just before Christmas. I am grateful, but I would have liked to know how it was arranged. I feel I am a piece in someone else's game."

And with that he sinks into a reverie from which I cannot arouse him to more damnations of himself. Well, perhaps there are enough already. Or perhaps they will let me have tomorrow.

17

And now it is tomorrow, and I am bewildered. My grief is a torture beyond the imagining of Lucifer, my joy divine. I know not which side to wear outermost.

Last night, when I came back to my room, I could not find my *Boudoir* manuscript. I hunted for hours, and in the end was convinced that the guards had taken it after arresting me, and the tribunal were even now wanking over it, before they killed me for it. I went to Laclos for consolation. He listened, and then he said, "Oh yes, I meant to tell you, I did you the favour of destroying the manuscripts I found in your room, after they took you away this morning. I thought it was the safest course."

I came back to my room unsure if I could survive.

Then, a great banging and shouting was set up in the Picpus, and no doubt throughout France. The news was that the Convention had indicted Robespierre. He was arrested at home and hauled off to the Luxembourg prison, where the warden refused to gaol him. While the argument went on at the gate, armed supporters were gathering around their hero, but he quietly bade them go home to bed. He would not lead an armed insurrection. He borrowed a pistol from one of them, put it in his own mouth and blew his jaw off. They kept him alive in hospital for the night, tried him this morning, and guillotined him on the Place de la Révolution. Thousands were there, cheering their throats out. More than a hundred of his gang joined him in the basket. The republic quite lacks any sense of good drama. To kill off virtually all your main characters is inept. I don't know where they find the actors to put up with it. It is very warm today, as well. The smell must have been hideous. I do hope they will find somewhere else to bury them than behind our hedge. Now the Convention has resolved that all further executions be suspended, while they take stock.

My stock is this.

First, I do not know if my life is worth living. My wife, and now Laclos, have idly destroyed my only treasures.

Second, the evidence I was eliciting for the tribunal to trap Laclos and Robespierre is redundant. Nobody will listen to Scheherazade. I am beside the point, if there is one. Therefore, the sentence of death passed upon me will no longer be suspended. However, presumably unsuspended sentences are now *a fortiori* suspended. Had mine still been suspended, it might now have been unsuspended. On the other hand, the death of Robespierre, which perhaps has saved my life, has perhaps saved Laclos's too, which mars my joy. I cannot describe the rapture it would have been to see him guillotined on my say-so. It would have been the criminal crown to my life, my books come true. I would have gone happy to the scaffold after him. I might never have another such opportunity.

Consider: he knew that eventually he would be guillotined, and so used me like a priest, to confess, with extreme unction. Or: he knew that his protection would always save his neck, so he used me like a clerk. In either case, he screwed me clerically.

And yet, now that Robespierre has gone, will Laclos not be the one who is terrified? Has he any protection left? Will he not be fed through the slicer as one of the Orleans gang? If, now, they give him an amnesty for that, he should be executed as one of the Robespierre gang. Having escaped the guillotine for so long he must have something to hide, and so deserves to be guillotined.

Would that I had Euclid's advice on whether to laugh or weep.

There is another dilemma. Now that we have apparently completed our work together on his memoir, it is his turn to scriven for me. I have been looking forward so much to watching his face as he takes down my regimen for the education of a young woman. I wonder how much I would be able to recapture of what he destroyed. And yet, he will certainly refuse to start that work until I have handed him the fair copy of his memoir. But I am not going to transcribe the coded parts into legible French, since their codification has already saved my life once, and I have seen far too much, in these years, to presume that my life might not need saving again. So I will not copy it, but dare not destroy it. I shall hide it well. That gives me all the power over him, except the only power I want.

18

This note added on the 11th day of July 1794, to the manuscript wherein I first recorded my blessed illumination concerning the number 11. It is two days since the death of Robespierre, and I have been avoiding Laclos. I spend every minute scribbling down all that I can remember of my *Boudoir* book, while the smell of it still lingers in my bereaved memory.

* * *

11th August 1794. Laclos and I remain distant. He was at first impatient, and is now suspicious, because I have not supplied him with his fair copy of these pages. *Don't worry, citizen,* I told him, *it is coming, like history.* "History doesn't come," he replied. "We make history." There's a *bon mot.* My delay, I explained, was caused by my imperative need to work on my own book, since I am short of money. He sniffed back that he had plenty to do himself, with notes for the Ministry of War on gunpowder magazines. Like me, I see, he is preparing for the worst, even though the Convention has already decreed that all held merely on suspicion should be released shortly. I pray every day that my sentence of death was lost in the turmoil after Robespierre.

* * *

11th September 1794. We are both still here. Coignard and Blanchard are full of apologies, but they dare not release us without authority. Suppose that, in drawing up the papers to be signed for my release, the tribunal chance upon the warrant for my execution?

Laclos's wife paid him a visit, the first for six months, ever since she was terrified by the lock of hair he sent her, poor thing. She has been living in Versailles all this time, he told me, and even now is in principle exiled from Paris. I was curious to see what so brave and devoted a woman looked like, and so peeped through the keyhole of his room. I am glad I did. While he bounced his narrow buttocks up and down on her, I could hear him reciting Rousseau from memory. "Goodness is beauty in action. Feelings are only what the heart makes of them." And in the pauses she would gasp, "Ah, the squirrel, the poor squirrel." And my inventions are thought outlandish.

* * *

11th October 1794. Still in the Picpus. It is intolerable. Even Mirabeau has been released. They found some papers at the back of a drawer in the Tuileries that proved the sly tricks he'd been up to with the King when he was posing as a dedicated constitutionalist. (There is a rumour that they implicate Danton, too.) So they went to the Pantheon and dug him up and dumped him somewhere else. How cross he must be. I can just see his face. Those cheeks of his will be flaming pink. *I know about you, Count of Mirabeau. I'm going to cut your ears off, do you hear?*

BRUMAIRE

A paper contributed by Zelda Butterworth PhD
to the 18th-Centuryist Colloquium at Potsdam, May 1991

De Sade was released from the Picpus on 15th October 1794. When Blanchard told him he was free, Sade was in such haste to go that he just walked out, leaving the door of his room ajar like the mouth of a corpse. He would send someone to collect his possessions. Did he take the Laclos memoir with him? His craving for security was obsessive, and we have his word that he believed the memoir allowed him a power of blackmail over Laclos which might one day save his skin, again. Was it with him through his few years of liberty and then his end back in the Charenton asylum? Or did he leave it hidden in the Picpus? If so, did Laclos find it? If not, did Laclos try to find Sade so as to demand it from him? We do not know, and unless the provenance of the manuscript becomes much less mysterious than it is so far, we cannot even guess at the answers. But there are two questions to which we can respond with some confidence, and they are both calligraphic.

One is the "code" that Sade often claims to have used to take down Laclos's dictation. Both to Laclos and to the tribunal, he declares that only he could decipher his own notes. Perhaps we are too sanguine, armed as we are with the scholarship that unravelled the notoriously cramped manuscript of the *120 Days*, but after scrutinising the whole script I have to say that Sade's so-called code is really nothing more impenetrable than a sort of speedhand – the omission of some vowels, a characteristic squiggle for certain recurrent morphemes such as *-ation*, and the use of initials for proper names, almost all of them unambiguous in their context.

Writing at dictation speed, his hand is not the tidy, well-formed and aligned script that we see in his letters, but a small scribble. In plain contrast are his own intrusions into the manuscript, which were written at his leisure. These, including the passages of conversation with Laclos, are invariably written out on separate sheets or inserted into the margin of the paper, strongly suggesting that they were in fact written after Laclos's narrative, as though to colour our reading of it, and our view of Laclos. And yet Sade repeatedly swears that nobody shall ever read any of it. If that confronts us with a paradox, or at least a contradiction, the solution may be no more riddling than a writer's need to write, the ingrained habit, the appetite that must be fed.

And so we have some evidence for the authenticity of the memoir, or for the virtuosity of a forger. The other question is potentially more damaging to the case for authenticity. Why are there no examples in the memoir of Laclos's handwriting, not even the pages at the start of Chapter 16 which he tells us, categorically, he is writing himself? We do not need forensics to tell us that those pages are written by the hand that writes the rest. Is it conceivable that Sade, loathing the labour of scrivening, was yet consumed with an authorial pride which drove him to make his own copy of Laclos's pages and destroy the original? Though most of the words were Laclos's words, still *he* was the writer of them − "if the story is his, the telling will be mine", as he says himself, near the start of the memoir. If that is so, we face virtually the same paradox as the one I have already mentioned, and the solution may be the same: the habit, the appetite. You might call it a completion neurosis.

Now I will leave the memoir, and come to my main theme, the end of Laclos's life.

Shortly after Sade's release, Laclos too leaves the Picpus. Alarmingly, it is at first only to be thrown into the squalid Luxembourg Prison, crammed a dozen to a cell − he is still a suspect man, the old Orleans puppet-master. But on 1st December he is standing on the sidewalk of the rue Vaugirard, after thirteen months of confinement.

A biting wind is rattling the tatters of revolutionary posters. It is another cruel winter. The Seine is ice, food barges can't reach the city, you wait in line for hours to buy anything to eat. The Bois de Boulogne is stripped for firewood. There are wolves in the countryside. Paris is dirty, and no one cares. The fountains have not played for months – they would be ice now, anyway. The warmest places are the theatres and the dance-halls. Hundreds of dance-halls have opened, because everybody wants to dance the new craze, the waltz. It is extraordinary. Without vestige of military formation, the dancers hold each other in their arms, they amalgamate, there are no dancers, there is only the dance. The men keep their hats on, the women are half-naked, with transparent corsages. One, two, three, one, two, three, keep the time, keep the rhythm, never stop. The theatres are verminous stews, where you cheer *The Death of Robespierre*. In the Palais-Royal Gardens, harlequins entertain the popinjays and strumpets, while the wind blows garbage around their ankles.

Laclos shakes his head. "Fear and servitude corrupt human nature," Rabelais observed. Laclos had always seen the *sans-culottes* as a mob, but during the revolution they were generally a respectable mob. Now, in the void, who is to shame them into decency? Not the Jacobins, with their daily baths and puritanical uniform that had so suited Laclos; they are a killjoy memory. Not Barras, the Chief Minister – he celebrates the ascendancy of the bourgeoisie in nightly orgies.

After Cromwell, the Restoration. After Robespierre – well, yes, in a crowd you may hear voices calling out for a king, but when there is a serious royalist revolt Barras quickly halts it. The young artillery officer who contemptuously shoots the rebels down is called Bonaparte. He had been a *protégé* of Robespierre, who spotted the coming man before he'd come. Bonaparte is made a General, he is winning brilliant victories in Italy and Austria, people in Paris drink toasts to him. Laclos raises his glass with the rest. And he remembers that name, Bonaparte. There were letters, from Valence, to the Correspondence Committee at the Jacobins. Laclos has a good memory. Perhaps he could even find those old letters from Bonaparte, if the

Jacobins' archive has not been destroyed.

Marie-Soulange was pregnant again. She gave birth to Charles nine months after her visit to the Picpus, when Sade mischievously claims that Laclos was panting Rousseau. The family had moved from Versailles back to Paris, into the faubourg Poissonière. Laclos was not well, after his incarceration, but he had to feed a growing family, and his army pension was not nearly enough. The price of flour was more than a hundred times what it had been five years earlier. Everyone received a ration of bread, but it was too little to fill the stomach, and on the open market a loaf cost 16 livres. People were starving to death, or committing suicide to end the agony of hunger. There were bread riots, with women in the vanguard again. When a deputy rebuked them, they paraded his head on a pike. Condorcet, a marquis on the run, betrayed himself at an inn, ordering an omelette. "How many eggs do you like?" "Twelve." (A misjudgment that cost him not only his life but also his reputation as an expert in probability theory.)

Laclos's talent for accountancy secures him a dull job in a mortgage house, where he likes the notion of decimalised currency that his old acquaintance Gouverneur Morris is proposing in Philadelphia. Now he has time to repair the web of connections he enjoyed before the Terror. He frequents Madame Pourrat's salon again, and meets Benjamin Constant. He resumes his development of an explosive shell. He writes again on the education of young women, recommending books that would promote the power of reason. Few of us, I dare say, would quibble with that, though I would do more than quibble when he holds up natural goodness and sweetness as the virtues most to be inculcated in a girl. His demand as a paterfamilias is that his home should be a Rousseauesque pastorale, and anyone who gets out of line is driven back with imperturbable clicks of the tongue. No wonder that Étienne grows up gentle and feckless, like a confused sheep.

None of it is what Laclos really wants. The financial world is tedious. He wishes he had lived through interesting times, not all this excessive squabble. If his novel is a text without an author, his life has turned out to be the reverse. At fifty-eight, he still dreams of commanding "Fire!" and seeing the enemy go down like wheat. Skirmishes with the British promise to turn, soon, into a proper war, an invasion of England. Now more than ever is it fine to be a soldier, in the brilliantly disciplined French army. With the help of Alquier, who is a member of the governing Directory, Laclos gets himself appointed as a reserve General of the line. It is not the artillery, nor is it active service. Trained by military discipline, his mind requires and respects order, orders, leadership. He lives, as he says himself, through others. Where, now, is the Other?

He still has friends in high places. Talleyrand is foreign secretary. His policy, Laclos tells him, should be expansionist, to sustain the revolution. Sieyès surfaces again to agree, and the newspapers hiss about a Jacobin resurgence. The expansion is pursued, with a campaign in the near east. The commander is Bonaparte.

Old Montalembert is still at large, now eighty-four. Over two decades, at his own expense, he has published his definitive treatise on perpendicular fortifications. "I wonder you didn't keep up your hobby of writing, Laclos. It is good to see eleven volumes with your name on every spine, I can tell you. It assures you a measure of immortality." But it does not assure Montalembert the vacant seat in the Academy of Sciences. He is passed over in favour of Bonaparte.

Sieyès joins the Directory. Laclos talks to him, and Talleyrand. The Directory is feeble, they agree, with people like Alquier on it. What is needed is the old Roman model, a triumvirate of consuls. Sieyès will be one, and will draft a new constitution. The pliable Ducos will do for a second. The third consul needs no discussion. They believe their coup on 18th brumaire, in November 1799, will be the last after-tremor of the revolution. But the third consul at once rewrites Sieyès's constitution, to install himself as First Consul Bonaparte.

One, two, three, one, two, three, conqueror, emperor, one,

two, three, one, two, three, Bonaparte, Bonaparte. Everybody wants to waltz. "Citizens," the First Consul declares, "the revolution rests on the principles that gave rise to it. It is finished."

* * *

Laclos is lunching at the Tuileries with the First Consul. Both are in dress uniform. Beneath his white jacket, Bonaparte wears his red embroidered waistcoat with the gold buttons undone. He has let his hair grow, so that locks flop over his dark brow, above the imperious stare, long nose and jutted lips. His posture is relaxed, but his voice is quick, nervous. Laclos, twenty-eight years older than the little Corsican, is in blue and white with red trimmings. When he arrived, on his wig sat the high bicorn with tricolour that has synthesised the old dispute between three corners and four. The two men agree that the artillery is the best corps in Europe. When Bonaparte describes Talleyrand as a pile of shit in a silk stocking, Laclos smiles in recognition. He smiles when the First Consul congratulates him on his novel. "I learned a lot," Bonaparte adds, his eyes sideways at Joséphine. Both have three degrees of nobility. They have much in common, including their correspondence when Bonaparte was a keen young Jacobin writing to the rue Saint-Honoré in favour of a constitutional monarchy.

Among the other guests is Minister of War Carnot, who asks Bonaparte what his plans are to have done with the Austrian army. The answer is, "I shall fall on Italy from the height of the Alps. The Austrians will come out from Genoa to meet me, but too late."

Laclos's neighbour, with a raised forkful of partridge, murmurs that it is imprudent to announce one's plan of surprise attack to a table where there must certainly be gossips at best, and probably spies.

"No," Laclos replies quietly. "You don't understand. He *wants* it to be known. When it reaches the ears of the Austrians, they will not credit it. They have no idea in Vienna of our

240

resourcefulness and resilience. They think us incapable of raising a decent army in France, let alone marching it through the snows of the Saint-Bernard Pass. So they will receive this news as a bluff designed to scare them out of Genoa, and it will be the one strategy for which they are unprepared."

His neighbour nods, and reaches for the sauceboat as a cover for turning to his opposite neighbour.

Berthollet is at lunch, too. He was in the Near-East campaign, from which Bonaparte returned to lay conquered Egypt at the feet of Joséphine, who turned and remarked to her maid, "Il est drôle, ce Bonaparte." Berthollet has kept the First Consul advised of the development of the explosive shell, in which he had assisted at Meudon. While Laclos was in the Picpus, the commissar Fabre had tried to claim credit for the invention, the more bitterly after blowing himself up. But the shell, we know, is Laclos's professional pride, and its mystery has served Robespierre as an instrument to save its inventor from the guillotine. Now it serves again. With Berthollet's backing, Laclos asks to be posted on active service as a General in the artillery. He has already bought himself a coach in readiness. Bonaparte nods. Some old heads at the War Ministry will be shaking when they hear about it. Some journalists will rehearse their parrot-shrieks against the Orleans puppet-master. But all will think better of it. The First Consul has nodded.

In an April dawn, in 1800, Laclos puts on his campaign uniform and sets off to join the Army of the Rhine, in Strasbourg.

* * *

The roads are dreadful: mire, cattle, brigands, tramping columns. Outside the inns, good-time girls are waiting for travellers. To win a customer they haul each other back by the hair and scratch with painted nails. Nightly, floating on champagne or the dream of action, Laclos writes home to Marie-Soulange about his journey, his meals, hopes, health, bedbugs. The author of an epistolary novel is writing novelistic letters.

"You should have more fantasy," he presumes to advise his wife, "not allow yourself to be so rutted in reality." Did she read that out loud to the children at her skirts? In Strasbourg Laclos rediscovers Louise Contat, once the lissom creator of Suzanne in *Figaro,* a revolution ago, now a handsome block of marble and mother of children by five men. Over the dinner table she chides him for having twice declined her invitations in those long-gone days. He reflects that the suspension of disbelief can persist charmingly even after the curtain has come down.

He orders horses from an ostler, and has to walk around Strasbourg asking if anyone can tell him where his army is. He finds it, and is told by the other generals, half his age, that he is to command the reserve artillery. He writes home winsomely, "If I do not deceive myself, some consideration attaches to my name." When the army goes off to take Freiburg, he has to follow later, because his horses are not ready. He catches up with them in Bavaria at Neuf-Brisach, where they are occupying a fortress designed by Vauban. The other generals have seen it all before. They like to tell him what they've done in battle, and what they will do. A thrill of envy runs through Laclos.

And then – let us note the place, Biberach, and the date, 9th May 1800 – he has fighting troops to command, and living, frightened Austrians for a target. After forty years, amid the percussion and screams, stink and fear of battle, he shouts "Fire!" and drops his hand. A 12lb shell is ejaculated from Bonaparte's master weapon, the Gribeauval cannon. Who knows where it lands, whose flesh it rips open? Who can count the children who were never conceived? Bliss was it. Blue smoke drifts across the sunlit field, and then the infantry charge into it with bayonets. The battle is soon won, two thousand prisoners taken, and the next step on the road to Vienna is Memmingen. But Carnot has come to ask for 25,000 men to be detached and sent to Italy. They will be under the supreme command of Bonaparte. And Laclos is to be one of their generals, commanding a siege force. It is a perfect text.

First, through Switzerland, *La Nouvelle Héloïse* to the life. He practises riding. Never happy on horseback, he must ride if he is to serve Bonaparte in a siege. He bumps up and down, his wig slipping on his skullcap. He persists, and it brings on piles. He has command of thousands of marching men, a long train of munition carts, horse-drawn cannons, he has to see them all provisioned, the officers lodged, the horses shod, guards mounted. He has not been prepared for this. Wheels come off, men fall sick, horses stumble and break a leg, squalls pelt down, and he cannot cope. Before they reach Berne he finds himself, one night, unable to give an order at all. He is shivering. The younger officers keep straight faces and sort out all the problems for him. The soldiers sleep under the stars, with giggling girls in ditches. Laclos says nothing. This is the modern army, Bonaparte's magnificence. Laclos stays in his lodgings and writes to Marie-Soulange. "To have loved you, and been loved by you, is achievement enough for one lifetime." A letter of hers, sent to Bavaria after he had left, reaches him with an endorsement in German: "Captured by the Imperial Austrian Army, opened in error, and forwarded forthwith."

By the time they reach Grenoble, he knows his mission is pointless. Bonaparte's victory at Marengo has already settled matters in Lombardy, and Laclos's beautiful siege sketches can be torn up. In Grenoble he spends most of his time alone, reading. When he meets people he is at his most taciturn. It is absurd, he tells himself, to have any bad conscience about this place. After three decades, how many of those I knew are still alive? And of those few, how many would my book have offended? In any case, it is summertime. The gentry are at their houses in the country. When he does encounter two old salon acquaintances, they pass by with a formal nod. Walking on, now he remembers the fierce indignation that ignited the book, and his conscience clears. He completely exonerates himself. France is immeasurably healthier now that the infection of aristocracy has been purged, and perhaps his book did play a part.

He feels so vindicated that he decides he will give a dinner for the leading citizens of Grenoble, and he will make a speech. He will speak about the revolution: "Those who hated it are still full of resentment, but all they have to resent now are the immense benefits that the revolution has brought all of us. Theirs is the resentment of those who see they were wrong. Bonaparte represents the fulcrum, the point of stability. He is a peacemaker. The wars he has to fight now are merely the final chapters of the revolution. May he live for ever. Let us drink a toast to him."

Rivière, whose garlic-drenched boarding-house Laclos had chosen thirty years earlier as the officers' quarters, is now the proprietor of the great Hôtel des Princes. "I owe it all to you, Captain Laclos, all of this. They tell me you wrote a book about the old days here. Ah, what days they were, eh? I must read it." When Rivière presents his bill for the dinner, everything is charged, down to the last sou for a broken glass.

Laclos receives new orders: to join the military administration in Milan, as deputy to General Marmont. When he gets there he finds that his commander-in-chief is twenty-six years old. Marmont was a stripling when the Bastille fell. There is little to do in Milan. Laclos sits in a box at La Scala and yawns at Cimarosa. "Nothing in the world is more mortally tedious than an Italian comic opera," he writes home. A young subaltern called Marie-Henri Beyle enters the box, insistent upon being presented to the author of *Les Liaisons Dangereuses*. Laclos unbends a little when he learns that Beyle is from Grenoble.

Another who expresses admiration for the book is the bishop in whose palace Laclos is lodging. "It is a deeply moral fiction," His Reverence asserts. Laclos concurs, pleased that someone has understood him. "Perhaps you could arrange for a copy to be sent to me?" the bishop asks. "It has always been on the Index, you understand. I would like to read it very much." He smiles. "I am by definition incorruptible."

In deepening boredom, Laclos's letters to Marie-Soulange become waspish. An aunt dies, but there is nothing for them in her will. "I didn't expect her to leave us anything. At least you inherit the hours which you would have had to spend in her tedious company." Alquier is promoted to the Senate. "He'll have nothing to do, an occupation he prefers to all others." Marmont is called away for a few days. "So I give all the orders and take the decisions. It is my destiny to function in the name of another." On a bookstall, he comes across a published copy of the Duke of Orleans's correspondence from London, which he had written.

Ulm, Augsburg, Munich, the advance on Vienna is remorseless. Laclos left Bavaria too late for Marengo and too soon for the great victory at Hohenlinden. He accompanies Marmont on an artillery mission to Monzembano, and at the Passage of Brenta is given command of an operation against an Austrian emplacement. He deploys twenty-five cannon methodically. The Austrians, who were all asleep, take to their heels at the first shot.

By February the war is over. There is some talk of Egypt, "a bit late in the day for me, though I'm not quite done for yet. All the same, I see my future as a rut of mediocrity." Bonaparte has offered him only military posts. "He's probably right to do so. For now I'll make no other demands of him." What other demands, we wonder, would the passionate soldier have had in mind? Who is the Other walking beside him?

* * *

Sade had grown grossly fat, though subsisting on scrumped carrots and beans at the back of a barn in Clichy, and cadging kindling. He earned a few sous as a prompter and stagehand. His chief preoccupation was the creation of a tapestry illustrating the most extreme trials to which he had subjected Justine. "Ah sir, it's an extravagant proposal," she sighs after eighteen chapters of it. Arrested and arraigned as the book's author, and confronted with the tapestry, Sade denied having written a word of *Justine*. He was also accused of scandalous libels about Bonaparte and Joséphine. Denying everything, surviving

everything – Robespierre's death saved not only him but also
Joséphine, who was scheduled for the guillotine that same day
– he was sent back to the Charenton asylum for good, or evil.
His improvisation never flagged. He lived on the margin.

Laclos, in contrast, now spends two torpid years in which he
is the author of a new design of gun-carriage, named The
Laclos Cannon-Cart. "Had I the courage left," he reflects, "I
would write another book. But I have grown stupid." When a
friend sends him the manuscript of a novel, his critical notes in
reply start to take on the lineaments of a fiction in their own
right. But he stops the fermentation. The theme would have
been that happiness is to be found only within married life, and
it would have served to catechise his daughter. But he stops.
Could he write only in hatred? Had he frightened himself with
his first and only book? Or was he discouraged by what
Aristotle knew, that the infinite variety of wickedness sprouts
more stories than the single bud of goodness?

The pattern of his life reasserts itself. He is given command
of an artillery expedition sailing to Haiti to put down Toussaint
l'Ouverture's revolt. But at Brest he is told there has been a
mistake. He is to return to Paris, where instead he is appointed
Inspector-General of Artillery. Étienne is found a diplomatic
job in Dresden, through Talleyrand's influence. His father
counsels him to be prudent ("Remember we are not well off"),
but Étienne runs up debts from the day of his arrival; and his
work provokes Talleyrand to ask, "How is it that the son of
Laclos writes like a fishwife?" Laclos frowns. A diplomatic
career was perhaps not the best choice. He will speak to
Marmont about a commission in the cavalry, or the artillery.
Marie-Soulange entertains her husband's associates (he never
had a friend) with broth, radishes, butter and gherkins, soup,
chicken, truffles, pâtés, cutlets, partridges, salad, cauliflower,
apple charlotte with Savoy biscuits, cheese, fruit, coffee,
liqueurs.

In his sixty-third year, Laclos is racked by a perception that
will kill him. He is perfectly alone. He has always wanted to

walk in the shadow of the Other, but nobody is beside him, never was. The Other, the image in the dark mirror, can never be anything but death. For a moment the perception is so terrifying that he is exhilarated. Then he resigns himself to what he has to do. Probably, when he leaves home, weary before he starts, rheumaticky, he knows he will never come back.

* * *

He is travelling again to Italy, a country he doesn't like. This time he has to go the whole way through it, to Taranto, in the south. The English have reneged on their agreement to vacate Malta, so Bonaparte, to control the eastern Mediterranean, is forming an army to be based in the Kingdom of the Two Sicilies. Laclos has successfully applied for command of the artillery. Above him in the military administration are Murat and Gouvion-Saint-Cyr, but where the artillery is concerned Laclos is at last his own man, the General of a fighting division. Accompanied by Captain Lespagnol as his *aide-de-camp*, he crosses the Alps at Chambéry in his coach.

He is subject to fits of weeping. Several times every day, inexplicably, his diaphragm sobs and tears trickle down his cheeks. A rash has flowered all over his body.

Turin, Milan, and to Piacenza, where his artillery is waiting for him. He inspects them and is pleased, then travels on ahead. He has to buy a map. Modena, Bologna, Rimini, and down the Adriatic coast. The news is that the English have broken off negotiations. There will be a war. Laclos no longer dreams of invading England. He can hardly remember what his present mission is. There is only the journey. At Ancona he rests, but his lodgings are 150 steps up from the road, several times a day. "You've put on a little weight?" he writes to his wife. "Good. The more of you there is, the better." Over the Adige, into the Kingdom of the Two Sicilies. Now the hills are so steep that sometimes the horses can't haul the load up them, and the two men have to walk beside the coach. The roads are pitted, the villages are wretched. In the country of Marcus Brutus, peasants copulate in full view and think nothing of defecating in the street. All day and night, his body streams with sweat. There are thunderstorms, but they don't clear the humid air, his clothes still cling to his skin, his breath is heavy in his lungs. The fleas and mosquitoes are relentless. Bari, and then inland, across the high heel of Apulia, tracking along the edges of ravines, the vegetation sparse and dessicated in hallucinatory heat. In Taranto at last, Laclos lies down on a bed, shivering and spare with fever. The smell of his own body is disgusting.

The next day, he forces himself to dress and inspects the artillery batteries, overlooking the Ionian Sea. They are not sited to his satisfaction, and the garrison is ill-supplied with munitions and provisions. As yet he has no funds. The King of Naples has ignored Bonaparte's request that he pay for protection.

Laclos spends a day in bed trying to sweat the fever out. Through Lespagnol, who serves him as a scribe, he writes to Marie-Soulange that soon, when he feels better, he will send for her and their daughter to join him. A doctor is called, a physician trained in Bologna. He treats Laclos as a malfunctioning machine, defective in its hygiene. The prescription is to drain off the dysentery, not struggle to control it. Laclos angrily dismisses him. He would rather have just Lespagnol there, to nurse the darkening body.

Word reaches Gouvion-Saint-Cyr that his artillery commander is ailing. When he calls on Laclos, one look is enough. He must be repatriated. Perhaps his wife could come as far as Naples to meet him? But Marie-Soulange has never made such a journey, let alone undertaking it without her husband to guide her. And she does not have the money it would cost, and she has two children to be looked after.

Through Lespagnol, Laclos writes to the Ministry of War. "I have used up 6,000 livres of my own money in subsistence, postal charges, horses, lodgings. Now I have the expenses of a sickness. To return to Paris will entail more than sixty overnight stops, since the doctors tell me I cannot expect to cover more than ten or twelve leagues a day. I shall die in Taranto if I do not receive 12,000 livres at least. When I left Paris, I did not suppose that I was embarking on the life of a beggar."

But it is all too late. Laclos is so ill now that he cannot travel at all, cannot even get out of his stinking bed. By early September, Lespagnol has to write in his own name to Marie-Soulange, since Laclos cannot find the words. "He is a bit worse, but we are doing all we can."

Laclos has withdrawn into his sickness. That is where he dwells now. Probably it is malaria, but the name of the sickness does not matter to him. He knows that it will soon be over. If there were any hope it would lie in the hands of others, and he expects nothing from them. He is scarcely aware of other people's existence. Why do we suppose that it is only in drowning that a dying body reviews its life? Laclos has suspended his belief in the present. He is visiting his ghosts.

The traditional last spasm of lucidity makes its cruel appearance. He uses it to dictate a letter to Bonaparte. "In the few moments of life that remain to me, I wish to inform the General and First Consul of my last concerns: the happiness of my country, your success in arms, and the fate of my unfortunate family. I die more peacefully in the assurance that you will be able to assist my wife and three children, who are absolutely without resources."

The First Consul received the letter at the same time as the news of Laclos's death, and told the Minister to bend a recently introduced law by which military pensions were restricted to the widows of men killed in action. Marie-Soulange enjoyed a thousand francs a year for the twenty-nine years she survived, and little Charles was later given a free place at a military college, where he was trained to be killed in the service of the Emperor Napoleon.

Alquier, now the Ambassador in Naples, attended to the disposal of Laclos's estate. He sold off the military effects, but sent the dress uniform home to Marie-Soulange. The next time he went to Paris it was on the pretext of seeing how proudly she had mounted the uniform on a dummy. He asked her to marry him, but she said No.

Laclos's final commitment to solitude was in refusing the last rites. It was a crazy gamble against Pascal, don't you think, *meine Damen und Herren?* What could he lose? You may answer: his dignity, his belief in himself. Dignity, in a dysentery-soaked bed? Belief, in a body thirty minutes from the death-rattle? I am, of course, inclined to agree with that answer. Most of us would, I dare say. But how can we *know?* A procession of choirboys sang at his interment between two artillery batteries. To save the cost of a tombstone a disused altar stone was turned and inscribed, but twelve years later Neapolitan soldiers vandalised the tomb and scattered the ashes. By then, Napoleon had been shipped off to Saint-Helena.

Glossary

Alquier. Mayor of la Rochelle when Laclos was stationed there; became a Jacobin, in positions of power on the Committee of Public Safety and the Directory, later an ambassador, and achieved lasting obscurity.

Bailly. Astronomer; president of Third Estate at the swearing of the Tennis Court Oath; the first mayor of Paris, after the storming of the Bastille, and so the civil authority presiding over the 1791 Champ de Mars massacre. Guillotined.

Barnave. Lawyer and orator from Grenoble; as president of National Assembly and secret adviser to King, a rival to Mirabeau; in favour of qualified monarchy and property-based suffrage; reordered Jacobins with his friends Duport and de Lameth. Guillotined.

Beurnonville. A general at the Battle of Valmy; later sent to take over command in Flanders from Dumouriez, who instead traded him to the Austrian army.

Billaud-Varenne. Lawyer; on Committee of Public Safety, one of those who turned the Terror on Robespierre.

Brissot. Leader of Girondins, denounced as enemy of liberty by Robespierre. Guillotined.

Brunswick, Duke of. Commanded Prussian army at Valmy.

Chamfort. Writer, wit, anti-monarchist, secretary of Jacobins, committed suicide in prison under Terror.

Chénier. Poet, posthumously considered France's greatest in 18th century, not that he had much competition; a zealous moderate. Guillotined.

Condorcet. Mathematician, philosopher who believed in human progress; Girondin, republican marquis, committed suicide in prison under Terror.

Corday. Assassin of Marat, a royalist with Girondin

sympathies. Guillotined.

Cordeliers. Extreme republicans, organised Champ de Mars rally in 1791 to demand deposition of King; later, growing still more radical, all leaders were guillotined.

Convention. Successor to Legislative Assembly.

Danton. Lawyer, Jacobin, adversary of Lafayette; as dominant figure in revolutionary government, led the call for war against Austria; suspected by many of devious dealing behind the scenes; sought to temper the Terror and so was guillotined.

De Launay. Governor of the Bastille, beheaded when it was stormed.

Desmoulins. Pamphleteer; credited with arousing popular anger that led to storming of the Bastille; undermined Girondins with accusation that they were in foreign pay; colleague of Danton and guillotined with him.

Diamond Necklace Affair. 1785 frame-up of Marie-Antoinette. She was innocent in it, but the scandal could not have stuck but for her known venality.

Directory. Five-man executive arm of government from 1795.

Dumouriez. At different times foreign minister, war minister; one of the generals at the Battle of Valmy; conquered Belgium, and planned military coup d'état but went over to Austrians after losing a battle to them in 1793, precipitating the crisis that led to the Jacobin dominance of the government.

Duport. Lawyer, colleague of Barnave, secret adviser to King.

Fête de la Fédération. First anniversary celebration of the storming of the Bastille; 400,000 gathered on the Champ de Mars. It poured with rain all day.

Festival of the Supreme Being. Acknowledging that the Republic of Virtue needed a civic religion, Robespierre presided over a ceremony celebrating the cult of Nature, on the Champ de Mars in 1794.

Girondins. Bourgeois republicans who vacillated on the main issues of the revolution, such as a constitutional monarchy, and wound up being guillotined, twenty-one of them, in 1793.

Jacobins. Political club dedicated to the retention of the constitution, and later to defending revolutionary gains against the aristocrats. Always moving to the left, its members came to dominate government, and the Committees of Public Safety and General Security during the Terror.

Kellermann. General who won the main battle at Valmy; later imprisoned by Jacobin régime.

Lafayette. The Hero of Two Worlds, so called because of his fighting for the colonists in the American War of Independence. A marquis, commander-in-chief of the National Guard after the storming of the Bastille. Advised the King on constitutional compromise, defended the Third Estate's property rights, ordered the shooting dead of fifty demonstrators at the Champ de Mars in 1791. After the 1792 insurrection, he chose to be an Austrian captive.

de Lameth. Count, fought in America alongside Lafayette. With Barnave and Duport, defended property-based suffrage and constitutional monarchy. After fall of monarchy, assisted by Danton to flee to England. Later joined Lafayette in Austrian captivity.

Lamoignon. King's strongest minister before revolution.

Legislative Assembly. Successor to National Assembly.

Lückner. General of German origin.

Marat. Doctor, journalist, passionate revolutionary leader, assassinated 1793. His corpse was exhibited to encourage patriotic heroism.

Mirabeau. Reformist count, orator and libertine. Constitutional monarchist, though distrusted by constitutionalists and the monarch, whom he secretly counselled.

Morris, Gouverneur. American ambassador, though royalist in opinion.

Mounier. Lawyer, leading member of Third Estate, sought compromise with monarchy.

National Assembly. Convened to draft first constitution after the 1789 revolution.

Necker. Swiss banker, several times finance minister, father of Mme de Staël.

Pache. Swiss protégé of Necker, minister of war 1792, then Jacobin mayor of Paris. Guillotined.

Riccoboni. Minor novelist.

Rivarol. Satirical journalist, monarchist.

Robespierre. The Incorruptible. Supreme Jacobin, republican democrat. Fastidious lawyer, committed to moral virtue as the basis of person and State. Driven by events, and deteriorating health, to harsh repression, including liquidation of Danton. Very popular. Executed with 107 adherents – the guillotine was brought back to the Place de la République for the occasion.

Sections. Administrative districts of Paris.

Ségur. Viscount, war minister under monarchy.

Servan. Girondin war minister.

Sieyès. Cleric, influential political theorist. (*What is the Third Estate? Everything.*) Later (1799) influential in overturning the Directory so as to bring in Napoleon, who sacked him.

Sillery. Girondin, husband of Mme de Genlis. Guillotined.

de Staël. Writer, with Girondin sympathies, holder of salon for intellectuals.

St-Just. Young republican, twenty-one when the Bastille fell. As he rose, at Robespierre's side, he became more unshakable in his views and more cruel. Guillotined.

Talleyrand. Atheist Bishop of Autun, diplomat, foreign

minister under Napoleon. Born with a club foot, a great survivor (till 1838) by dint of reversing his position whenever it was prudent.

Tilly. Scandal-mongering Jacobin.

Vigée-Lebrun. Portrait painter to royal family.